CRITICAL PRAISE FOR
KATE WILHELM
The Nebula and Hugo Award Winner

For *Smart House*
"A taut, high-tech mystery abounding in ingenuity!"

—*Publishers Weekly*

For *Dark Door*
"Wilhelm is in top form as the thriller plot races along while characters teeter over an abyss of insanity!"

—*Publishers Weekly*

Pitting likable characters against a monstrous phenomenon, Wilhelm creates an engrossing thriller!"

—*Locus*

SMART HOUSE

In this skillfully crafted mystery, Charlie Meiklejohn and Constance Leidl were called in to investigate the murder of a computer genius who had invented the fully automated home of the future. Although they had no shortage of suspects, the detectives soon began to wonder if Smart House was smart enough—and vicious enough—to kill.

KATE WILHELM

SMART HOUSE

A CHARLIE & CONSTANCE MYSTERY

LEISURE BOOKS NEW YORK CITY

A LEISURE BOOK®

May 1991

Published by

Dorchester Publishing Co., Inc.
276 Fifth Avenue
New York, NY 10001

1

THREE things happened that week in April to make Beth Elringer decide to attend her husband Gary's birthday party. The first was losing her job, which came about because of a broken press at the company where she worked as editor. Beth and Margaret Long, her employer, sat opposite each other in a booth at Taco Time. Beth pushed a tamale around on her plate while Margaret talked.

"I just can't take it any longer," Margaret said. She looked exhausted. "We were up all night, and then the damn press went blooey and we have as much chance of meeting our deadline as we have of finding pearls in oysters."

"Why didn't you call me?"

"You know how to fix the damn press? A pulley broke. Three weeks, Mike said, to get a new one installed, if we had the money to do it in the first place."

"What will you do?"

"I wish to God I knew. But, honey, you'd better be thinking of another job. I just don't know if this is the last straw. I have a feeling it could be."

Beth liked her job as editor; she had a book of poetry in the works that she especially liked, by an author who might never get it published if the Long Press went out of business.

The second event came two days later when her brother Larry asked for a loan. She gasped when he told her how much he needed. He had been out on strike; he and his wife had gone into debt and they would lose the house and everything else if he couldn't pay off some bills.

The third thing was finding her cat dead a few nights later. She wept over that. She knew she could get another job, and she had taken out a bank loan to help her brother, but there wasn't a damn thing she could do for the cat. If she had not been so preoccupied with jobs and loans, she would have noticed that it was sick, poisoned maybe; she would have taken it to a vet instead of finding it stiff and cold on her kitchen floor.

That night she examined the agreement she had signed with the Bellringer Company when Gary had given her a share of stock. There were only nine shareholders, and the company was said to be worth millions of dollars. Even one share was worth a fortune, she knew. And she owned one share. The agreement stated that if ever she wanted to dispose of her single share, she must first offer it to Gary without telling anyone else it was for sale. She read the paper twice, then nodded. Gary's party, she decided. That was the time to tell him. He would be in a good mood, happy with a weekend party going on around him, pleased that she was attending. He had predicted that she would be back, had infuriated her with his self-assurance about her penitent return. She read through the agreement one more time. If she and Gary could not agree on a price for her share, she could then present it at the next shareholders' meeting and accept the highest offer that met or exceeded Gary's offer. That would be the day after his weekend party. If still no satisfactory price could be agreed to, an independent accountant would assess the market value of the share, and she would be paid that amount by the company, the payment to be assessed among the shareholders according to percentages of ownership; they would then divide the share. But she knew it would never come to that. Gary would snatch it up. And if he didn't, then his brother Bruce would.

Two weeks later she boarded the small commuter plane in San Francisco on her way to Smart House. The invitation had said simply somewhere on the Oregon coast, and the airplane ticket had been for the town of North Bend. "Don't worry about it," Gary had said on the phone, "we'll meet you." Now Beth stared bitterly out her window at the great expanse of ocean, all gray and frothy near the shore, with deep shadows and gleaming highlights beyond that, and then flat gray to the horizon. She could make out fishing boats, small boats closer in, a large ocean-going cargo ship, all dipping and swaying and passing from sight above and below her tiny window on the world. She could feel her stomach rise and fall in time with them. She clutched the arm of her seat and closed her eyes, but that was even worse. When the plane went down, she wanted to know it. She could not understand why it mattered, but she did not want to plummet into the sea with her eyes closed. The plane was buffeted from side to side, and it rose and fell with an unpredictable motion that did not allow for compensation. Just when she braced for a downward plunge, the plane rose alarmingly, then dropped again.

Damn Gary, she thought over and over. Damn him. Gary had scrawled on the invitation, "You'll love the plane ride. I can't wait to show you Smart House!"

Thirty, she thought morosely. Who would have gambled on Gary's surviving this long? The plane lurched and dropped at the same time. She hung onto the seat and muttered, "Damn him! Goddamn him!" Staying married to Gary Elringer for ten years, she thought, gave her privileges; who had a better right to damn him to hell?

On the ground, waiting for the plane from San Francisco, was Madelaine Elringer, Gary's mother. Maddie was sixty-two, and after fighting plumpness for most of her life, had finally given up the battle, only to find that when she stabilized again she had a new figure, not altogether unpleasing, she thought secretly. She was busty, with a waistline still defined, and shapely legs, nice wrists and ankles. Not bad at all, she had decided, and had colored her hair strawberry blond—pink champagne, the shop called it. She used makeup with a deft hand and bought very nice clothes, all in keeping with her role in life as mother of a millionaire genius. She sat in her B.M.W. smoking cigarette after cigarette waiting for the arrival of her daughter-in-law. A front had come in, bringing erratic winds that were frigid, not at all Maylike; the small terminal was dreary, and she was too worried to be pleasant to the few others who were awaiting the plane. The weekend was a ghastly mistake, she had known that from the start. Bringing together nine of the shareholders, even Beth, and heaven alone knew what was on *her* mind these days, and Bruce being a real shit about the whole thing. She dreaded the shareholders' meeting on Monday more than she had dreaded anything in years, or maybe ever. She lighted another cigarette from the butt of the last one and flicked that one out the window, then felt a start of guilt and looked around hastily to see if anyone had noticed.

At last the plane was down and three passengers appeared on the tarmac; she left the refuge of her car to enter the terminal. To Maddie's eye, Beth looked exactly the same as she had when she and Gary had first met. Boyish, with short dark hair that was instantly windblown, she was too lanky and long-legged to be really pretty, and made no effort to pretend anything else. She was wearing black jeans and a gray sweat shirt, for heaven's sake, Maddie realized. She had not approved of her daughter-in-law, but neither had she caused Beth and Gary trouble, so why did the girl seem to go out of her way always to look just a little wrong? Not quite proper . . .

"Beth, I'm so glad to see you! I'm so glad you changed your mind!" They both stopped advancing simultaneously, suddenly awkward with each other.

"Hello, Maddie. You look great! How are you?"

To the considerable surprise of both women, Maddie burst into tears.

Now Beth closed the gap between them and embraced Maddie; she rubbed her back gently, making soothing nonsense sounds. Maddie fought to regain control, aware of eyes watching her in amazement. People often cried at meeting after a long absence, or at parting with a loved one, she told herself. Let them stare. She took a shuddering breath.

Beth had only her carry-on bag and an oversized canvas purse. They left the small terminal. Beth whistled at the sight of the new automobile and Maddie said almost apologetically that Gary had bought it for her for his birthday. She groped for her keys and sighed when Beth pointed to them in the ignition. "He thinks all children should give their parents presents when it's their birthday, the children's birthday, I mean. To say thank you, I suppose. Bruce was furious about it." She blinked back tears. "Oh dear, I didn't realize I was this upset with it all.

Maybe we'd better have a little drink before we go back."

Beth said grimly, "Bruce always was a pain in the ass, even if he is your son. What's going on, Maddie? Why a three-day get-together? What's Gary up to?"

Maddie started to drive jerkily, then jerked even harder when she hit the brake. "A bar, a tavern or something," she said. "We have to talk about it all. Then you can drive. The car hates me."

Maddie drove them to a tavern that also served seafood. The odor of frying fish, rancid oil, and onions was stifling. Beth ordered coffee and listened to Maddie ramble as she gulped bourbon on the rocks. Everyone else was already there, she said. Bruce, her other son, six years older than Gary, the boy genius. Rich, Harry, Laura . . . She did not know what Gary was planning; no one did, but Bruce was trying to organize a palace coup, she said ominously. He would approach Beth, she warned. And he might even have the votes.

Beth listened and tried to rearrange the nearly incoherent information. There were too many bits and pieces, with too much left out. The Bellringer Company, Incorporated, had nine shareholders, but it was Gary's company undisputedly, and he ran it as he saw fit. During the last few years he had been totally preoccupied with creating Smart House, a computerized, automated house that until this weekend no one had seen except those who had worked there.

"I hate it!" Maddie cried. "It knows where you are every minute! It spies on everyone all the time, listens to everything you say, turns the lights on and off, and heats the bathwater and the temperature in the greenhouse. It does everything, and I hate it!"

Beth nodded in sympathy. Bruce had called her months ago, had wanted to meet for lunch, and she had turned him down. She wished now that she had gone. A coup? It did not seem bloody likely, she decided, and tuned Maddie in long enough to know she was still going on about the house. The house must be the rabbit hole where all the money was vanishing, she realized. After Smart House had got underway, the company had stopped showing profits. All the others, except Maddie and now Beth, were also employed by the company, and she had assumed their salaries had been adjusted upward when profits dried up. Now she doubted that such was the case, and it explained Bruce's fury. Enough votes to override Gary? Beth's one share gave her a single vote in whatever came up at the meeting on Monday, hardly worth anyone's while to capture.

She was jolted from her own thoughts suddenly when Maddie put her hand on Beth's and said, "Please promise you won't tell him you want a divorce until after the weekend."

"Who told you I want a divorce?"

Maddie looked about vaguely, as if searching for the informant. "You do, don't you?"

"Has he been spying on me? Have you? Bruce?"

Maddie drained her glass and set it down hard. "Darling, it's not a secret that you aren't living together in any way. And it's not a secret that Gary's a little eccentric. I just want you to wait until after his party, that's all. Don't spoil his birthday party, please."

"Eccentric! Maddie, he's crazy! Your darling boy is a nut!"

Beth drove along a curving road lined with small buildings, shacks, frame houses weathered gray, auto shops, bait stores. . . . Neither spoke now except for the directions Maddie provided from time to time. The ocean was not visible, but its presence was there; the gusty wind off the sea was fresh and cold, bringing news of the East, news of the deeps, of passing ships and whales, shrimps and crabs. The sun made a brightened area in a thick cloud cover, then the woods closed in on the road, and even that timid bright patch was blocked. She turned off this road at Maddie's instructions, onto a much narrower blacktop road with no markings, a private drive without shoulders, just woods that came to the edge of the black surface, that met overhead and turned the early evening into night. Still no sea. The road climbed steeply, became more crooked.

She slowed down more when she saw a sign, Stop Ahead. Around a curve there was a mammoth gate that looked like bronze. She came to a stop. No one was in sight; a high chain-link fence vanished among the trees on each side of the gate. A lighted sign asked her to open her window, and as soon as she did, a crisp male voice said, "Please identify yourself and your passenger."

She looked sharply at Maddie, whose face had become pinched.

"Beth Elringer, Madelaine Elringer," she said, raising her voice slightly.

"Thank you." The gate swung open silently; the lighted sign went off.

"See what I mean?" Maddie whispered.

"I see that Gary's being cute," Beth snapped. "Is this what's bugging Bruce? That Gary's sinking company profits into toys?"

"He's spent millions and millions," Maddie said. "I don't think anyone even knows exactly how much. That's what's bothering Bruce, I suppose, that there's no real accounting. A talking gate! Talking doors! An indoor waterfall!" Her voice rose to a near wail.

Someone knew where the money was going, Beth thought, ignoring her mother-in-law again. Milton Sweetwater was the company attorney; he must know. Or Jake Kluge, a whiz kid in business affairs.

Or, for heaven's sake, Harry Westerman, the accountant. Someone, maybe all of them, knew. If Bruce didn't, it had to be because Gary did not want to tell him. The road started down, still narrow and as winding as before, but now the greenery looked planned, not the wild growth of the other side of the fence. Landscaping on a macrocosmic scale, she mused, that was her boy, her husband, Gary. Masses of rhododendron in bloom formed immense blotches of scarlet, rose, gold, fringed with lacy ferns that were so deeply green they looked black in the darkening shadows. She made another turn, and finally there was the ocean, a couple of hundred feet down, on three sides of this point that jutted out from the mainland like the prow of a ship. She had to drive another quarter mile before she got a glimpse of Smart House. She gasped and stopped the car in order to gaze at it.

Although the building was tall, apparently it had only two stories, with a gleaming dome on top and walls of glass and redwood and metal broken by a continuous balcony at the second-story level. The building appeared to be curved all the way around the front, with a straight clifflike back wall made of stone. The dome did not cover the entire roof area; there were plants up there, a terrace? She drove on. The house was eclipsed by trees and shrubs; she drove past a tennis court, formal gardens that looked imposing, and finally a broad concrete approach to the house. Apparently every room in it had a vista of ocean. Behind the house a cliff rose almost straight up.

At first the house had appeared almost grotesque, then it had looked like a curious hotel, a resort perhaps, and now close up it loomed monstrously, like a madman's vision. A red-tiled verandah curved out of sight as she and Maddie left the car and approached the front entrance.

"Good afternoon," a pleasant female voice greeted them when they walked across the verandah. "Please identify yourselves."

Beth looked for cameras, but they were hidden too well. Maddie stopped before the high entrance door, intricately carved and polished, and said in a meek voice, "Good afternoon. I'm Madelaine Elringer, and this is Beth Elringer. We're expected."

"Yes. Please come in. If you'll leave your bags, we'll have someone collect them." The door swung open.

Maddie glanced at Beth, as if to say, see?

The foyer was thirty feet by thirty feet, with a curving staircase to the left, and a wall full of museum-quality art on the right. The floor was a continuation of the red tile. There were several black pedestals with statuary. Beth kept thinking that at any moment a uniformed guide would appear and start a spiel.

"I can't actually show you around," Maddie said in her new, subdued voice, with a nervous glance over her shoulder. "I'm supposed to show you your room, that's all. Or you'd never find it." Her voice became shriller, and she caught her breath sharply and clutched Beth's arm. "Up these stairs."

Beth held back a bitter comment. Maddie was acting as if Gary had become Attila the Hun. They went up the stairs. "Do you know what he's planning for the weekend?" she asked.

Maddie shook her head. "No one seems to know yet. He'll tell us after dinner. Drinks in the garden at six, dinner at seven."

They reached the top of the stairs and Beth gasped. Across the corridor was another glass wall, and this one looked onto a jungle. She moved closer and saw that the interior of the house contained a mammoth atrium enclosed in a circular glass wall that was as high as the house. Beyond the glass there were trees, and a swimming pool at the end. The space appeared to be a grotto, with entrances at the second level, stairs that looked like natural rock formations leading down, other entrances at the ground floor; there was a clifflike wall of various rocks behind the pool, with a path, and a waterfall that appeared, vanished, then plummeted down to the swimming pool.

"For God's sake," Beth muttered finally.

"It's . . . just grotesque," Maddie said, and tugged her arm. She seemed in a hurry now. "Your room's all the way around on the other side."

There were closed doors on one side of the corridor, the glass wall on the other, and as they moved Beth had always-changing glimpses of the scene below. There were rattan tables and chairs, a bar, and half a dozen people standing, sitting, drinking, talking. That must be the garden, she decided. How like Gary to order no tours, to force them to explore the house without a clue. Okay, she thought grimly, she would go along with that; she would not show any more surprise than she had already shown, just accept whatever the damn house had to offer and find a chance to talk alone with her husband. They stopped before one of the closed doors.

"This is your room," Maddie said. "I can tell you this much: No one but you and the staff can open the door. Watch." She put one hand on a panel with the number two on it, and tried to turn the doorknob with the other hand. The door remained closed. "You try. Don't worry, it already knows who you are and what room you've been assigned. And where you are, and what you're doing . . ." She bit her lip and moved aside, her hands twisting together as if with a life of their own now.

Beth put her hand on the panel and turned the knob; the door opened.

"I'll leave you alone to freshen up. We'll all be in the garden. Come down when you get ready." She fled back through the hallway, apparently toward her own room. Beth watched her only a moment, called out her thanks, and entered the room.

She realized that she was moving as quietly as possible, almost holding her breath, and she knew that no one would want to talk in this house, not really. Was it listening, recording everything? She closed the door hard, but it was virtually soundless anyway, and now she saw that her suitcase had been brought up already, just as the house had said it would be.

She spent several minutes exploring her room and bath. The colors were dusty rose and a pale yellow. Twin beds, a good desk with a computer that was on with no visible way to turn it off, some magazines, books obviously from a used-book store—well read, some pages even dog-eared. She picked up a beautiful rose quartz statuette of a mermaid, carefully replaced it on the table; there were two lamps with bases of the same rose quartz, and a massive, matching ashtray. In spite of herself, she was feeling overwhelmed. Angrily she marched into the bathroom, to see an assortment of soaps and shampoos, a blow dryer, many nozzles in the tub/shower, and a panel of push buttons for water temperature, perfume, and bubble bath mixes, all expensive, selected by someone who had known what to buy. And she had to count pennies every day, she thought with fury.

Her room faced south; the outside wall was glass, with a sliding door to the balcony, ceiling-to-floor drapes. She stood gazing at the ocean for a long time. The sun had come out and was low in the western sky at the edge of the vista her room provided. She was startled by the sound of four soft, melodious, clear bell tones, the audible logo of the Bellringer Company. She turned to see the notes displayed on the computer monitor.

"It's six o'clock, Beth," the pleasant female voice said. "Would you like to bathe before dinner? If you will tell me the temperature you prefer, I'll be happy to draw your bath."

"Can I turn off the audio signal of the computer?" Beth asked in a strained voice.

"Yes, Beth. I'll signal if there is a message for you." A message appeared on the monitor: *The audio signal is now off. Please indicate if you wish any service.*

Without moving, Beth said, "Close the drapes." Soundlessly the heavy drapes drew together, shutting out the ocean view. Beth nodded. Her lips were tight as she began to unpack her suitcase, shook out a long skirt and sweater, and yanked off her jeans. No wonder Maddie looked like that. Actually, Maddie had been showing considerable restraint. Beth showered and dressed and left her room to find her way to the garden.

Laura Westerman waved when Beth drew near the small group clustered by the bar in the garden. Laura was in her thirties and very beautiful. She wore a pale green silk dress that showed her perfect figure at its perfect best. She had chestnut hair, tumbled model fashion, and wore makeup so adroitly applied that few people suspected it was even there.

At Laura's elbow was Jake Kluge, over six feet tall, gangly, with limp, straight brown hair. He was the most powerful man in the company, next to Gary, of course. She wondered if Gary had consulted him about Smart House, if he had approved. It used to be that he was the only person Gary even pretended to listen to. This passed through her mind swiftly as she tried to understand what it was that was so different about Jake. Then it came to her. He used to wear oversized glasses that magnified his pale blue eyes eerily, but now he seemed to have gone to contacts and looked younger than when she had last seen him. She knew he was five or six years older than Gary. He came to meet her with his hands outstretched.

"How are you?" He gripped her hands firmly and examined her face, then kissed her on the forehead.

"I'm fine," she said, wishing he were not quite so earnest all the time, wishing he would not show concern for her, for Gary, for everyone he came across. She pulled loose and looked beyond him at Milton Sweetwater, the handsome lawyer who groomed himself to look like a lawyer, or like Gregory Peck playing the role of a lawyer. She had always felt a great reserve concerning him, never certain what he thought of her, if he actually disapproved. He was too well mannered to let anything except civility show. But then, she thought, he would never mention it if Gary had a limp either. Suddenly she felt as if she were Gary's limp that Milton Sweetwater was too polite to notice. She nodded to him and went to the bar, then hesitated. Automated, damn it, she thought in disgust.

"Let me," Milton said, joining her. "I take it that you feel as uncomfortable as I do talking to a machine."

"You take it just right," she admitted. "Is there wine? If I drink anything harder than that, I might pass out. It's been a long time since breakfast." She glanced around as he opened a refrigerator and brought out a bottle of white wine. "Where's . . . everyone else?"

"Inspecting the marvels of the new age of electronics, I think. In the basement."

He handed her the wine. "It's all something else, isn't it?"

She nodded. The wine was excellent. "Forty-eight degrees, I bet," she said, holding the glass up. "Bet?"

He laughed. "It's good to see you. How long has it been? Four, five years? You look exactly the same. Wonderful."

"You too," she said, and she felt as if something had clicked off, or perhaps on. When she first met him, ten years ago, he had awed her with his impeccable manners, his expensive clothes, an obviously superior education—his elegance, she summed it up now. She had been timid, almost tongue-tied, in his presence because she could not see past the highly civilized facade he presented; she never once had glimpsed the person behind the smile. For the first time she felt at ease with him. Not that she would be able to talk to him, even now, but it no longer mattered. Back in San Francisco he had an elegant wife and two superior teenage children going to superior schools and making superior grades. She wondered what people like that talked about. Laura sauntered to the bar.

"Are there ice cubes, Milton, darling?" Her voice was the caress that Beth remembered. Laura turned to her and smiled. "I heard what he said, and it's true, dear. You do look very nice. I always did like that skirt."

Beth gripped her glass harder and nodded, then looked past Laura at the garden and did not speak. At first glance she had assumed that they had brought in loads of dirt and dumped it to make a hill, but she saw now that all the greenery was in planters arranged in a semicircle on wide stairs that rose to the second floor, where there was a balcony. The illusion of being at the bottom of a hill was magical, and although she had been able to see into the garden, she could not see out. The illusion was that it went on and on. There were banana plants and palm trees and climbing philodendrons with leaves three feet long. There were orchids hanging from trees, growing in baskets, growing on trunks of trees. There were blooming orange trees and lemon trees scenting the air, but overriding all the other fragrances was the smell of the swimming pool, a tinge of chlorine; the air was heavy and humid, junglelike, and always there was the sound of the waterfall splashing into the pool.

Then at the far end of the atrium Gary and Bruce Elringer appeared. Tweedledum and Tweedledee, she thought distantly. The brothers were arguing, their voices loud and carrying, neither listening to the other, neither intelligible because of the other. They both had dark curly hair and blue eyes; Bruce was an inch or so taller than Gary. Both were chubby with legs a little too short for their torsos.

"What a lovely sight," Laura Westerman drawled.

"Shut up," Harry Westerman said.

Beth looked around in surprise; she had not seen Harry enter, but suddenly he was at Laura's side. More startling to Beth was the expression that crossed Laura's face; she became rigid, and even looked afraid for a moment before her customary mask reappeared. Beth looked from her to her husband. Harry Westerman was hard all over, wiry gray hair, wiry hard body, hard black eyes. He was not a large man—both Jake Kluge and Milton were taller and broader—but Harry gave the impression of great strength. He looked like a pole vaulter in the instant before a leap; he had that kind of tension about him, a furious energy that was being consciously suppressed. It was said of him that he never saw a mountain he didn't covet and eventually climb. If he saw Beth, he did not acknowledge her in any way, but kept his gaze on the approaching brothers, watching them with a remote, unreadable look.

Beth turned to watch them also; their voices were

still raised in argument. She could make out some of the words, but before they made sense—going over budget, going broke, going for broke, whatever—Gary spotted her and abruptly cut off what he had been saying. He hurried to her and seized her arms, shook her.

"It's about time you came back," he said. "You know I want your input. My wife belongs at home."

2

IF it had not been for Laura Westerman, Beth might have hit him, but she knew it would vastly amuse Laura. She gritted her teeth and yanked away, spilling her wine on him in the process. He wiped at it halfheartedly and turned to Laura.

"Come up with any ideas about the campaign yet?"

"Gary, darling, you put it in my lap two hours ago! Come on!"

"Okay, okay. But, listen: Alice in Wonderland, how about that? A ballet dancer exploring Wonderland, Smart House." He took Laura's hand and pulled her toward a table, at the same time drawing a notebook from his pocket. "Greatest character in English lit exploring the greatest house ever built . . ."

Beth realized that Milton was taking her wineglass from her hand, and she breathed deeply. She was shaking. The others drifted in, chatting or talking with intense concentration, or maintaining a sullen silence, and she paid hardly any attention. She sipped wine, grateful to Milton, and decided to leave the next day. It had been stupid to come in the first place, to have expected any changes in Gary. She would get a lawyer to handle the entire matter, including a divorce, she thought with surprise. Actually she had not come around to that decision until just now, but having arrived at it, she knew it was part of her reason for being here this weekend.

At dinner she was seated with Alexander Randall on one side and Jake Kluge on the other. Alexander was twenty-seven, painfully shy, painfully thin, so adolescent in every way that it was an ordeal to have to spend any time at all with him. His fingernails were bitten off, his fingers red and sore. He was terrified of women. When the talk wound back to computers, as it did repeatedly, he became statue-still listening, then withdrew again when any other subject was raised. He ate with furious energy, barely glancing away from the food before him. Jake Kluge appeared to be preoccupied, either in deep thought or else totally absorbed in the conversation at the far end of the table, where Gary was going on about his plans for advertising Smart House. TV, of course, national magazines, tours. Jake's gaze was on Gary, but Beth didn't really believe he was listening any more than she was. She felt almost a malicious satisfaction seeing Laura squirm as Gary demolished her one reason for being in the company at all. If he took on advertising, along with every other phase of company business that he had already assumed, Laura would be as valuable an asset to the company as Maddie was. And that was zilch.

Beth paid no attention to the food, or the two middle-aged people who served it—husband and wife presumably, Mexicans maybe. She was vaguely aware that the food was good, the service excellent. She was thinking: They would finish dinner by nine; she would follow Gary and speak to him about her share of stock, if he would listen. If he would not listen, she would still follow him out, wish him a happy birthday, and tell him she was leaving first thing in the morning. He would have a tantrum, and

Maddie would cry again, but she no longer cared. Coming here had been a mistake, staying would be a bigger mistake; she knew with certainty that if he manhandled her ever again, she would hit him. Clobber him, she amended.

Across the table from her Bruce suddenly threw down his spoon. "What the fuck makes you think you'll have another million or two for advertising, you asshole?" he yelled at Gary.

Maddie cried, "Bruce, behave yourself!"

Milton said coldly, "This is hardly the time or place for a scene."

Others said other things, but at the end of the table Gary laughed. His laughter always had been too loud, a braying, animal-like noise. Beth flinched at the familiar sound. "We can pour our own coffee," he said to the man servant. "Take it and cups and stuff to the living room and then you and Juanita beat it as soon as you clean up here." He stood up and walked out.

The rest of them began pushing chairs back, and in an awkward silence they trailed out after Gary.

The room they entered was as big as a hotel lobby; and like every other room so far, beautifully decorated. In here the colors were a deep rich maroon and pale blue with gold accents. There were several groupings of couches and comfortable chairs and low tables. Gary was already in an armchair before the window wall. The woman servant was arranging a tray with coffee and cups and the man was busy with another tray with pastries. They finished and left soundlessly before the shareholders were all settled. Maddie stationed herself at the coffee service and started to pour, a nervous, if very proper, hostess.

"By Monday, I'll have the votes," Bruce said. He sounded less angry now, more in control, but his eyes were cold and fierce. He accepted coffee and sat down with it.

Gary smiled. One by one they all were served by Maddie, and seated themselves on the twin couches, the various chairs that made up a semicircle before the window wall. The sun had set, the sky was now deep violet; the sea a leaden gray with white-capped waves rolling in. Crashing, Beth thought, but the house admitted no sound from outside.

"By Monday," Gary said as soon as they were all seated, "you'll have seen Smart House in operation. It won't matter who has how many votes by then. And, in fact," he went on, regarding them all with the smile that seemed too amused, too superior, as if he were looking at idiots at play, "to show you how sure I am of your confidence on Monday, I have planned a little entertainment for this weekend." No one moved. "A game," he said, "called Assassin."

Maddie clattered a spoon on the table; it was the only sound. Gary laughed and put his cup down. "The rules are very simple. I'll state them briefly, and if you want to study them, they're on the computer in your room. The idea of the game is to kill off a designated victim in front of a single witness, record your kill with the computer, and get a new victim. Each player starts with one vote that his killer will gain. If a victim already has collected other votes, his killer gets them too."

"You're crazy," Bruce said harshly.

"It's just a game," Gary said with a shrug. "A way to force everyone to experience Smart House. As I said before, by Monday I don't think it will make any difference who does or doesn't have the votes. You'll all see Smart House my way by then, but someone could pick up a few extra votes and swing things his way on Monday. Of course, if you don't dare risk anything, you don't have to play."

But he did have to play, Beth thought, chilled through and through. They all had to play. When

Gary said eat, they ate; when he said walk, they walked. Now he had said play, and they would all play.

"Gary, this is ridiculous," Maddie said nervously. "Grown-up people don't play such childish games. This is a game for children. I read about it. Teen-agers play it."

He looked sullen. "Kids play a lot of things that work for grown-ups. I never had a chance to try most of their games, remember. I want to catch up. One vote each. The weapons will be in the showroom downstairs. You can only have one weapon at a time, and you have to register it with the computer or your kill won't count. The computer will keep score, and its decisions are final."

"What weapons?" Milton Sweetwater demanded.

"Squirt guns, poison darts, poison capsules, poison gas balloons, things like that. Key in *Weapons* on your computer. It'll show you what's available. They all are down in the showroom in a case with a com-puter lock. After you use a weapon you can't use it again, even if you don't make a killing with it the first time. You have to turn it in and get a different one. And you can't tell anyone anything, not who your vic-tim is, or what weapon you have, or if you've been killed yet. Nothing!"

Maddie was shaking her head. She stood up. "No, Gary. I won't have anything to do with this."

"Then your vote can go to Laura. She's the only one with nothing to lose." He looked at his watch. "The game starts now and will end Sunday night at ten. You all know already that no one can enter your rooms except you. Those are safe places, the only perfectly safe places unless you invite your killer in. Remember, you need one witness—anyone, dead or alive, playing the game can witness, but no more than one. And as soon as you make a killing, you and the victim and the witness have to report in to the computer. It will instruct you further."

He stood up and looked them over. No one voiced an objection. Abruptly he laughed his insane laughter, too unexpected, too loud, then cut off so totally that it was as if it were controlled by an on/off toggle, not an emotion. He walked from the room.

"He's really crazy," Bruce said in an intense, low voice. "I mean certifiable!"

Milton Sweetwater turned to Alexander Randall. "Is this what he's been up to? Programming a damn game?"

Alexander fidgeted. "I didn't know anything about it until right now. He was afraid that no one would really give Smart House a chance. I guess it's like he said; if you play the game, you'll know what it can do."

"You already know, you little jerk," Harry Westerman snapped. He glared at Alexander, then at Rich Schoen. "And you. What do you know about all this?"

Rich Schoen was the architect. He and Alexander and Gary had lived in the house for months, had worked on it together from the beginning. Beth had met Rich only one other time, and he had been distant, abstracted then. He seemed just as distant and abstracted now. He was a heavily built man, thick through the chest, with large hands, big wrist bones, an especially large head that was nearly bald. His wife and daughter had been killed in an accident a few years before he went to work for Gary on the house. Very calmly he regarded Harry and said, "I never heard of this game before tonight. You don't like it, don't play."

Watching him, Beth thought, that was what he would do if he didn't want to play. He would say no. He had nothing more to lose. What she had regarded as abstraction and distance had been the veneer over emptiness. Gary had told her that for Rich there was nothing on earth except work, and God help anyone who got between him and his work. She watched silently as he stood up and left the room without a backward glance.

"He's going to look up weapons and get one," Laura said, and stood up. "And so am I." She left the room also.

With some embarrassment, some hesitation, the others began to get up, to mill about, and gradually to leave the spacious room.

In her pink and yellow room again, Beth paced for a long time. Was Gary really crazy? At length she had to conclude that she did not believe that. She suspected that he had told the exact truth: He had not had time to play as a child, then as a teenager, and he wanted to catch up. What did he mean *experience* Smart House? She glanced at the computer monitor and was not at all surprised to see a menu displayed. *Rules, Weapons, Victims, To register a point, Layout of Smart House, Kitchen.* She sat down and selected the first item on the menu and read through the rules of the game. Gary had stated them succinctly, without any obvious omissions or additions, as far as she could tell. Next she examined the weapons, each one displayed on the screen, with a brief text about its use. *Water gun. Range of four feet. Will not fire through glass or through any solid material such as a door or wall.* There was a section of plastic rope. She read: *Electrical line, assumed to be plugged into a power source. May be used any way that a real electrical line could be used.* There was a self-sticking dagger made out of soft plastic. Three "poison" capsules, quarter-sized discs the color of chocolate. A ribbon with Velcro on both ends—a garrote. It had to be secured to the victim's neck, the Velcro fastened, to count. An open-weave net bag to be used as if it were plastic film. She went down the entire assortment of weapons, and then selected the house layout. When the basement level was displayed, she asked if there was a printout. She typed the question.

In the top desk drawer there is a printout, the computer responded on screen.

What else was it programmed to serve up? she wondered, but did not pursue the question. She took the printout and spread it on the desk to study. Beautifully executed house plans. Rich's work? Probably. There was an elevator, and two flights of stairs, front and back, to all levels, and there was a terrace surrounding the dome on the roof; it could be reached by elevator or stairs.

After looking over the house plans, she reluctantly returned to the menu and selected *Victims.* The computer displayed: *Your first victim is Rich Schoen. Good luck.* The message vanished and she was back in the menu again. She bit her lip. One of the others had just done that, she thought, and her name had come up. One of them would be selecting a weapon, making plans. She blinked when the computer flashed a new message. *Would you like to see the weapons displayed again?*

"No," she snapped. "Do you know where Gary is?"

Yes, Beth.

"Where?"

I'm sorry. I am not allowed to give out that information.

"Fuck you," she muttered, and turned toward the door, belatedly realizing that she had been talking with the damn machine, not going through the keyboard. Okay, she thought, so Gary had a genius computer on the job, one that understood spoken language that had not been programmed in. She realized this was one of the things he wanted them to experience for themselves. What else?

She opened her door and started to leave her room, just in time to see someone on the far side of the curving corridor duck back inside a room. She had not been able to identify the person. Unexpectedly she felt a jolt in her stomach—fear, anxiety, nerves, something. "For God's sake," she muttered, "it's just a game!" But in that moment she knew that others might be playing the game seriously, with every intention of winning, of garnering points in order to sway decisions at the business meeting on Monday. For the first time since the founding of the company, her one vote was important to someone, important enough to "kill" for. For the first time she was perceived as a menace to someone else. She felt a giggle start to rise, and drew in a deep breath. Damn Gary, she thought again, as she had so many times over the years. Damn him.

She wandered for a while but did not find Gary. She tried the elevator, looked at the terrace on the roof, glanced into the kitchen, and finally she found the basement showroom with the case of weapons on display. Silly water guns shaped like dragons, a pea shooter and pellets, the "poison" discs. . . . Each weapon was in a section that obviously was under observation by the computer, otherwise how could the computer keep up with who took what? She could not locate cameras. She turned away from the display case and looked over the rest of the room. Here were all the Bellringer computers, from the first one—it now looked tacky, more like a toy than a working machine—to the most recent one, which cost over a hundred thousand dollars and looked it. Each system was set up on a flawless acrylic pedestal. Hanging on the walls were pictures of silicon chips magnified, blown up to four by six feet; they were very beautiful.

"Impressive, isn't it?"

She whirled to see Harry and Laura Westerman at the doorway. Neither was carrying a visible weapon. Then she saw Alexander behind them and released the breath she had drawn in. One witness only, she remembered. They would be safe in groups of four or more.

Laura laughed. "We decided to roam in packs. It's like finding a fourth for bridge. Have you picked your weapon?"

Beth shrugged. "Maybe. Have you?"

Alexander shuffled his feet and looked from Laura to Beth to Harry Westerman. "There's four of us now, so let's get the weapons and then I'm taking off. Things I want to get done tonight."

Beth stared at him, then at Laura and Harry. They were all going along with it! Helplessly she nodded, and she and Alexander moved to the door where they stood facing the basement playroom. The central portion of the basement had been given over to Ping-Pong, pool tables, electronic games, hockey, pinball machines. . . . Gary really was making up for a lost childhood, she thought bitterly. No one was in sight among the many amusements. Behind her she could hear Laura tell Harry to turn his back, not to peek; then the computer voice said, "Thank you, Laura. Your weapon is registered." The process was repeated with Harry. She and Alexander moved inside the room once more when the other two were finished.

Alexander waved her ahead and turned his back when she approached the display case. She could not tell what was missing. There had been multiples of everything she had noticed before; there still were. Since she had not made a selection on the computer in her room, she was not even certain she would be allowed to take anything now. After a moment's hesitation she lifted the lid of the display case and picked up one of the balloons. The voice thanked her by name, as it had done all the others. When she closed the lid, she tried to lift it again; it did not budge. Okay, she thought. She stuffed the balloon in her skirt pocket.

"Your turn," she muttered to Alexander. He was fidgeting with impatience.

"Later," he said. "I'll pick out something later. Look, I really have work to do . . ."

Laura laughed her throaty laughter again. "Hold it a second, will you? Give us a minute to get out of here. I want the dessert we missed before. Coming, Harry?"

Two were safe, Beth thought distantly, or four, but not three. She stood with Alexander until Laura and Harry had vanished, and then Alexander was galvanized and nearly sprinted across the game room, to disappear in a corridor on the far side. Slowly Beth made her way to the stairs and the first floor again. The balloon felt like lead in her pocket.

On the first floor a cluster of people had gathered in the hall near the kitchen door. As Beth drew near, Milton nodded to her, and Maddie said she had taken the tray of cakes to the kitchen. She was carrying a glass of ice cubes. She waved vaguely when Laura invited her to join them. "Watching a movie," she said. "Good movie." She wandered into the atrium, leaving the door open after her. The smell of chlorine drifted into the corridor. With a scowl Laura pulled the sliding glass door shut again. She looked at Milton and Beth and held up four fingers. Harry looked disgusted and entered the kitchen ahead of them.

The kitchen had a fifteen-foot oak worktable, a

double-doored refrigerator, a walk-in freezer, the biggest microwave Beth had ever seen, and on and on. Wearily she stopped examining it all and turned to the table for a cookie. Laura demonstrated a cleaning robot that detached itself from the wall to wipe up milk she had deliberately spilled. Milton watched her intently, nodding now and then; Harry ignored her and went to the refrigerator for ice cubes. Self-cleaning windows throughout, Laura said, munching a cookie. You want coffee? Press a button. Milk? Another button. Harry poured himself a drink from a decanter on a sideboard.

"I'm taking this up to our room," he said.

Laura jumped up. "You know I won't stay here with two others," she said. Then she laughed. No one laughed with her.

"A whole damn weekend of this," Beth muttered, watching them leave. "I wish I could find Gary. I have to talk with him."

"He could be anywhere," Milton said with a slight shrug. "Swimming, in the Jacuzzi, working, sleeping, watching the movie with Maddie, killing someone, getting killed. He thinks you're here to demand a divorce, you know. He asked me if there's any way he can prevent it."

Beth drew in a deep breath. "What did you tell him?"

"That it's not my field. But you should have an attorney represent you, Beth. Don't take him on alone." He went to the door. "See you tomorrow. Goodnight."

Beth finished her milk, thinking about Milton and the disquieting feeling that he was not at all concerned about her, but that he simply did not want a scene this weekend when he was part of the captive audience. Nothing had changed, she thought wearily; they were all still afraid of Gary and his tantrums. She put the glass in the dishwasher. Gary was still up, she knew. He never went to bed until two or even three in the morning. He never got up until after noon and was barely human until 2 P.M.; if she did not talk to him that night, she would not see him until late in the day tomorrow. She felt tired enough to fall asleep standing up. Five minutes, she told herself. If she didn't find him in five minutes, she would give up and go on to bed. But if she found him, they would have it out. She smiled grimly; she and Rich, she thought, the only two with nothing to lose.

She left the kitchen and headed for the television room. Before she reached it, she heard Maddie's voice raised angrily.

"I told you to count me out! I meant it! Leave me alone!"

Beth stopped at the door to look inside. The room was lighted by an oversized screen where Ginger Rogers and Fred Astaire were dancing; the sound was off.

"You saw it! I got him and you know it!" Gary yelled. Bruce shoved him out of the way and stamped to the door; Beth moved aside. He continued, with Gary at his heels. "You son of a bitch! Don't you walk away from me! I got you!"

"Gary!" his mother wailed.

"You got nothing, you asshole!" Bruce's voice rose to a screech.

Beth clamped her hands over her ears, turned, and fled to her room. By the time she got inside it with the door closed she was shaking, not with fear, but with a rage she hadn't known she was capable of.

3

Beth could not sleep until she draped a towel over the computer monitor, and even then she fantasized that she heard footsteps for a long time, first on the balcony, then in the corridor, in the room next to hers. She knew all this was due to an imagination working overtime, but she strained to hear again and again. When she woke up shortly after seven, she was headachey and sore. She emerged from the shower to hear the four notes of the Bellringer Company, and snatched the towel away from the monitor. There was a message: *Good morning, Beth. Breakfast will be served in your room in a few moments. The highlighted items have been chosen for you. If you would like to make changes, please select from the menu.*

She was looking over the menu when the drapes opened behind her; she whirled around. It was a sunny morning, with a bank of fog or low clouds out to sea. Closer, the ocean was brilliantly blue and appeared calm. "What's the forecast for today?" she asked aloud.

Do you want me to use the audio mode today, Beth?

"No." Just testing, she thought, and turned to look

at the monitor. It was showing the forecast—sunny with late-afternoon clouds, high sixty-eight, low forty-five, wind out of the northwest at ten miles an hour, gusting to twenty. She turned back to the window; when she glanced at the screen again, it was cleared. Watching, she thought. It was watching, recording every motion. She decided to eat and get out, and stay until afternoon.

It was after one when she returned to Smart House. Her face was windburned, and she was ravenous. She washed and followed the sounds of voices to the dining room where a buffet was laid for lunch: salads, sliced meats and cheeses, a chafing dish with something steaming. . . . Rich Schoen and Alexander Randall were at the table eating, Jake Kluge was serving himself. Everyone looked up when Beth entered; there was a momentary lapse in the talk; then Rich shook his head and speared a bit of ham on his plate.

"Not a good weekend for ulcers," he said. A large roll of blueprints was on the table; he moved it closer to him as if to make room for someone else.

"Sorry," Beth muttered, joining Jake at the buffet. She was instantly aware of his size again; she tended to forget it when he was seated, or standing across a room. He was over six feet, broad through the shoulders, with a deep chest, but he didn't use his size as a weapon, she realized suddenly. That made the difference. She felt a little confusion about what it meant to think that, and couldn't sort it out at the moment, but it was important, she knew. God, what if Gary had size like that to go along with his ego? The thought alone was enough to bring a shudder.

Jake grinned at her, made room, and then looked over his shoulder at Rich and resumed speaking. "At least four modes, so far. It's pretty damn impressive.

Security. Housekeeping. Maintenance. Plants? Sure, why not? Automatic watering, fertilizing, creating a dozen different microclimates. Rich, Alexander, my God! Hat's off!"

Rich was grinning widely and Alexander was twitching with embarrassment and pleasure. Jake could do that to people, Beth thought. He was lavish with praise and apparently did not have a trace of jealousy concerning the accomplishments of others. She had watched the end of a chess game between him and Gary once. Gary had won, and crowed over his victory until it had been ugly, but Jake had reconstructed the last ten moves to show her the beauty of the final trap. Naturally he would go along with the insane game and find it exciting and fun, just like Gary, but she realized, watching him, his exhilaration now was over Smart House. Again she was struck by how much younger he appeared with contacts than with the thick glasses she had become used to. That change and his excited animation made her feel almost as if he had become a stranger, no longer the avuncular guest who never quite saw her. His excitement and pleasure enveloped Alexander and Rich now, and she felt out of place, unable to share it with them.

They were all experiencing Smart House, in their own peculiar ways, just as she was, Beth realized, making a sandwich, listening but paying little attention to the words.

"So," Jake was going on, as he joined the other two men at the table, "you have to have both boards in tandem. The good old BOS and the new arsenoid celsium, and that costs a mint, but my God, it's worth every million!" His laughter was genuine, unaffected. Rich chuckled in a low rumble.

Beth finished assembling her own lunch and left them talking. At the door she glanced back, trying to tell by looking if any of them had been killed yet. Not Rich, she knew. She had his name, and upstairs in her skirt pocket she had a murder weapon, a balloon.

For a moment she stood uncertainly in the corridor, then went into the atrium to eat. It was peaceful there, and coffee was available at the bar. She took her lunch to a small table off to one side.

Now she could appreciate the glass dome on top of the building. It allowed the sunlight to enter and light up the stone wall behind the pool. The stones were varied, some gray, some black, obsidian she guessed, a pink that might have been sandstone. . . . Mosses and lichen grew on the rocks, and the waterfall trickled, vanished, reappeared to make the plunge into the pool. She finished eating and stretched out on the chaise, watching the shifting light at the far side of the atrium.

She had slept, she realized, and felt disoriented, unsure where she was. Then she heard a man's deep chuckle and a curse. Gary's curse.

"I think your computer called this a blunt instrument. You're dead. Harry? Witness?" It was Rich speaking.

"Sure thing," Harry said. "We can use the computer at the bar."

They moved into her line of sight. Gary was scowling. One by one they keyed in something on the computer; it thanked them by name.

"Now, off to collect a new victim, new weapon. Fun game, Gary. See you guys."

Rich sauntered toward the rear door. Harry followed after a moment, and Gary began to move in Beth's direction. He stopped when he saw her.

"I want to talk to you," she said, joining him near the bar.

"Next week."

"Now, Gary. Let's sit down a minute and talk. You're out of the game."

He shook his head. "The only thing that matters is that you came home again. I knew you would. They'll all be gone again by Monday evening. We'll have all the time you want then."

"I'll be gone, too, Gary. I'm not staying. We have to talk!"

"Not now!" he yelled shrilly. "Why do you do this to me? You won't be gone, damn you! Haven't you looked around Smart House? Don't you understand what I've done here, you idiot? I'm putting you to work. Everyone's going to be working from now on. No more free lunches for you or anyone else. Monday!" He wheeled and left.

She leaned against the bar weakly. Her hands were clenched, her entire body felt clenched. Suddenly something was wrapped around her throat and she clutched at it reflexively.

"Sorry, Beth. I'm afraid you're dead."

Her heart was crushing thunder in her chest; her knees were giving. If she had not been supported by the bar, she would have fallen. The thing at her throat was taken away again, and she turned to see Jake Kluge looking at her anxiously. He held up a ribbon with Velcro at both ends. "Garrote," he said. "Harry?"

"You got her," Harry said in a voice charged with irritation and even anger.

Beth had not heard them enter. She felt her neck, then nodded. "My God," she whispered, "this is an insane game!"

Jake nodded, at first glance apparently as upset and unhappy with the game as she was, but then she realized that his face was too rigidly set and that behind his show of concern, he was laughing. He was having fun with the crazy game. She looked at Harry; at least his anger and impatience were visible and honest. For the first time since she had met him, she felt more allied with him than with any of the others in the company. Jake moved around her to the other side of the bar and keyed in information to the computer. When he motioned to her, she went to the keyboard silently and confirmed that he had strangled her with the garrote. Harry confirmed the kill. The computer thanked them all in the nice low female voice. It congratulated Jake and told Beth it was sorry she had become a victim. All of them by name.

She read in her room until she was too restless to sit still. She had explored the entire house and had no wish to meet any of the others, and she felt too wind-scoured to go down to the beach again. Finally she left by way of the balcony and made her way to the greenhouse. When she entered, Jake and Gary scurried out the other end.

The greenhouse was forty by sixty feet with rows and rows of vegetables, strawberries and melons, ornamentals. There were glass-walled rooms within the structure that simply baffled her. Little greenhouses inside a big greenhouse? Why not? No one else was there now. Slowly she wandered up and down the aisles. Summer fruits, ripening tomatoes, cucumbers. A room without a season, controlled in every way. She spotted a misty area and went to investigate. Watercress in a tray of circulating water.

Dinner was a dismal affair that night. Everyone was edgy, even the dead ones, Beth realized. Gary snapped at Maddie and Bruce, and Harry told Laura to shut up when she laughed and started to say something. Gary glowered at Beth. Bruce muttered to Jake and Rich and ignored everyone else. Milton looked pained, as if there were at least a million other places he would rather be; he said nothing and ate little. Maddie was drinking steadily. Even Laura became subdued and her stunning beauty suddenly seemed painted on, and not a very good paint job at that. She would look old suddenly, Beth thought, studying her. The lines would start, the flesh sag, and it would happen all at once. She was that type. Beth poked her food around on the plate with no interest and was relieved when Gary jumped up and left the dining room abruptly. No one else lingered after that.

"Some of us are watching movies," Maddie announced. "We'll have coffee in the television room."

"What movie?" Laura asked.

"Who cares?" Maddie said with a shrug. She took her glass out with her when she left.

And that was right, Beth knew. No one cared. If they could get through this evening, all day tomorrow, it would be over. Anything on the screen would serve.

The problem was that no one could sit quietly and watch a movie, no matter what it was, she thought a while later. They had argued at first about *The Yellow Submarine* or *Topper*. They would watch both, they decided, but then people kept getting up and going to the bar at the end of the room, or leaving altogether and returning. One of the times it was Laura who left her chair, and Beth heard her stifle a scream, then laugh too shrilly. Killed, she thought. Another victim bites the dust. She did not turn to see anything going on behind her. Maddie left and came back. Rich drifted in, then drifted out. Beth went to her room and paced a few minutes. When restlessness drove her out again, she saw Jake closing his own door, and she hesitated a moment. He appeared as self-conscious as she felt, and apparently had as little to say as he caught up with her and they went down the stairs side by side in an awkward silence. She was relieved when they parted in the wide corridor and she returned to the television room. Bruce muttered something that she did not catch, and she looked away from him, closed her eyes. A moment later she heard Gary's laughter and a vacuumlike silence when he stopped. There was the odor of chlorine and popcorn, she thought without wonder. Why not? Press a button, *voilà* popcorn! She wandered to the kitchen for no real reason and got a drink of water that she did not want.

When the Beatles came on singing, Maddie left again. "Save my chair," she said in a loud voice. "I'll be back, just not soon. Maybe they'll get that out of their system. I didn't know it was cartoons!"

Maddie heard Laura say something unintelligible as she walked out, no doubt something snide or crude. She was tired, tired of them all, of the silly game, of Gary's tantrums and Bruce's sulks. Just tired, she thought. Getting old maybe. Used to be able to stay up as long as anyone, drink as much as anyone, joke, laugh, tease. But this was a hellish weekend and she was plain tired. She waited for the elevator. Lie down a little while, rest. Too early to actually go to bed, but rest a little, that would be nice. The door slid open silently, and she started to enter the elevator, then stopped.

"For heaven's sake!" she muttered. That damn game! That goddamn game! Rich Schoen was lying on the floor, taking it too far, too damn far. "Rich, get up. Stop that." Then she knew. She took a halting step backward, another, and she screamed again and again and again.

Things happened, too many for Beth to track. He couldn't be dead, she wanted to explain to anyone who would listen. That thing on his head was an open weave net bag; it couldn't hurt him, not really. Milton told them all to go to the living room and stay

and no one argued with him, and that would make
Gary furious, she thought. He couldn't bear for anyone else to give orders. That was his prerogative, no
one else's. Bruce took Maddie to her room because
Maddie would not stop yelling, and that was silly. It
was a game, Beth thought at her, just a game. Rich
was playing the game. Then someone was shaking
her slightly and she focused her eyes to see Jake.

"Hold on, kid," he said. "Just hold on. Okay?"

She nodded, and she was okay suddenly. His face
was ridged, with hard lines down both sides of his
cheeks, like a wood carving, she thought, as if he had
put on a mask. "Is there something we should do?"
she asked then. "Call the police? An ambulance?
Where is everyone else?"

"Milton's trying to find everyone now. He called
the sheriff's office already. Can you help me get
some coffee? I'm afraid we're in for a long night."

She nodded. Laura was on one of the couches looking like a zombie. Bruce was there, and Harry.

"We're going to get coffee," Jake said to them.
"Milton wants everyone to wait here. We'll bring it
back when it's ready."

Milton Sweetwater was the company attorney,
Beth thought distantly. Perry Mason taking charge.
She followed Jake from the room. They had barely
got started searching for the coffee when Milton appeared at the kitchen door and asked them to come
back to the living room.

"We can't find Gary," he said. He was pale and so
somber it was like another mask. They all had masks,
Beth thought almost wildly. Milton turned to Alexander and said, "Get on that computer and unlock his
door."

Alexander Randall was biting his fingernails as he
faced Milton. "He'll kill me if I unlock his door," he
protested.

"And I'll kill you if you don't."

Alexander looked at the others beseechingly, then seated himself at the computer terminal in the living room and started to key in something. He stopped and looked up at Milton. "There's a better way, through security. At least I can find out if he went to his room."

They all watched the screen as Alexander typed in instructions. No one moved. Finally Milton said, "In the Jacuzzi."

They started out together and, without volition on her part, Beth followed. They went around the atrium, to a narrow hallway backed by obsidian, through another short hall to a closed door. It opened at a touch. The insulating cover was over the Jacuzzi pool. The room was hot, the air foul with chlorine, dense with steam, more like a steam bath than a Jacuzzi room. For a moment no one moved, then Milton found a control panel on the wall and studied it for a moment; he pushed a button. The cover of the pool slid open, releasing clouds of steam, and there in the water, face down, was the fully clothed body of Gary Elringer.

4

CHARLIE Meiklejohn brooded about the weather. The end of August, two more weeks of hell before they could expect real relief. And what the devil caused the haze that hung between the trees and followed the contours of the hill out back like a London fog? Not rain. The grass was browning nicely and he'd be damned if he would water it. There was too much. Constance watered a patch surrounding the terrace behind the house, but that was because it bordered her flowers, and no drought would be allowed to detract from the riot of colors. They had a green backdrop, and then the grass turned brown. So much the better. It might not need mowing again this season, and if there was anything Charlie disliked more than shoveling snow, it was mowing grass. You water it, and fertilize it, and then you cut it down, he thought, and shook his head. Dumb.

"Dead cat," Constance murmured, joining him on the back terrace, shaded by purple clematis and wisteria. She pointed to Brutus, on his back under the lilac bush, his head twisted to one side, his feet splayed out in what looked like a joint-breaking position.

"We should put in air conditioning," Charlie said in

a grumbling way. It wasn't fair, he thought aggrievedly; Constance always looked cool. She was ivory pale and never looked flushed, never tanned very dark, and always seemed to have the right sort of thing to put on for whatever weather they were having. Now she wore a loose cottony dress that touched her at the shoulders and nowhere else and was exactly the color of her eyes, light blue, cool blue. She was slender, with long legs the color of honey, just enough color to be interesting. Charlie was dark, with unruly black hair speckled with gray, and he was thickly built, heavy in the chest, thick arms and legs. He was very muscular, but he knew he could lose ten, fifteen pounds and maybe take the heat better for it. Thin people didn't know what it was to suffer from the heat, he decided, and it wasn't fair.

Constance smiled and sat down in a chaise longue. She did not say, "Yes, dear," about the air conditioning, but her look said it almost as clearly as words. They had talked about it last summer, and the summer before that. They had talked about it years ago when they bought this place in upstate New York, while they were still living in New York City and could only make it up here on weekends and holidays. And they would talk about it next summer, she knew. Her smile was contented. They had a window unit in the bedroom, and a fan that they moved from living room to kitchen to dining room. Always before when they talked about it, when they had reached the point of actually doing something about it, a cold front had come through bringing cooling rains, or autumn had come along, or they had had to leave for something or other.

"Those poor bastards," Charlie sighed, and she knew he was thinking of people in the city.

"Rather be here," she said.

If it had not been so hot, he would have turned to give her one of his looks, but he didn't bother. That's what came of living together so long, he thought. They could speak in code by now, speak by number, and have perfect understanding. Sometimes he missed the city. He had lived there all his life until retiring after twenty-five years of service, first with the fire department, later as a city police detective. Constance had taught psychology at Columbia for most of those years. On days like this they used to meet after work, both of them exhausted and wan, and plan for the time when they could chuck it all, move to the country where it was cool and fresh. Hah! But he knew what it was like in the city now. His memory of Manhattan during an August heat wave was clear in his mind—hot buildings, hot pavement, hot metal smells, hot tempers. God, those tenements! He stirred restlessly, willing the memories away. He did not miss New York in August.

"After what's-his-name leaves, let's go to Spirelli's and eat."

"Maybe we should talk out here," she said. "It's better than inside."

He nodded. "Probably won't take long. Look." He pointed. Another cat, Ashcan, had spotted Brutus playing dead and was sneaking up on him. Brutus would slaughter him, Charlie thought. But Brutus opened his yellow eyes when Ashcan got close, glared at the meeker gray cat, and closed his eyes again. Ashcan began to clean his tail.

"Have you read through all that stuff he sent?"

"There's not that much. A computerized house went bananas and killed a couple of people. Case closed. Evidently the house is guilty as hell."

And Milton Sweetwater had asked for an appointment to discuss it, she thought, and almost felt sorry for Mr. Sweetwater, although he was a stranger.

Where computers were concerned, Charlie was a hanging judge; sentence first, questions later, if ever. For two weeks Charlie had been doing battle with the telephone company over an error in their billing. "Let me talk to a person!" he had yelled into the telephone finally. Then he had banged down the phone and turned a stricken face to her.

"What happened?"

"It was a computer pretending to be a person," he said in a near whisper. "By God, it was passing itself off as human!"

Milton Sweetwater did not hesitate a second about taking off his jacket. He handed it to Constance with gratitude, followed her to the terrace, and shook hands with Charlie in the ritualistic manner of men, eyeing each other carefully. He accepted a beer and sat down. Very handsome, she thought. Movie star looks, like Gregory Peck. And he was obviously studying both her and Charlie as much as she was studying him. Charlie, she also thought, was not being helpful.

"Hot day for driving," Charlie said; Milton Sweetwater agreed, and now there was silence.

Abruptly Milton Sweetwater laughed and leaned back in his chair, obviously relaxing. Until that moment Constance had not realized that he had been tense.

"I got your names from Ralph Wedekind," he said and drank his beer thirstily. His glass was covered with condensation, so heavy that it dripped like a shower when he moved it. "Actually I have three names. I already talked to someone else and didn't like him. You're the second. If you turn us down, there's another man in New York that I'll talk to. I was ready to reject you for making me drive out to your place, instead of your coming in to the city, but after a couple days in New York, I'd be the first to admit you'd be crazy to live there. And the last thing we need at Smart House is a crazy detective."

"Why a New York detective?" Charlie asked lazily.

"We don't care where our person is from, as long as he's good, with good references. Wedekind gave you his highest recommendation. So I'm here."

"Did the computer kill those two men?" Charlie asked, but without any real interest.

"Of course not. But the shareholders are in a bind. We've had three meetings so far and no one knows exactly where to go next, what to do next. The company's in a tailspin financially and the management is in a tailspin psychologically. Beth Elringer is crying murder, and her brother-in-law is screaming for action. It's a real mess."

Charlie sighed and poured himself more beer. "I read the news stories you sent. What else is there to know? Were the stories accurate?"

"To a point," Milton Sweetwater said after a pause that was hardly noticeable, as if in that brief moment he had come to a decision. "Can we all accept that our conference today is confidential whether or not you take on our problem?"

Charlie waved his hand. "That's the way we play it."

Milton Sweetwater leaned forward. "There's a major part of that weekend that we decided not to talk about with the press or the police. I don't think it has a bearing, but at our last meeting, we decided to tell a detective all of it and go on from there."

Charlie nodded, then regarded the cats under the lilac bush again. The leaves of the bush were drooping dispiritedly; the cats looked dead; he felt wrung out.

"You should know something about Gary Elringer and the company or that weekend won't make a bit of sense," Milton began. "Gary was a prodigy. I guess the news stories went into that. He built his own computer before he was ten, went to Stanford at fifteen, Ph.D. by twenty, with half a dozen innovations or outright inventions or discoveries under his belt already. He had a couple dozen patents before he could legally take a drink. He also had a difficult personality. Spoiled rotten as a kid, spoiled as an adult. He was chubby and had the social graces of a polecat, snarling, taking what he wanted, and generally making people miserable. In college he met Beth MacNair, shy and very bright, and undeveloped physically. Somehow they hit it off and got married. That was ten years ago. Bruce Elringer, Gary's brother, meanwhile had come up with a program to write music on a computer, some kind of breakthrough, and they decided to start the Bellringer Company. They had a new computer—hardware— and a lot of software to go with it. Gary had already made a lot of money—not enough, but a lot. They rounded up a few others, including me, and we launched the Bellringer Company, Incorporated. It was a spectacular success from the start. That was eight years ago."

He finished his beer and lifted the bottle to read the label.

"Local company," Charlie said. He went inside and returned with two more bottles. Constance was having iced tea. She drank beer with Mexican food. He began to think of Mexican food—pork with green sauce, chicken breasts with chilies in a creamy sauce . . .

"Well," Milton went on after pouring more beer, drinking again. "The company was Gary's from the start. He kept controlling interest. And no one objected. We all knew that without him there wouldn't be a company. Even after he started handing out shares to buy loyalty, he kept control, no doubt about it." He went on at length explaining the articles of incorporation, the shares that had been distributed, how the company functioned. "And until three years ago it didn't make a lot of difference who had control," he said presently. "In the first years there weren't any profits to go to shareholders; we were all on salary. Then there were profits to parcel out, but when Gary started Smart House, the profits vanished."

Charlie didn't actually yawn. He wasn't that much of a boor, he told himself, but neither could he work up any interest in the corporate structure that the lawyer was going on about. Mexican or Italian, he deliberated. Hot, spicy food was said to be more cooling than nonspicy food in the long run. And a pitcher of margaritas. He was leaning more in that direction. Maybe Milton Sweetwater would finish in another few minutes and go away, and he and Constance could discuss the matter of food until it was time to go eat the food.

"You have to understand some of the background or you'll never understand why we all went along with Gary's game of murder," Milton said then, not at all unaware of the effect his words would have.

Charlie blinked at him. "Tell me about it."

By the time Milton had finished describing the game, Charlie was regarding him with disbelief, and Constance was looking at him with horror.

"You're a lawyer and you went along with that?" she asked.

He shrugged. "You had to know Gary. It would have been worse if we hadn't gone along with it. I decided that it was relatively harmless, and it did exactly what he predicted: It made each of us find out for ourselves what a marvel Smart House really is."

"Such a marvel that it wanted to play, too," Charlie

muttered. "Go on. I take it this is what your game players failed to tell the cops."

"Exactly. We just didn't see the point. Think how it would have looked all over the newspapers, the tabloids. And the game had nothing to do with what happened. It might have been any game, or no game at all. What difference could it make to their investigation?"

"I don't know," Charlie said. "You tell me. What difference did it make?"

The lawyer looked uncomfortable now. "For one thing everyone became paranoid. It seems incredible now, but we were all paranoid almost instantly when the game started. The other thing is that because of the game we knew that the house, the computer, I should say, appeared responsible for both deaths. You see, it kept track of everyone's movements all that weekend, and when that portion of the program was displayed, it clearly showed that Rich had been alone in the elevator, and that Gary had gone into the Jacuzzi alone. The police determined that there were glitches in the program, as we all agreed; after all, this was its test run, the weekend, I mean. And no one came forth with any information to contradict that, so although the case wasn't officially closed, it's at a standstill, a dead end. An unfortunate accident—two of them. And Bellringer makes killer computers," he added bitterly.

Charlie was shaking his head. "The police had more than a lousy program with glitches. What else?"

"Yes," Milton admitted. "There was more. You see, the way the game was set up, and everyone so paranoid, no one was staying for any length of time with just one other person. For the most part we were all staying in groups of four or more, and keeping a sharp eye out for each other. If you were with one other person, a third person might join you looking for his victim, you see. One victim, one witness, one killer. I think we all had our suspicions about who had been killed already and who hadn't, but even an apparently nonchalant attitude could have been an act." He spread his hands in a curiously helpless gesture. "Anyway, we knew Rich was alone, not with just one other person, and we knew he wasn't in a group of four."

Very patiently Charlie asked, "Exactly how did you know that?"

Milton looked more uncomfortable than ever. Sheepishly he said, "I was stalking Laura Westerman. She was in a group watching a movie. There was a bar set up in the room, and she was drinking. I thought it was just a matter of time before she wanted to refill her glass, so I waited near the bar. Sure enough, she came back. Rich was near there, too, and I spoke to him, to get his attention, so he would be my witness. When Laura got within range, I shot her with a pea shooter." He did not look at Charlie or Constance, but frowned into the distance. "It was listed as a poison dart, an instant kill."

Charlie watched his glass sweat and Constance swirled her ice in her tall glass. Finally Milton glanced at her, then at Charlie, and continued.

"I motioned Laura and Rich to come out of the room where others were watching the movie. We stepped into the next room, the library, where I used the computer to register the kill. Rich witnessed, and Laura confirmed it. She and I both saw him leave alone. I suspected that he needed to report in to the computer in his room to get a new victim, or else go downstairs for a weapon. That's how we were all thinking. I kept a close watch on him because for all I knew, he had my name. That was the last time anyone saw him alive."

"No wonder you didn't want to discuss this with the police, or reporters either," Charlie muttered. "Of all the goddamn foolishness! What time was that?"

"Ten to eleven. He was found at eleven-forty, and they estimated that he had died between eleven and eleven-thirty."

"The story I read mentioned a net bag over his head," Charlie said. "Another deadly weapon?"

"Yes. I think he went down in the elevator to collect his next weapon and that was it."

"A net bag?"

"It was supposed to be a plastic bag, like a laundry bag, I guess, the kind with the warnings not to place them over your head. Anyway, it was supposed to suffocate the victim. It was loosely woven, soft cotton netting."

"That suffocated him," Charlie said dryly. "Did the police even try to explain why it was on his head?"

Milton shrugged. "How could they? They think the automatic vacuum system came on while he was in the elevator, that it sucked out the air, and he collapsed before he realized what was happening. Maybe the elevator locked and wouldn't open. Anyway, since he was alone, and he died of suffocation, that was all they could come up with. There weren't any marks on his neck, no marks at all to indicate otherwise. None of us could come up with anything better," he added.

"Okay. How about Gary Elringer? What's the story on his death?"

"No one saw him after dinner. A couple of people watching the movie heard him laughing at one point, but no one even noticed what time it was then. The police say he walked through the Jacuzzi room for some reason and fell in, and the computer closed the cover on him. It had overheated the water drastically; why not also cover it by mistake?"

"Nothing was in the news story about overheating. How hot?"

"By the time anyone thought to check the thermometer, it was one thirty-five, but I think it had been quite a bit hotter. Clouds of steam rolled out when we opened it. The heat made it impossible to tell exactly when he died. Maybe even before Rich. His death was attributed to drowning."

Constance shivered in the August heat.

"And you say the computer had tracked both of them all evening? It can do that?"

"I tell you it's a true marvel. I've never seen anything like it. It kept track of everyone in the house, by name, from the time of arrival until Alexander stopped the program. According to the display, Gary went into the Jacuzzi room alone. No one else went in until the search party entered."

Charlie regarded the lawyer morosely, then turned away to observe the third cat, the fluffy orange and white Candy, wend her way through the dying grass. She walked with her tail straight up, twitching at the end. Some hunter, signaling by semaphore to any prey within range, *Here I come.* Her eyes were the color of butterscotch. Ashcan gathered his legs under him in a spring-ready position; Candy ignored him, and he became interested in something moving in the grass, pounced at that. Candy continued toward the terrace until she spotted a stranger; she stopped, her fur rose along her spine, her ears flattened, and she yelled obscenities at Constance and Charlie in a hoarse, raucous voice. Ashcan fled in terror and Brutus heaved himself to his feet and stalked away in disgust. Finally Charlie brought his gaze back to Milton Sweetwater.

"What did the computer do to convince the police that it had really gone berserk?"

Milton drew in a long breath and nodded, as if to

say, *good for you.* "Not a word of this was in those news articles, but you're right, of course. They had been there an hour perhaps when lights here and there went off or came on. Doors that had opened at a touch were locked; other doors opened. Alexander Randall was beside himself. Then, the final touch: An insecticide was released in the greenhouse, enough to have killed anyone exposed to it, I gather. It set off an alarm. Fortunately no one was inside the building at the time. I think that was what convinced them that the house is a killer."

"Uh-huh. And you. What do you think?"

"It can't be," Milton said without hesitation. "If it is, we're ruined."

Charlie raised an eyebrow at him and reached for the bottle of beer that had very little remaining in it. "What do you want? Why are you here?"

"Right. That's the scenario we're working with, pretty much as I've outlined it for you. After the funeral, after the formalities, things were supposed to get back to normal, as normal as possible, with reorganization and replanning for the future, and so on. Suddenly Beth Elringer, the widow, started to voice objections. And Bruce Elringer backed her. Well, by now there's a schism as broad and deep as the one that parted the Red Sea. No one has enough votes to do anything at this point. The company will go under if it doesn't move forward. That's the way it is in the computer industry. No one can simply stand still. We had a shareholders' meeting last Thursday and everyone screamed at everyone else for three hours, until finally I said we should bring in an independent investigator to clear the air. Bruce has another idea, and in the end, we decided to work with both."

"Bruce Elringer? What's his scenario?"

"He thinks Beth killed her husband."

Charlie whistled softly.

"It's ugly as hell," Milton said with some bitterness. "Anyway, Bruce has invited everyone back to Smart House next weekend, to reenact the last day, to demonstrate that Beth had the opportunity to murder Rich and Gary. He's talking about her motive, and circumstantial evidence, and so on. Enough of us protested that he had to allow for you, or someone like you, to be there also. And that's why I'm here now." He took a deep breath.

Silently Charlie left, returned with two more bottles of beer. Constance poured herself the rest of the tea, and for a long time no one spoke.

At last Charlie said thoughtfully, "If we go to Spirelli's we won't be able to talk because that damn accordian player starts at eight. I say it's El Gordo's and margaritas. How about you two?" He added, almost kindly, to Milton, "I have a hell of a lot of questions to ask, I'm afraid."

5

LATE that night Charlie and Constance talked in the cool bedroom, both of them propped up on pillows, the television on, the sound off. Outside the bedroom door, Brutus screamed for admittance. The cats hated it when they closed the door all the way, and with the air conditioner on, they kept it closed.

"If I let him in, he'll prowl around five minutes and then yell to get outside again," Charlie said. "Pretend you don't hear him. What do you think of Sweetwater?"

"Awfully slick, and smart. Charming. He looks like Gregory Peck, and, unfortunately, he knows it. Your turn."

"He's a computer nut," Charlie said as if that defined his entire impression.

"From what he said, they all are."

"I know," he grumbled. Brutus raised his voice, and Charlie cursed him. For a moment there was silence, then Ashcan screeched, and cats galloped through the hallway. With a sigh Charlie left the bed and went out into the hall. He could hear Constance's soft chuckle behind him.

He led the three cats to the sliding glass door to the terrace and shooed them all out, then stood outside for a minute. Lightning played with clouds in the west, too distant for the thunder to reach this far. The air felt heavy, ominous, and too damn hot, he decided. Then thunder rumbled closer, the lightning flashed to the ground, and thunder boomed.

"All right!" he said, and went back inside to call Constance. Three times that summer they had had electrical storms that had taken out the lights. One of the neighbors, the Mitchum family, had had a television and an electric stove ruined by a power surge.

They went through the house together pulling plugs and then sat on the terrace waiting for the storm to drive them inside. A fitful wind was rising. The temperature seemed to go up, and the air smelled of ozone. Charlie hoped it would be a good storm, a freshening change of weather, an end to the heat wave that was turning him into jelly day after day.

"If the house, or the computer in the house, actually did kill two people, don't you think it might be a dangerous place?" Constance asked between two rolls of thunder. Moving away, she thought with regret.

"We'll stay out of elevators and away from the Jacuzzi. Nervous about it?"

"Not really. It just occurred to me. It also seems that if they were all that disturbed because of a game before, just imagine what they'll be like this time when they get together. Now they know there's a killer house, or else a human killer among them."

"Damn storm's going to stay south of us," he said, disgruntled. "At least it'll be cool on the Oregon coast."

For a moment she had the distinct feeling that he had agreed to look into this insane affair simply to escape the heat wave. She opened her mouth to protest, then closed it again. If those people were as bothered as she would be in their situation, he might wish he were back here very quickly.

"Charlie, after talking to Milton, reading the material he gave us, do you think the computer is to blame?"

"You know, when a guy wants to kill someone, usually he reaches for a weapon he's familiar with—a gun, a club, a brick, poison, whatever it might be. Or else he grabs what's at hand, a skillet say, a dandy weapon. Good old black skillet meets head, head gives. But an open mesh bag? Drowning a guy in a whirlpool? Well, like I told Milton Sweetwater, we'll have a looksee, keep an open mind as long as possible, and hang the computer in the end. Let's go to bed. No storm here tonight. It's hotter than it was an hour ago."

People on the coast went inland to warm up in the summer, the gas station attendant had told Beth that morning, a few miles south of Bandon, Oregon. The day was misty, gray, and cool. Earlier, there had been dense fog, but it had lifted by the time she reached this area. From there to Smart House had been less than an hour.

Crazy, she told herself, shivering when she drove up to the house, suffering from déjà vu, her stomach in a hard knot that she could not relax no matter how many deep breaths she sucked in. Crazy, crazy, crazy.

The front door opened before she had her suitcase out of the car. Jake strode out to meet her. He stopped short of actually touching her this time, but examined her face closely, then nodded. "Why didn't you return any of my calls?"

"I don't know. There didn't seem much point, I guess."

She turned from his searching gaze and opened the back door and now he moved past her and brought her suitcase out. Silently they entered Smart House. Neither suggested taking the elevator up. As they mounted the stairs from the foyer, the house seemed uncannily quiet. In the upper hallway she looked down into the atrium, as beautiful as before, with no one in it. The waterfall was working, the splash of water reflected one of the hanging lights, sparkled, and broke the sparkles in an endless kaleidoscope effect. Someone must have left open one of the doors, she thought distantly; the unpleasant odor of chlorine was everywhere. She had forgotten how it filled the house when the doors were left open.

She wished that someone other than Jake had met her, or no one at all. She could manage her one suitcase. It was true, he had called quite a few times, and she had listened to his voice on her machine, and turned it off each time. What was the point? she repeated to herself. They reached her door.

"Is . . . is the computer turned on?" she asked, hesitating now.

"No," he said brusquely. "That damn thing's off for good." He reached past her and turned the doorknob. "There's a lock inside, a plain, old-fashioned mechanical chain lock. I installed it a while ago."

"I'll have to open my own drapes and regulate my own bath—" Beth started. At the sound of laughter she became rigid and felt the world going out of focus—Gary's laughter. She clutched the door frame.

"Take it easy," Jake said; he held her arm in a firm grip. "He's been practicing."

Bruce yelled from the elevator at the end of the hall, "It's about time you got here! We're having a family meeting in the garden in five minutes."

"Oh, my God!" Beth breathed, staring at Bruce. Always before he had stressed the small differences between himself and Gary: He had worn suits, Gary sweaters; he had worn polished shoes, Gary sneakers; his hair had been relatively neat, Gary's unruly, a mop of curly hair that he had cut only when it got down to his eyes. Today, Bruce was in a sweater and slacks, untied sneakers, his hair wild and bushy.

Even the words, she thought, he even remembered what Gary had said the last time.

"As I said," Jake muttered savagely, "he's been practicing." He carried her suitcase on into the room; she followed and stood by the door.

Now Jake looked awkward. She moved aside for him to pass, but he didn't move yet. "Beth, don't let him get to you. Okay? You've got friends in the company, you know. Milton, me. Bruce is being ugly, but he doesn't have any power, and he knows it. He can't actually do anything. So take it easy."

She nodded. "Thanks, Jake. I appreciate that."

"Yeah. I'll see you later." He left swiftly.

Beth closed the door, and after a moment she put the chain lock on, and only then advanced into the room, the same pink and yellow room she had had the last time. She opened the drapes and gazed at the sea. There was no horizon, just the gray sea and the gray sky that became one. No escape there, she thought. You could sail out that way only so far and then you would be sent back by way of the sky. She turned away from the ocean and found herself gazing at the computer, silent and blank. She was shivering. Walking quickly she went to the bathroom and got a towel, brought it out with her, and draped it over the monitor. *There,* she breathed at it. In no hurry, she unpacked, washed her face and hands, and pulled on a sweat shirt, not sure if her chill was due to cold or to an internal malfunction. It didn't matter; she was freezing.

Maddie and Bruce were in the atrium garden at the lowest level near the bar when she arrived. It was hot and humid here. Something new must have come into bloom, she found herself thinking, something heavy and too sweet. Gardenias? She embraced Maddie, who looked glassy-eyed, tranquilized, and smelled of gin and tonic. A coffee pot and cups were on the bar counter. She nodded briefly at Bruce and poured herself coffee.

"All right," Bruce said. "Here's the program. The company's in a hell of a spot. We've got to raise money enough to pay for forty-five shares of stock, and frankly, there's no way on earth we can do it. The others are going to opt for a sellout, naturally, take ten cents on the dollar and be done with it."

"Bruce, stop it!" Maddie cried. "We agreed not to have a business meeting unless everyone is present."

Bruce went on as if he had not heard. "Milton says we have to reorganize first, before any decisions can be made. You know who will take over if we go along with that! Jake. And then Milton will get in line and they'll vote to sell out. So we have two choices. We can serve up the murderer, clear the computer of all charges, and then the shares go a different direction. Mom and I split them and we both waive payment for now. Or you can defer payment for an indefinite period," he added, glaring at Beth. "Deferred payment is acceptable, Milton said."

"What are you talking about?" Beth demanded.

"A murderer can't benefit financially from her crime," he said almost petulantly. "You know that. I checked it with Milton. That means that Mom and I will split Gary's estate. The money stays in the company and we'll start showing Smart House—"

Beth felt distant, an observer of a scenario she had no understanding of, with no means of arriving at an understanding. She stood up.

"Sit down!" Bruce yelled at her. "I'm giving you a choice, goddamn it! You sign a waiver about payment for now and we let it rest there. I don't say a word about what I know."

She felt herself moving before she realized she had willed motion. She walked blindly toward the sliding door to the hall, hearing the shouts and curses behind her as if Bruce were on a stage rehearsing for a production she had no interest in.

"You'll do what I tell you! Or it's your ass!" Bruce screamed.

Because she was walking in the direction of the foyer when she left the atrium, that was where she found herself a moment later, and she kept going to the front door, and on outside. She did not see the man and woman approaching until she nearly bumped into them.

"Hi," Charlie said, "I'm Charles Meiklejohn, and this is my wife, Constance Leidl. Who are you?"

"You're the detective?" she said, and blinked several times.

"He is," Constance said briskly. "And from Milton Sweetwater's description, I'd guess you're Beth Elringer." Beth nodded. "Look, we were just debating whether or not lunch would be possible inside. Arriving at this time of day is a little awkward, isn't it? We said we'd arrive in the afternoon, and, of course, officially it is after noon. About one, isn't it? But still, we did not say we would come for lunch. Will you have lunch with us somewhere? Maybe you could direct us."

Charlie raised his eyebrows at her, but she was already taking the young woman's arm, steering her toward the rental car they had just driven up in. Lying like a trooper, he thought happily about Constance, and took Beth's other arm; the three of them went to the car and got in.

"I'd better go somewhere," Beth said, between them on the front seat. "If I go back inside right now, I might kill Bruce, and that would really look bad for me, wouldn't it?"

"That would look bad," Constance agreed. "What on earth did Bruce do?"

"He accused me of killing Gary."

"Did you?"

"No."

"I thought they all said the house killed both men," Constance said.

"They said it, but I don't believe it. I guess Bruce must have done it, after all."

"You thought he did, and then you changed your mind, and now you think it again," Constance said thoughtfully, as if they had discussed this before.

"Yes. I couldn't think of a reason before, but he just gave a reason, only he didn't seem to realize it. Actually I don't know this area," she said then, looking at Charlie. "I don't know where there are restaurants or anything else."

"That's all right," Constance said reassuringly. "We passed a lot of them on our way in. Charlie knows where to go. What was the reason Bruce just revealed?"

She would get away with it, Charlie knew. She had moved in when Beth was practically in a state of shock; she had said and done exactly the right things at the right time, and this poor kid had no more resistance to her than he himself did. No sound escaped, but he was humming under his breath, listening to every word, and searching for a restaurant.

"It's pretty complicated," Beth said after a brief hesitation. "I thought I understood it just a minute ago, and now it seems confused again. It has to do with the company and the way it's set up." She lapsed into a troubled silence.

"I never studied economics enough to get a decent grasp of business affairs," Constance said. "That's a closed corporation, isn't it?"

"That's it," Beth said, and now her words came in a rush. "When they started it all, Bruce was still married to Binny. They got divorced a couple of years ago. Two kids, perfectly awful little monsters, all whining and smeary and clinging. It's sad for Maddie, her only two grandchildren turning out to be monsters. Anyway, Gary couldn't stand Binny, and no one else could either as far as I could tell, except Bruce, and that didn't last. She isn't very smart, doesn't know anything about computers, or anything else, I guess. So when Gary was starting the company, he had Milton write up the articles of incorporation in such a way that no stock could be inherited in the case of death of the shareholder. He was terrified of letting someone like Binny get any shares, having any voice, input, he called it. You can't just sell a share, either," she added in an aggrieved voice.

"So the shares of the deceased revert back to the company, which has to pay the estate the market value of them and then divide them up using a formula based on the percentage of shares they already own. The company has to buy back Gary's shares, and Rich's, now and redistribute them."

"But weren't you named his primary heir?"

Beth looked at Constance, puzzled, then nodded. "I don't get the shares, that's the point. They have to pay me their value, and they don't have enough money. I think the courts will force a sale, or something of that sort. That's my motive, according to Bruce." She no longer seemed able to get from that to the reason she had found for Bruce to have done it. She frowned in thought.

Charlie slowed down and clicked on the turn signal. He glanced at Constance; she grinned back, her look telling him she had known all along that he knew perfectly well where a good restaurant was. He parked and they all got out in front of Ray's Clam Chowder and Other Fine Food restaurant. Charlie took a deep breath of the cool, misty sea air. Back home it was closing in on a hundred degrees, he thought with satisfaction.

The restaurant was small, with only two other parties in booths. They seated themselves in a booth overlooking the parking lot and consulted the menu, and suddenly Beth said, "Oh, yes. That's it."

"First we order," Charlie said firmly. "You two can have the other fine food. I want chowder."

They all did, and as soon as the waiter left them alone, Beth said, "If he can convict me of murder, I can't inherit. The stock still goes back to the company, but he and his mother will inherit the estate. They will be owed for the shares. He'll make Maddie accept a deferred payment plan, and he will too, and the company won't have to raise millions of dollars to pay for Gary's shares. And the company won't be under the cloud, either, of having a crazy computer that kills people." She nodded. "That's his motive."

"Is the company really broke?" Charlie asked.

"Practically. A cash flow problem, as they say. I guess there's operating money, money due on back orders, and so on, but nothing more than that. Gary sank every cent he got his hands on into Smart House. If they can clear the Smart House computer, they have a new gold mine, of course. God alone knows how much they'll make when they start selling the advanced programming, the computer systems, everything to do with Smart House."

Charlie was studying her thoughtfully. "It seems to me that if there is a human killer, he cut his own throat by casting suspicion on the computer. Everyone there is involved with the company, even if you do say 'they' when you talk about it."

She blushed and ducked her head. "I guess I never thought of any of it as having anything real to do with me," she mumbled. "It was always Gary's, and theirs, not mine."

"How long were you married to him?" Constance asked, and although that was not the question

Charlie would have put to her then, he leaned back to see where Constance was heading now.

"Ten years," Beth said in a low voice.

"You were both children," Constance said, also softly, with great sympathy.

"Yes. We were nineteen when we met. He was getting his doctorate already, and he was so shy and funny looking and awkward. I was the only girl he ever went out with. And I didn't have any social life either, until he came along. In my own way I was just as funny looking and awkward and shy. Two misfits. We got along somehow. No one understood what either of us saw in the other, and now I don't either, but then . . . All those years, for the first seven years, I did exactly what he wanted. He was hardworking, determined to make his mark in the world of computers, full of ideas, some of them wild, some simply wonderful, and he made his mark. He really did. He wanted to redesign the architecture of the machine so that he could develop half a dozen software packages that would be totally compatible and require a minimum of available memory. He did it, too."

The waiter came with their chowder. His frank appraisal of Beth was oddly reassuring. He was young, probably younger than she was, but interested. She was oblivious. Constance watched her eat a few bites, and as soon as she seemed to lose interest in the food, Constance asked, "You could work with him on computers at that depth? I'm awed. All I know about computers is that you plug them in, insert a program, and hope for the best."

Beth laughed politely. "Actually I only worked with him for the first few years. I took my degree then, and four years ago I told him I wanted to go back for my master's in English. For the first year that I was back in school, I kept working with him, but it was too much and gradually I gave it up. Three years ago I moved all the way out to go to Berkeley. I had an apartment, and after that I saw very little of him. I don't know how far he moved during those four years; pretty far, I guess."

"Did he object?" Charlie asked. "Did you fight over leaving him for school?"

She pushed her spoon around with one finger and shook her head. "We never fought," she said. "Never. He said at first that going back to school was a good idea, and later he said he didn't really have time for me anyway, not then. He was too immersed in the work on Smart House. He agreed to help me financially, of course, until the money ran out anyway. We never were separated the way people thought we were. We just weren't together. He believed right up to the end that one day I'd be fed up with trying to support myself, and I'd be back."

"And you? Did you think that?" Charlie asked, baffled by her in a way he could not fathom. Didn't she know she was a damn good looking young woman? And smart as hell?

She looked at him candidly and sighed. "I don't know. Probably I would have gone back eventually, if he insisted. Once he said that he knew computers would do anything you wanted them to—the trick was to find the right language, the right method and sequence of commands to tell them what you wanted. He believed that about people, too. And he was right, at least about people. They always did exactly what he wanted them to. Always."

Charlie shook his head at her gravely. "One of them didn't, Beth. Either a computer or a person did not do exactly what he wanted at the end."

6

"Dessert," Charlie announced, "is loganberry pie, and I intend to have it. Ladies?" They both shook their heads. "Good. I eat. You, Beth, talk. Thumbnail sketches of the players at Smart House."

She looked toward Constance, as if for help, and got only an encouraging smile. Did this mean they trusted her, or that they were testing her? She felt her confusion rise and shook her head, but Charlie was motioning the waiter over, and Constance was watching him. He finished with the waiter and turned expectantly to Beth.

"First, the brother, Bruce," he prompted, when she did not speak immediately.

"Bruce," she said after a lengthy pause, "seems to equate genius with insanity, but he's acting. Gary wasn't crazy," she added hurriedly, not certain why she was defending him even now. She stopped in confusion, then said carefully, "He wasn't aware of what he did to the rest of us . . . them." She had to stop again, because that wasn't right, either. Charlie made a noncommittal noise, and Constance simply waited; Beth tried again. "His priorities were different," she said finally. "Anything to do with problems, puzzles, games, anything intellectual, I guess, came first, people second." She thought a moment, then nodded. "Look, it wasn't that he was unaware of people, it was rather that he had a way of delegating importance that left them behind other things. Once," she hurried, wondering again why she was trying so hard to make them understand Gary, since it no longer mattered, "when Jake was still married, his wife gave him an ultimatum. He could keep working eighteen-hour days forever, or he could be married to her, but he couldn't do both. Gary understood exactly what was happening, and he gave Jake even more work. He tested him. In full awareness of the consequences, the cost to Jake, his wife. It was another problem, nothing more than that. He had a good understanding of human problems, but he filed them under a different category than most people."

The waiter brought coffee, and they were silent until he left again. Then Charlie said, "Harry."

Beth blinked and regathered her thoughts, tried to encapsulate Harry. "He's driven," she said slowly. "It's as if he got a glimpse of something he never used to believe was attainable, and suddenly began to believe he could have it. Like a mountain peak," she added, and looked from Charlie to Constance. "You know, he climbs mountains. I mean, almost obsessively." Charlie nodded. "Sometimes I get the feeling that he's climbing a mountain all the time, even if he's on level ground just like the rest of us. I wouldn't want to get in his way. He'd push anyone out of his way, and if you fell over the side, tough."

"Even Gary?"

She shook her head. "You don't understand. Gary was at the peak already, urging him on, encouraging him. He was the role model, the goal. Probably no one admired him more than Harry did."

"Poor Gary," Constance murmured, when Beth

lapsed into silence again. "Didn't anyone care for him as a person?"

Beth flushed and ducked her head, watched her spoon whip the coffee in her cup into a whirlpool. "Maddie did, of course, and I did, a long time ago. Jake cared for him."

The vortex in her cup spun higher and higher until it reached the rim and sloshed over the side in a torrent. She was remembering the day of Gary's funeral. They had all gone back to Maddie's house to find it full of people, curious people, friends, strangers, some malicious, some caring, some huddled, held together by whispers, some wanting to touch, to pat, soothe, feel. She had fled upstairs to Maddie's tiny office where she stood with her back to the room, head bowed, both hands pressed hard against the door as if the mourners might follow and try to gain admittance.

She stiffened at a touch on her shoulder, spun around, and found herself being gathered into the arms of Jake Kluge. He held her and stroked her hair as if she were a child, and she had been overcome by guilt, guilt at not feeling bereaved, at not suffering, at not caring; guilt that she was alive and Gary dead and maybe she was even glad he was dead; guilt because she did not know what she should be feeling and was as empty as the guests downstairs, as cold as ice. Jake murmured nonsense words and she wept, not for Gary, but for herself and the ruins of her life. The guilt doubled, redoubled, until she shoved Jake away, unable to bear his touch. He was wearing his glasses, so thick they distorted his pale eyes but did not hide the reddened eyelids. His very real grief made her more ashamed.

She had run from him, all the way out of the house, to her car, had driven for hours. After that, when he called, she had listened to his voice on her machine and turned it off, turned him off. She had understood that he wanted to share her grief, assuage their mutual grief, and she had none, unless for the girl she had been ages ago.

She looked up from the mess in her saucer, and now on the tabletop as well, and put her spoon down. "They'll be wondering where I am," she said quietly. "We should go now."

When they drove back to Smart House, Charlie had Beth show him where she had stopped to wait at the massive bronze gates, which were standing open now. He drove on, and waited for her to go through the motions she had gone through the day of her arrival. He looked for the camera eyes just as she had done that day, and with as much effect. They were hidden too well.

He rang the bell then and the four clear notes of the Bellringer Company sounded. Seconds later the ornate door opened and a middle-aged woman stepped aside.

"This is Mr. Meiklejohn and Ms. Leidl," Beth said. "Mrs. Ramos."

She was a handsome, sturdily built woman, graying hair in a soft chignon, no makeup, no jewelry, not even a watch. Charlie remembered that she and her husband had been on a long-distance call from a few minutes after eleven until nearly eleven-thirty the night of the deaths. Mrs. Ramos was a new grandmother. She inclined her head fractionally. "I will show you to your room. Do you have bags? If you will please leave your car keys, we will bring up your bags and park the car in the garage. Mr. Sweetwater asked to be notified on your arrival." Her voice was very pleasant, musical even; she had no trace of an accent.

Beth said, "If I see Milton, I'll tell him. See you

later." She waved and went around them, through the spacious foyer.

"Would you like to take the elevator up?" Mrs. Ramos asked.

"Yes indeed," Charlie said, and she led them into the wide corridor with the glass wall of the atrium. Charlie whistled.

"We can go that way," Mrs. Ramos said. "Most people do. It's the shortest way through the house."

They examined the garden, the pool, the arrangements of chairs, tables, the bar, the way the room was built up to resemble a rocky hill covered with jungle greenery. The air was heavy.

"You know why we're here?" Charlie asked, pausing to study the rock wall where the water plunged down into the pool.

"They told me."

"I feel like I'm in some damn pasha's palace," he said, and started to walk again. "Will you be here all weekend? We'll want to talk to you at some point. You and your husband."

"Of course," she said. "We are in a cottage on the property. Whenever it's convenient."

The unflusterable, perfect housekeeper, Charlie thought, and wondered what lay behind the serenity of her expression, the wise black eyes. She stopped again almost immediately on leaving the atrium.

"The elevator," she said.

The elevator was at the end of the corridor, with a narrower hallway leading directly away from the pool area. The doors to the elevator were bifold, open. They stepped inside. On the wall next to the doors the control panel was a music staff with notes, the controls flush with the wall. Gold metal strips divided the walls into random sections, each a different pastel—blue, green, yellow. . . . Rich burgundy carpeting underfoot seemed almost too deep. The ceiling was ivory colored, luminescent, the light source. The cage was eleven feet deep, five feet wide, with a ceiling eight feet high, Charlie knew from the reports he had read.

"Where's the automatic vacuum?" he asked Mrs. Ramos.

"The center panel on the rear wall," she said, nodding toward it. "I can't show you on this floor. It only operates on the basement level. These are the floor indicators," she said then and touched one of the notes. "The first one shuts the doors," she said. The doors closed soundlessly. "The next one opens them, and of course the rising notes are for the floors. We're on one, and your room is on two." She touched another note. There was no sensation of motion. "When the computer is operating, there's no need to remember to press any buttons, you just tell it what you want. It's automatic."

She led them into the hallway on the second floor, the glass wall on one side, the bedroom doors on the other between long expanses of wall with very nice art, each picture illuminated with its own light above it. They passed several closed doors before she stopped and opened one. She did not enter, but held the door for them. "I hope you will be comfortable. Number six on the phone rings in the kitchen, if you want anything. And I'll make certain that Mr. Sweetwater knows you have arrived."

Throughout the minitour and minilectures Constance had remained silent and watchful. Now she asked, "Did you work for Gary Elringer?"

"No. I work for the company. Sometimes he was here, sometimes not; I work in the house for the company."

"Do you like it, Mrs. Ramos? Smart House, I mean, the computer controlling things?"

For an instant there was something other than the

pleasant well-trained-housekeeper face, an expression stony and cold; it was so fleeting it might not have been noticeable if Constance had not been watching closely.

"The computer is turned off; it isn't running anything anymore." She glanced inside the room in a professional way, then turned and left them.

While Constance crossed the room to open the drapes, Charlie examined the door lock and the numbered panel on the outside and tried to fathom how the thing worked when the computer was operating. He could not understand it, he decided, and closed the door, looked for a lock that he did understand, and failed to find that, too.

"This isn't a house!" Constance exclaimed, standing at the wall of windows. There was an ocean view, misty and gray and beautiful. The room was decorated in orchid, lavender, and navy blue, with exquisite cloisonné objects here and there—lamps, a statuette of a crane, an ashtray. "This is like one of the four-star hotels you read about."

Twin beds, a desk with a computer, a television, chests of drawers, large closet, extravagantly fitted bathroom, like an expensive hotel, Charlie agreed, after looking through it all. Except there was no way to lock the door. He knew he would use the old chair-under-the-doorknob trick.

When they left their room, it was to find Beth in the corridor. "I'll take you to the living room," she said. "Milton's waiting for you. And Bruce and a couple of the others." She looked gloomy as she motioned down the hall. "No elevator. I wouldn't get near that thing again." She led them down the back stairs.

"You really need a guide," Constance said.

"They handed out floor plans last time. There must be some around still. Milton will know."

They entered the living room and she introduced them: Alexander Randall looked nervous and uncertain of what to do with his hands. Milton nodded to them. He was carrying a large manila envelope. Maddie Elringer nodded to them both and did not speak. Her makeup was a mess: too much lipstick not very well applied, and her mascara had run and had not been repaired; as if she had not looked at herself in a mirror since morning. She was holding a tall drink and every sign said that it was not her first although it was then only four in the afternoon.

As soon as the introductions were over Milton Sweetwater held out the envelope to Charlie. "I managed to get everything you asked for, and Alexander here worked on the house from the start. Anything you want to ask about the place, he should be able to fill in."

"Thanks." Charlie tucked the envelope under his arm.

From behind him a new voice demanded harshly, "What did you give him? Dossiers on all of us?"

"That's Bruce," Beth said wearily.

"And that's not an answer," Bruce said in a truculent tone. He joined the group near the window, looking over Charlie, ignoring Constance. "I know who you are. What I want to know is what he told you we hired you to do."

"Bruce, you're making a fool of yourself," Milton snapped. "I told him exactly what we discussed at our last meeting, and I supplied him with the forensic reports, the police reports, the articles of incorporation, the terms of Gary's will, a summary of the company's financial statement of the past year, a floor plan of the house, and perhaps one or two other documents, a list of which I can and will supply at our next meeting."

Constance was watching with an interest that was

nearly clinical. Maddie's hands had started to shake so hard she had to put down her glass, and now each hand gripped the other so tightly that the ends of her fingers were scarlet, the knuckles white. Alexander was edging toward the door, ready to bolt.

"I already told them what you're accusing me of!" Beth said coldly, looking at Bruce with icy disdain.

He made a grab for her arm and she twisted out of reach.

"Don't you touch me!" Her voice was choked with fury.

"Stay and listen to me tell it. I don't want you accusing me of saying anything behind your back. I was watching her," he said to Charlie. "We heard Gary laughing. I was watching her. She heard it, just like I did. And she got up and went out after him. She'd been trying to get him to talk to her all day, and that was her chance, while everyone else was watching the movie. He was going to make her work for some of the dough he was shelling out on her, and she wanted a divorce and a fat settlement. I know the signs, by God! That night I saw her go after him. Who else would he let anywhere near him in the Jacuzzi? Who else could turn off the computer so it wouldn't track them into the Jacuzzi? He was mad because she didn't show any interest in his new toys. He would have shown it to her; he wanted to show off to her. He turned them both off the tracking program and said he'd talk to her and they went into the Jacuzzi. She got her hands on it." He raised his voice to a falsetto and went on, "Oh, Gary, let me see it. How clever of you."

Beth made a strangled noise and shook her head. "You're insane!"

"Then you shoved him in the pool and pushed the button to cover it. He never had a chance! And you had the control computer in your hand. You could go anywhere without any record. He wouldn't have let anyone else touch it, just you!"

"What do you mean, a control computer? How big was it?" Charlie asked.

"Little. Like a pack of cigarettes."

"How do you know?" Alexander asked in wonder. "He said he wasn't going to show anyone until our meeting on Monday."

Bruce looked at him in contempt. "Everyone knew, you asshole. You think he could resist showing off?"

"I didn't know," Milton said slowly, shaking his head. "I don't think anyone did. It would have come out before now."

"Neither did I," Beth said.

Bruce looked from one to another in disbelief. Maddie was near tears, raising her glass again, her hand trembling visibly. "You all knew," Bruce said harshly. "Nothing else made any sense. I figured it out and so did all of you. What are you trying to pull off? A frame? It won't take! She did it! No one else had a reason except her!"

"Did you people tell the police about this little gadget?" Charlie asked blandly.

Alexander shook his head. "I thought I was the only one who knew, and I couldn't find it later. I didn't even think of it at the time because Gary was playing the game, same as everyone else. He wouldn't have used it during the game. He was going to demonstrate it on Monday. The whole house was on a trial run that weekend, a demonstration. Everyone here was a Beta tester for the weekend, even if they didn't know it. Anyway, that was just a safety device, a backup in case something went wrong, a door stuck or something like that, and nothing did. Go wrong, I mean. I never gave it a thought until later."

Charlie said easily, "I wonder if you would mind

giving Constance and me a guided tour, explain things about the house as we go, since you're the one with the most complete knowledge of what it can and can't do."

Alexander moistened his lips, glanced at Bruce, at Milton, back to Charlie, and nodded.

Bruce glared at the others in the room, then stamped out, yelling over his shoulder, "Any hacker in the world would have figured out that he had such a device. You all knew!"

They started in the lowest level—computer laboratories, offices, the playroom with billiards, pool, and arcade games, and finally the showroom with the glass case that had held the toy weapons used in the game. Charlie gazed at it with brooding eyes. The case was empty now.

"How did it work?" he asked finally. "Beth said it wouldn't open unless you were due a weapon, and then it thanked you by name. How?"

Alexander shifted uncomfortably and mumbled, "By visual identification and the original visual scan at the entrance, and the weight of the object itself. It was pretty good, but not perfect, not yet. We were still working on it."

"So I approach the case and I'm recognized by the computer." At Alexander's nod, Charlie moved to the case and stopped. "I could open the top now?"

Alexander went to his side and pointed toward the ceiling. "There's a scanner up there, and one on this side," he said. Neither showed even though he was directing Charlie's attention to them. "It's up there," he said. "And outside the bedroom doors, and the front door, and at the gate. By the time you get inside the house there are two pictures of you, and at the front door and the bedroom door your weight is registered. The carpet runners in the halls are wired, of course, but not the interiors of any rooms, except the elevator. After that it's a matter of matching data, that's all."

"The toy weapons were on a scale of some sort?"

Alexander nodded. "They were registered by number, and as soon as one was lifted, it was recorded. Then the case wouldn't open again until someone else tried, or you registered a kill and could take another weapon. That part was simple."

Charlie and Constance exchanged glances. Hers said, *Simple as any magic.*

As Alexander led them through the corridor, Constance asked almost meekly, "What's a Beta tester?"

Alexander looked at her suspiciously, as if he thought she was teasing him. "End user tests," he mumbled. "Someone who's not supposed to know how the program works, just if it does."

She nodded gravely. The next room they entered was Gary's former office and laboratory. A maze of wiring, computers without cases, some wholly encased, test boards, extra keyboards, disk drives, and monitors appeared arranged haphazardly, but obviously there had to be a method, Charlie assumed, without being able to discern it. On the back wall were shelves, a filing cabinet, a workbench with what looked like more testing equipment . . .

"What's behind that wall?" he asked after surveying the room a few moments.

"A fruit cellar. You can get to it from the pantry upstairs."

"Onward," Charlie muttered. "I want to see how the vacuum system works in the elevator."

Alexander explained that it was simplicity itself, one of the best features of the house, as far as marketing was concerned. The units fitted into the walls of every room. Each room had a control, or they could be put on a timer, individually or as a complete system. He touched the control button, a small bar under the musical staff that had looked merely decorative. At his touch the back panel detached itself and slid to the floor on casters that were hidden by the body of the machine. The whole unit was only a few inches high, about twelve inches by sixteen; the top was the same material as the elevator walls, a pastel blue plastic with a soft sheen. It began to move along the floor of the elevator; when it reached the end of the wall, it made a right-angled turn, continued, and repeated this at the next corner, humming softly.

On the wall that had housed it were two strips of metal to guide it back into place, and a round hole. Charlie nodded toward the housing. "It's emptied there?"

Alexander reached down and picked up the humming vacuum cleaner and turned it over. It stopped its operation. There was a brush visible, and the four ball-bearing type wheels, and a round hole for the dirt to enter. Part of the mechanism was hidden by a metal plate. "See," Alexander said, pointing. "When it's cleaning, this hole is opened; the cover slides over it to expose the other one when it's in place to be emptied into the system. Here are the air vents to assist the suction phase."

The vents were almost invisible along the metal strips that edged the machine on both sides. Charlie studied the whole machine dubiously. "They actually think enough air could have been pulled through there to cause anoxia?"

Alexander put it down and touched the bar button again. The vacuum moved silently to the wall and slid back into place. The humming increased for a few seconds and then died out.

"That's how it should work," he said. "They had people measure the elevator and calculate the cubic feet of airspace and how much air can be pumped out in a minute, all that, and they said it could have happened, if the machine malfunctioned."

"And the man simply waited and died."

"They said that's what happened."

"You don't agree, I take it."

Alexander Randall bit his thumbnail and shifted on his feet, glanced at Constance, at Charlie, at the vacuum cleaner, and back at his thumb. "I don't know," he said at last.

"Okay. Can we get to the back of the elevator, the pipes, whatever?"

He looked relieved. "Sure. Best way is through the heating plant." They went back through the game room to the other side of the basement, into another large area.

They passed an oil-burning furnace, an equally large air conditioner, other oversized machines. There were rows of tanks on one side of the wall, with pipes from them vanishing behind panels. Chlorine, algaecide, other pool chemicals, carbon dioxide.

Charlie looked from the last tank to Alexander. "What's that for?"

"The root cellar, cold storage for apples, grapes, things like that. Carbon dioxide helps keep them longer. And some goes to the greenhouse. One part per thousand increase raises the yield by some incredible number. I don't know much about that. Rich knew, and there's a horticulturist working on the greenhouse."

Charlie's expression was murderous. "A man dies of anoxia, you have tanks of carbon dioxide handy, and no one thinks to mention it! Why not?"

"The police tried to make a connection and couldn't," Alexander said, his nervousness making his voice almost shrill. "No one could see how it got from here to the elevator, or anywhere else. There's no way."

"I bet. Where do the pipes go?"

Alexander led them from the room into a narrow passage between the back of the house and the concrete wall of the swimming pool. The wall was a maze of pipes and ducts. The carbon dioxide pipe was thin stainless steel tubing near the top. In the center of the passage a steep flight of stairs went up; the pipes continued straight ahead. The largest duct stopped at the back of the elevator wall; other pipes went on through the end of the passageway.

"And that?" Charlie said, pointing to the end. "What's behind there?"

"The cold-storage room. You can't get to it from down here, only from the pantry off the kitchen."

Charlie examined the tubing again and could find no way the gas could have got from it to the elevator. It was unbroken, without a valve, without a seam. He turned and led the way now, up the narrow, steep stairs that took them to the back of the house near an entrance to the rear garden. Opposite the stairs was the door to the Jacuzzi room.

The whirlpool was ten feet long, six feet wide. There was a taut plastic cover over it, a roller at one end, grooves along the sides where the plastic cover was secured.

"Open it," Charlie ordered, and watched the unhappy young man go to the wall with a control panel. He touched a button and the cover slid back, rolled itself up, and vanished.

"Close it again." Charlie grunted, his eyes narrow as he watched the cover slide over the pool. Although it moved fast, it was not fast enough to keep anyone in who wanted out. But once in place, it would be almost impossible for anyone under it to move the cover out of the way. Less than an inch of space separated the cover and the surface of the water. He looked closely at the groove and tested the cover, and finally said with a scowl, "Let's move on."

"The cold-storage room?" Alexander asked. He had started to chew on the other thumbnail. The rest of his nails were bitten to the quick.

"Naturally." Charlie took Constance's hand and squeezed it a little, reassuringly, he hoped. She had not said a word since their tour started, but she had seen everything he had, he knew, and later they would talk about it, compare notes. Her hand was cool in his.

They passed a dressing room and a lavatory, then found themselves in the corridor by the elevator doors again. Another hall led to an outside door. Alexander went down that one. Near the end of this passage there were doors on both sides, one to the kitchen, one to the pantry, which he opened. Just inside the pantry was another very heavy, insulated door. A draft of cold air flowed from below when he opened this one.

"It's really a refrigerator," Alexander said, leading the way down. "Gary called it a root cellar, but it's a refrigerator."

It was like entering an ice cave. The room was so heavily insulated that no sound penetrated; the walls were stainless steel, the floor plastic. Bins lined one wall, shelves the other. Two fluorescent ceiling fixtures cast a bluish light. Constance shivered and hugged her arms about herself. At the far end of the room were two stainless steel carts on wheels and another door, this one only about five feet high. Charlie spotted the steel tubing; it dipped down in this room and went behind the bins.

"Explain all this," he said brusquely, waving at the bins, the other door, the room in general.

"It's Rich's experiment," Alexander said. "The

room is a low-oxygen, high-CO_2 environment. Not dangerous," he added hastily. "Fifteen percent oxygen, one percent carbon dioxide, it won't hurt you, at least not very fast. The bins are meant to hold special produce—grapes, pears, whatever, each in its own environment most ideally suited for long keeping. The bins are airtight, and the carbon dioxide mixture is controlled by the computer."

Charlie reached for one of the bins, and Alexander caught his arm.

"Don't do that. Look." There was a panel with symbols that meant nothing to Charlie. "That says this bin has a concentration of twelve percent carbon dioxide, and the temperature is forty-two. You don't want to open it until you exhaust the gas, you see."

Charlie examined other bins with other panels, all slightly different, all containing carbon dioxide. He pointed at the end door. "And that?"

"A dumbwaiter up to the pantry. The idea is that you can hang a side of beef down here, or bushels of fruits, stuff too heavy to lug down the stairs. So there's a dumbwaiter."

Charlie was looking at him with incredulity. "I hope we can open that," he said.

"Oh, sure. I know what you're thinking, Mr. Meiklejohn. I really do. But the police swarmed over this room and the bins and everything, and they couldn't figure out a way to make it add up. Look, this bin is empty." He pulled it open. It was about two feet deep and just as wide, narrowing at the bottom. He closed it again and went to the back of the room and opened the door to the dumbwaiter, a stainless steel box, two by three feet, about five feet high. The control here was simple: one black button for up, one for down. There was a bar handle on the outside of the door; the inside space was completely smooth without controls or handle.

Charlie was glaring at Alexander by now. "Let's have a look at it from upstairs," he growled. They left the cold-storage room gladly. Constance was shivering, and Charlie felt chilled through and through. The dumbwaiter in the pantry was behind another insulated door, and there were two control buttons on the wall. Alexander started to reach for one and Charlie shook his head. "In a second." He pulled the door open and examined the space. There were vents in the ceiling of the enclosure. He looked at Alexander questioningly.

"A duct leads to outside. In case of a leak, you know. Carbon dioxide is heavier than air, so it wouldn't go out the door at the top of the stairs, but it could flow into the dumbwaiter. If the dumbwaiter gets up here with any carbon dioxide inside it, it's automatically vented out before the door will open. At least, that's how it works when the computer's controlling it." He pointed to what looked like a thermometer without mercury on the side of the up and down buttons. "A safety backup sensor," he said. "It determines if there's carbon dioxide in the cage."

Charlie nodded and pushed the up button. Nothing happened.

"It won't work with the door open."

Charlie closed the door and tried again. The mechanism was soundless. In a moment the box had arrived; the door opened.

7

Neither Charlie nor Constance objected when Alexander began to hurry to finish the rest of the tour. He showed them how each doorway had been under observation during the game, and where the sensors in the floor were concealed under the carpeting so that no one could enter any of the rooms without being registered.

"It's sure to revolutionize security systems," the earnest young man said.

"Big Brother is alive and well," Charlie said sourly.

"If you have to have security, you might as well have good systems. Gary's room was upstairs. You want to see that?" He sounded defensive and a little belligerent.

"Is it stripped?" Charlie asked.

"You mean his personal things? Yes, but the furnishings are just like they were, and the computers he used are still there. It's not locked or anything."

"We'll manage by ourselves, but before you vanish, tell me something about the gadget Bruce was talking about, the control computer. He said as big as a cigarette pack. Is that about right? Exactly what could he do with such a small device?"

Alexander brightened again. "There were several

of them, actually, each a dedicated computer." He looked from Constance to Charlie, as if testing if they could follow, then looked despairing again. "You know garage door openers? The hand-held signaling device that opens and closes them? That's a dedicated machine. Made to do one thing only. That's sort of like the hand-held computers for Smart House. Suppose someone fell down in one of the bedrooms and couldn't get to the door, or there was a fire, or any number of emergencies arose. One of the hand-held computers worked sort of like a master key, a skeleton key. It could open doors. Any of them. Another one could intercept, alter, or add to some of the basic functions of Smart House, like if the lights were timed to go off at eleven and you wanted them to stay on until later, you could do that. The basic instructions would still be functional, and the program would revert back to them, but temporarily you could control some things."

"What besides the lights?" Charlie asked patiently when Alexander's voice trailed off.

With a vague gesture Alexander indicated the entire house. "Just basic things like lights and the climate-control system, bathwater temperatures, things like that."

"Swimming pool temperature? Jacuzzi temperature?" Charlie asked softly.

Alexander fidgeted, his glance darting all around them. They were standing at the foot of the stairs, the glass wall behind him, Charlie and Constance facing it. Nervously he glanced over his shoulder. When he spoke again, his voice was nearly a whisper. "Mr. Meiklejohn, I honestly don't know what all he programmed into them. There were three of them, and I haven't been able to find a single one. They were always kept in the office downstairs, but after Gary decided to play the game, he kept them in his bedroom, and I haven't even seen them since last spring sometime. He could have added features, macros, I don't know anything about, or he could have put them somewhere and forgot about them. I just don't know. But no one else could have used them, sir. I mean, our program is unique, and each of them was programmed in a language that is brand-new. No one else here could have used them."

Charlie studied him with great curiosity. He could not decide yet whether this young man was simply ingenuous or extremely clever. "We'll talk more later, Alexander," he said then. "Right now I don't know enough to ask many questions. I'm sure I'll think of some."

"One question," Constance said, as the young man turned away in evident relief. "First, you said he could have programmed in features or macros. Would you explain those terms?"

Alexander shifted as if in agony. After a pause he said, "Let me describe one of the things we programmed in, to give you an idea. Suppose someone in room number three is a smoker. In each room there's a smoke alarm, of course, but they're all set to register minute amounts of smoke—cigarette smoke or pipes, whatever. We put in a conditional macro that says in effect that if the smoke detector is activated at a certain minimum level, then certain other steps are taken. I mean the air conditioner is reprogrammed to exhaust smoke, and change the air more often, things like that. That's a feature activated by a macro—it's a string of commands in a permanent file that is started by a signal, in this case the smoke detector. Of course, smoke from a real fire would cause other things to happen—the fire alarm, sprinkler system to start, things of that sort. But any string of commands can be activated by a key, or combination of keys, or any signal you program in.

That's what the hand-held computers could do, send the signal."

Constance nodded thoughtfully. "I see. So the little computer could have been used to erase someone playing the game, just as Bruce suggested?"

He shrugged his thin shoulders. "Sure. That's the point. Gary could have programmed that in, or a number of other things. I don't know if he did, but he could have."

"Thanks for being our guide," Charlie said, taking Constance's arm. "Onward and upward. See you later."

Alexander darted away, and they went upstairs without speaking. At the top Constance said, "Charlie, you know carbon dioxide poisoning isn't the same as anoxia."

He grinned. "I thought I would have to explain that to you."

"But why did you go on about it down there?"

He put his finger on her lips. "I want them all to talk as freely as possible. If our killer needed inside info, who's a better bet than Alexander? Good God, he must have chips instead of gray matter in that skull of his. Look, there's someone new. More than one, in fact."

He was looking down into the atrium. Constance joined him and saw Milton with three people they had not met, two men and a woman. The woman was very beautiful.

"Let's take a quick look at Gary's room, and a quick look at the roof, and then go meet the newcomers."

Gary's suite was a disappointment. Without his possessions it was just another luxurious hotel suite. There were two rooms: a small office with two computers, and his bedroom. There was a walk-in closet, and a bathroom twice the size of the one in the room Charlie and Constance had. Charlie gazed around with dissatisfaction. "We'll get back to it," he said. "Now the roof."

This was a disappointment also. The mist had grown so dense that the ocean had vanished into it. Little of the grounds was visible. The dome was glass, the flooring plastic, and, Charlie realized, it was constructed of solar collectors. A small redwood building housed the elevator and held many outdoor collapsible chairs and several small tables. It was cold and wet up there; they did not linger.

They took the elevator back to the ground floor and entered the atrium where a small group had gathered and was having drinks at the bar. The odor of chlorine and gardenias and blooming orange and lemon trees made the room stifling to Constance. As they approached the bar, she realized that she hated Smart House. As beautiful as it was, as modern and comfortable and convenient, it was also too inhuman in scale, in expertly selected furnishings and colors, and in spy eyes everywhere that might or might not be watching.

"Constance, Charlie," Milton Sweetwater greeted them. "Laura and Harry Westerman, and Jake Kluge, and now you've met us all."

It used to be, Charlie thought almost aggrievedly as they all shook hands and made quick, mutual assessments, that businessmen going into middle age had certain similarities, a bit of a paunch for example, or a receding hairline, or something. Here were two more healthy specimens—Jake Kluge was gangly and strong, with straight brown hair that could stand cutting and was a bit limp. His eyes were pale blue behind contact lenses. Harry Westerman was a mountain climber, according to Milton, and he looked it. He was rock hard all over, wiry, with the sort of muscularity that never turned to flab because there was absolutely no fat coating the muscles and underlying the skin. His eyes were piercing and dark, and now looked irritable and impatient. And Laura Westerman was a knockout. She kept his hand less than a second too long, but he knew it and she knew it. He had seen her, or women who could pass for her, for years in New York, usually carrying hat-boxes, makeup bags, hurrying to meet this photographer, or make that modeling event, denying themselves any calories more than an allotted number carefully arrived at with the aid of a nutritionist. And he had seen the husbands, he thought soberly; either they were eaten alive by jealousy, or they were so involved in their own endless affairs that they were oblivious to the fact that their wives were saying yes to every man they met.

"You aren't afraid of the house, I hope," Jake Kluge said to Constance. "We agreed at our last meeting that except for basic systems that we're all familiar with, nothing would be turned on this weekend. There's no more to worry about than the elevator in any building in Manhattan."

Before Constance could reassure him, Charlie said, "That's a damn shame, in a way. I'd love to see this joint in operation."

Harry Westerman turned abruptly and went behind the bar. "We're having martinis. What would you like?"

"That sounds fine," Charlie said, after glancing at Constance who nodded. He looked about the garden and waved at it all. "How about the lights in here? On a timer, or do you have to go around and flick them on and off?"

"There's a light switching board," Milton Sweetwater said, glancing uneasily at Harry who was shaking the drinks. "Or you could do them individually."

Harry poured two more drinks and put them on the bar counter. "Usually they're under the control of

Smart House," he said. "Like everything else." Charlie handed a glass to Constance, lifted his own, and sipped, and Harry asked in a voice as hard as everything else about him, "Exactly what do you think you can learn in a weekend, Mr. Meiklejohn? The police held us here for days, and they've been coming around ever since. I voted against bringing you in, you should know."

"I already know some things the police weren't told," Charlie said easily. "I know about the game, and I know about the hand-held computers that could override the main system. And now I know that the decision wasn't unanimous to open yet another investigation. I'd say I'm making a certain amount of progress."

Harry's expression darkened, his eyes narrowed, and Laura laughed softly. "Harry did come around," she said. "By the time we thrashed it all out, he agreed along with everyone else."

Harry motioned for her to stop, and Charlie filed away the fact that in spite of her feigned disregard for him, she seemed uncommonly aware of his gestures, his frowns.

"What hand-held computer are you talking about?" Harry demanded.

Charlie looked from him to Jake, who shook his head. "Gary didn't demonstrate one for either of you?" He looked at Laura. "Or you?"

Her laughter was brittle this time. She moved to stand by Harry behind the bar and began to look over bottles there. "You might as well add something else to what you know that we didn't mention to the police. Gary loved secrecy more than anything else in life. If he had such a toy, he would have guarded it very jealously, at least until he was ready for the big production, which was to take place on Monday. Isn't that about right, darling?" she said to Harry mockingly.

"All I know is that he didn't tell me about it."

"I'll be damned," Jake Kluge murmured. "Of course he would have had such a thing, a number of them. Where are they? Have you seen them? Does Alexander have them?"

Charlie shook his head. "'Fraid not. Alexander says he can't find them. Why do you say, of course?"

"We should have figured it out," Jake said. "Obviously you'd have an override control. Another ace in the hole for Gary. But they must be around somewhere. Did Alexander search for them?"

"He said he couldn't find them. Why are they important, Mr. Kluge?"

Jake started, then grinned. "Jake," he said. "And you're Charlie, and she's Constance. Okay? You've brought us something already, Charlie. You see, some things the damn house was doing we haven't been able to figure out, and this could explain why. If he was overriding the main system, he could have made it perform in certain ways. Harry, let's go find Alexander. Thanks, Charlie."

Harry came out from the bar and they started to walk out together.

"Before you take off," Charlie said. "Just one thing. You weren't eager to open this can of worms, I take it. Either of you. Why did you change your minds?"

Jake shrugged. "I never said I was against it."

"But weren't you?"

He regarded Charlie curiously for a moment, then nodded. "I think we just want to put it behind us, get on with company business. And, as Harry said, we have little faith in anything coming of a new investigation."

"Did the house do it?" Charlie asked very softly.

"For Christ's sake!" Harry snapped. He started to move again, but Jake caught his arm.

"Wait a minute," Jake said. "We hired him. The company hired him to ask questions, and we agreed to answer them. No, Charlie, not in the way you imply by your question. The house couldn't have intended to kill anyone."

"I didn't bring up intentions," Charlie murmured. "But, Jake, Harry, if the house didn't do it, then a person did. You want to put that behind you, too? Leave it alone if we determine that a person killed two men?"

Harry looked murderously at Milton Sweetwater, as if the lawyer had been responsible for making him change his mind. "Bellringer could go under," he said sharply. "I don't give a damn who did it. I just want it settled for once and for all so we can get on with things. Does that satisfy you?"

Charlie nodded. "Yes indeed. Jake?"

"You didn't bring up intentions, but neither did you bring up accidental deaths. That is the third alternative."

"I'll keep it in mind," Charlie said agreeably. "And if we decide it was a person? What will that do to the company's outlook?"

Jake shook his head. "I don't know. None of us knows. We could all be ruined one way or the other, but we do know that if we don't clear up this mess, we'll certainly be ruined. We'll cooperate, Charlie. Is that the real question?"

"Partly. Partly. See you later." He turned to Constance. "Let's go unpack and wash our hands."

Milton mentioned that dinner would be at seven, and Laura watched Charlie take Constance's hand with a slight smile. She looked at him and wiggled her fingers in farewell.

Going up the stairs, Constance chuckled softly and Charlie made a snorting sound. "You won't think it's funny when I sling her over my shoulder and take off for Mexico."

"No, dear," she said.

*   *   *

In their room again, she unpacked while Charlie went through the contents of the envelope Milton had provided. He studied the beautifully drawn floor plans for a long time. The articles of incorporation looked intimidating, and the forensics reports chilled him too much to dwell on before dinner. He pursed his lips over the list of toys that had been designated murder weapons, then folded that paper and put it in his pocket. When he looked up from the papers on the desk, Constance was standing at the window gazing out at heavy fog that rose and fell, revealed, concealed, teased. He joined her and put his arm around her waist.

"What do you think?" she asked.

"They're like passengers on a ship that was being tossed in a storm with a mad captain. Any of them might have wanted Gary overboard, I guess. Milton must want the company to be as stable as IBM or Ma Bell; he doesn't like disorder. Jake is in line for power, money, prestige, whatever goes along with being head honcho now. Harry could be hiding a case of terminal jealousy under that Mount Rushmore exterior. Bruce? A nut, also jealous for other reasons, in debt. Beth wanted out from slavery. Laura? We'll see. I don't have a doubt in the world that she had a case, too." He squeezed her shoulder. "How'm I doing?"

She laughed softly. "A-plus. They're a strange group," she said thoughtfully. "I don't think they would do a thing about either death if it weren't for company profits."

"Want to bet that one of them will bring up the possibility that a stranger got in that night, and at least two of the others will back up the idea?"

"You know very well that I am morally opposed to gambling," she said primly. "Besides, I already picked Bruce to raise the possibility, and his mother to back it. Charlie, don't you think it's strange that Alexander didn't mention the little computers before? Of the three men who really worked on the house and understood the entire system, he's the only one left. He probably can make the computers do whatever they're capable of doing without any effort at all. Don't you think so?"

"I think," he said grimly, "the only way you're going to get anything out of that twerp is by nailing him down and poking him with a sharp stick from time to time. Well, ready for another go round with them all?"

Bruce said at dinner, "You know, it's quite possible that someone actually got in that night, someone not invited, I mean."

Maddie nodded emphatically. "Of course, it's possible. I never believed in that total security system."

Constance looked at Charlie brightly; he sighed.

"Jake, Harry? Would it have been possible?" he asked, pretending to be unaware that Alexander had stopped his fork midway to his mouth, that he had started to speak.

Jake shook his head. "I doubt it. The police spent hours trying out the system, first at the gate on the hill, then at the various entrances to Smart House proper. You just couldn't get in and out unregistered. There's a log of every entrance and exit that was made. They tried to get around it, just to see if anyone could have done so."

"How about the roof?" Bruce demanded.

"The balconies," Maddie said. "All those balconies! Anyone could walk in!"

This time Alexander spoke before Charlie could interfere. "No way! That's one of the systems we were ready to market, practically."

"Practically?" Charlie asked. "You mean it wasn't complete?"

"It was still too specific," Alexander muttered. "We were in the process of generalizing it before we actually showed it. A few more months, that's all it needed. It was working back in May for the specific conditions, though."

"That's the hitch," Harry said angrily. "It would have to be custom tailored for each individual or company, and that means time and expense. A few months? I think a year or more."

"Do you think it might have failed to register an intruder that night?" Charlie asked him.

"Sure. Especially since Gary had the override system. He could have turned the whole thing off. We're talking about a system that controls this whole house, the grounds, the greenhouse, everything, and whatever the main system can do, the hand-held computer can start or stop."

"Someone could have come up from the beach," Maddie said with a touch of desperation in her voice.

"Maddie, stop it!" Milton said, but his voice was gentle. "We all know no one got in here that night!"

"Why not from the beach?" Charlie asked thoughtfully.

"Because we're on a headland here, and at high tide you can't get around it," Milton said. "There's a cove with rocky cliffs on the both ends, completely cut off at high tide. The police looked into that."

Charlie turned to Bruce. "You said the roof. How could anyone get up there?"

Bruce glanced at Harry, who collected mountains, then away quickly. "I examined that rock wall today. It's climbable. A good climber could go right up the back wall to the roof."

Harry nodded. "That's true. I looked at it too, from a different angle, of course. Not just a good climber.

Anyone who wanted to go up could do it. But once on top, Bruce, you still have to pass through a scanner and a sensor in the floor." His voice was vicious. "Okay, Gary or Rich, or someone else, could have turned off security, but they didn't. There's a record of movements that would show an intruder. And don't even pretend an outsider could have got his hands on the system, and not just that, but have time to learn the system and reprogram it."

"It's been my experience," Charlie said comfortably then, "that practically every action made by people in close quarters is noticed by someone, even in a house as big as this."

"We were taken over that whole evening by the police several times," Laura snapped. "I am sick to death of thinking about it all, who was where, when. No one saw anything!"

"I think people saw more than they realized then. The police accepted your statements because they had not been let in on the fact of the game, and I have been. You were all watching each other closely, I'll bet. In fact, if you had admitted how closely to the police, it might have appeared suspicious. Now you can, all admit it freely. What I propose is that you reenact the game as it developed back in May. Going through the movements probably will stimulate memories in a way that just talking didn't do."

"No!" Maddie said, and she started to get to her feet. She groped for the table and knocked over her glass of wine and sank down again staring at it in horror. "Look what I've done. Look what you made me do!"

Gently Constance said to her, "You didn't play the game then and you certainly don't have to play it this time."

"No one has to play it," Laura Westerman said. "If that damn computer is turned on again, I'm going home." She glared at her husband. "I'm not even a shareholder. I don't have to agree to anything."

"But we need you," Charlie protested. "You have to take Mrs. Elringer's one vote. Isn't that what you did before?"

"Gary insisted," she said sharply. "He didn't give anyone a choice, and another thing you might as well know is that no one here dared cross him in any way. No one! He wanted to play his insane game and everyone said good, let's kill each other for fun! If I had turned him down, Harry would have bitched for months! Does that satisfy you? You, I'm afraid, don't have that kind of power over us."

"Of course not," Charlie said in a placating way. "I wouldn't want that kind of power." He regarded them all broodingly. "I confess I'm still trying to figure out why you all went along with it, why you all played for votes."

There was a lengthy silence. Finally Jake cleared his throat. "It was an important meeting. Gary and Rich, and Alexander, of course, and a few others in the company were researching artificial intelligence in their computer systems in Smart House. Making some real breakthroughs, apparently. But others among us saw it as a black hole that would suck the company dry in no time. It's the sort of research that needs government grant money, big money, not a small company like ours to back it. It was an important meeting. The idea of gaining enough votes to have an influence was irresistible to many of us."

"He was willing to risk so much?" Charlie asked. "Would he have gone along with a negative vote? One that forced him to stop his line of research?"

"It wasn't a risk!" Alexander cried. "He knew that if they all just gave it a chance, they'd see what he had accomplished here. He had done most of the things he had set out to do, and that weekend would have proven he was on the right track. Whoever makes the breakthrough in linking a digital computer with an analog computer in a comprehensive, parallel system that is both logic-directed and goal-directed will be the intellectual hero of the century. Gary was doing it!"

"That sounds like big bucks," Charlie murmured.

Jake laughed suddenly and tossed his napkin down on the table. "Charlie," he said, "that must be the understatement of the century. And that's why we never seriously considered that any of us could have murdered him. That's what you're talking about, of course. Murder. By one of us. But he was the goose who could produce the golden eggs, you see. And while the rest of us don't match him in intellectual capacity, neither is there an idiot at this table. We're in the process now of reviewing all the work he did here, trying to debug some of it with Alexander's help, and the help of others who came in very skeptical and are true believers now. If we can stay afloat, the systems in this damn house right now will mean big bucks, very big bucks, and there wasn't a one of us who didn't know that by midafternoon of that Saturday, many hours before Gary died. That's our dilemma, Charlie, in a nutshell."

"Then there shouldn't be any real objection to going through the motions of playing the game again, just to see if someone spots something not quite in line with what memory serves up."

Bruce shoved his chair back. "Okay. Now we go to the living room for coffee and hear the game rules, just like we did then. You going to chicken out, Laura?"

She raked him with a contemptuous look. "I meant it. If that computer is turned on, I leave."

"We won't use the game program," Charlie said. "What I propose, actually, is that I'll take the part of the computer. Coffee, you said? In the living room? I'll tell you what I have in mind over coffee."

8

THE coffee service was on a sideboard in the living room; this time they all helped themselves. Charlie waited until they were settled and then said, "I asked Mrs. Ramos to bring out the conference notebooks and pencils, and here they are." A stack of yellow legal pads and a pewter mug of pencils were on an end table. He picked them all up and began to hand them out. As he moved along, he asked pleasantly, "Whose idea was it to erase the game from disk, by the way?" No one spoke. "Let's try it this way," he said. "Was it before the cops came, during, or after?"

"After," Alexander said. "They were gone by then."

"I see. So while they were here, you simply kept mum about the game and the record of movements." He finished giving out the note pads and sat in a deep chair the color of midnight; it was so soft, so comfortable, it was almost too sensuous. He resisted the impulse to stroke the arm. "Where were you when the decision was made to erase everything having to do with the game?"

"The library," Alexander said. "They said they would send someone down from Portland, a special detective, and we should all stay here until he came and asked questions. We had a meeting. We didn't know where we stood legally, the company and all, I mean."

Charlie nodded sympathetically. "I can imagine. So you were at the long conference table. Where Mrs. Ramos got the note pads, I understand. And someone said, let's get rid of evidence of any game. Is that how it was?"

"You know it wasn't like that!" Laura Westerman cried shrilly. "No one thought of it as evidence of anything except stupidity. I said we'd be on every front page of every tabloid in the country. They'd make us all look utterly ridiculous."

"So they would," Charlie agreed, and waited.

Jake shrugged. "I could have been the first to voice the suggestion. I simply don't remember. I do remember that suddenly we were all talking about it. The police had the disk with our movements, remember, from the Smart House security program, a totally different system. But we all thought all our movements were on it. At least," he added flatly, "that's what I thought. And, at our meeting concerning you, we agreed to provide you with a printout of the record the police took." He looked questioningly at Milton, who nodded.

"I have it," Charlie admitted. "But if Gary had an override system, I wonder how accurate it can be. Anyway, to get to our reenactment of the game, what I want you to do is try to retrace your movements that had anything to do with the game. When you found out who your victim was, when you got your weapon, what it was, when and if you used it."

"Starting when?" Harry demanded. "I for one can't provide you with a minute-by-minute account of my movements for the whole twenty-four hours. Who could?"

"Just the highlights for now," Charlie said soothingly. "Victim, witness, weapon, time. You'll be surprised how much you recall once you actually start something like this."

"What difference does it make?" Harry insisted. "This is more damn nonsense!"

Charlie regarded him soberly. "Someone was playing the game for very high stakes. Someone found out about the override gadgets and used them. Do you know who that was, Harry? One of you knows for sure, and others know more than you realize. If there was a murderer here, someone, or more than one of you, saw enough to point at that person."

"My God!" Beth said with a moan. "We were paranoid then, but this . . . this is monstrous!"

"Murder is monstrous," Charlie agreed. He surveyed them coldly. Maddie's face was chalky, her hands shaking too hard to hold the pencil, coffee, anything else. At Charlie's words Laura had put her hand on her husband's arm, and Harry had shrugged it off again and was contemplating his shoes with a distant hard look. Jake was watching Charlie closely, his expression remote and unreadable. Alexander twisted his pencil, bit the eraser, twisted it again and again. Only Milton Sweetwater looked resigned. He broke the silence.

"Charlie, what do you suspect? What do you know already?" he asked.

"I know that something's wonky with the printout of movements starting with the opening gambit. If you hadn't withheld evidence from the police, they would know it, too. Gary had you all in here Friday evening and outlined the game rules, then he left. The printout shows him going up in the elevator, then into his room. It does not show him leaving it again that night, and yet I know he was on the first floor later, playing the game, trying to kill Bruce." He laughed harshly. "A magic act. The printout shows him entering his room a second time that night." He looked them all over again. No one had moved. "Unless you people have secret clones that you haven't bothered to tell me about yet, either the system didn't register all his movements, or else he pulled off an impossible stunt. Didn't the police ask to see the entire printout?"

Alexander shook his head. Suddenly the pencil snapped in his fingers, making a cracking sound that was too loud. He cleared his throat. "I didn't look at the entire printout a single time. No one thought of going back to Friday. What for? The police wanted it from Saturday from after dinner until they arrived. No one asked about any movements before that evening. Why would anyone?"

"Exactly," Charlie said dryly.

Harry jumped to his feet, flung down his note pad, and glared at Jake. "The whole thing's a fucking lie! That record doesn't mean a goddamn thing! Proving that no one was on the elevator with Rich, that no one went into the Jacuzzi with Gary! All a fucking lie! See what keeping our mouths shut about the goddamn game got us!"

"The program's full of bugs," Bruce said murderously. "I knew it! That bastard! That goddamn bastard! All that money down the drain! You can't trust any of it! I knew it from the start."

"It isn't!" Alexander yelled and leaped to his feet, his hands clenched. "If Gary turned it off, that's one thing, but the program didn't make a mistake or lie. It works, damn it!" His voice was shrill.

Constance was watching them all. When Maddie took a deep breath and got up, she stood up also.

"I don't feel very well," Maddie said faintly. "I'll just go lie down a bit."

"Let me go with you," Constance said. "I want to go up for a few minutes, too."

The voices continued to shout as they left the

room. As Laura's high-pitched voice chimed in, Constance wondered if Charlie had pushed them too hard. She had flashed him a message—she would try to get Maddie to talk—and had been acknowledged by such a brief, tiny nod that it would have passed unnoticed by anyone else, she knew. All those geniuses, she thought then, had performed exactly as Charlie had planned, and now he would sit back and watch and listen and when the time was right, he would prod them again. And one of them would say something meaningful. At the stairs Maddie turned without hesitation and started up. No one appeared to want to take the elevator in this house.

Halfway up the stairs, out of sight and hearing of the others, Constance said, "Mrs. Elringer, you can stop acting now."

Maddie paused and looked at her sharply.

"I mean the drinking act," Constance said, and took her arm. They started up again. "I've been watching you all evening. You haven't had as much alcohol as I've had, I'd say."

"They all keep wanting me to take sides," Maddie said in a low voice. "Gary's been dead for under three months, and they're fighting like dogs. Like dogs."

Constance nodded. "As long as they think you're feeling the alcohol, they leave you alone, is that it?"

"I guess so," Maddie admitted.

"Can we talk a few minutes?"

"I really am tired," she said. They stopped outside a door; she reached for the knob.

"And you're terrified, too," Constance said gently. "Perhaps you should talk a little."

Maddie's face crinkled and tears welled in her eyes. Constance leaned past her to open the door and they went inside the bedroom.

"He should have been an only child," Maddie said a few minutes later. She had gone to the bathroom and washed her face and was in one of the chairs at the table before the windows. Constance was seated in the opposite chair. The drapes were drawn, the room lighted only by a dim wall lamp. "He was a difficult child. Very difficult. So precocious, of course, but Bruce . . . He was only six and didn't understand. A bad age to bring in a new baby, they tell me. He had been the baby of the family so long, and he was brilliant, of course, but suddenly there was someone new who was even more brilliant. There wasn't a thing Bruce could do that Gary couldn't do better, from the time he was three or four. He was Bruce's equal at first, and then surpassed him. In all ways. They fought so much. Car trips were hellish, staying home with them was worse." She shook her head, her eyes closed, her forehead furrowed.

"He didn't realize how much he could hurt people," she said. "His father, me, Bruce, then Beth, everyone eventually. It wasn't malice. He wasn't evil. He just didn't know. He took what he needed from people and when he had all there was, he turned his back on them without another thought."

She sighed deeply and became still now, wrapped in memories that twisted her face in pain. After a moment, Constance said, "Yet you all remained loyal to him. You all went into business with him, kept protecting him even after he was grown up."

"He was always so vulnerable," Maddie said. "He just didn't know what effect he had on people. That night when he talked about the game, he was sincere. To him it was a game. I had a premonition," she said nearly in a whisper. "I don't even believe in premonitions, but suddenly I knew there would be a tragedy because of the game. I just knew it. Everyone had so much hurt, I just knew they'd all want Gary to be their victim. But it was more than that. I had the feeling of horror. I said I wouldn't have anything to do with it. I wouldn't. Tonight when your husband began talking about the game again, it came back, that awful feeling of horror, of terror."

When Constance went down to the living room again, Charlie looked up at her questioningly.

"She's resting."

His look said, you did fine; hers asked how it was going. He nodded slightly and she went to the sideboard for coffee. Apparently no one else had left yet. There were sheets of the yellow note pads on tables, on the floor by chairs, several on the coffee table Charlie was using as a work surface. It did not surprise her at all to find them doing it Charlie's way.

"Okay," he said, consulting his own notes. "It's after one. Gary has just tried to kill you, but your mother can't witness since she's not in the game. Right?"

Bruce's expression was petulant, his voice a whine when he said that was right. Constance watched him, wondered if he had developed that attitude in reaction to a genius brother. Was this the real Bruce, or the man who shouted and cursed and screamed obscenities almost randomly?

"Jake didn't cooperate," Bruce went on. "He ducked out when he saw what Gary was up to."

Jake nodded at his account and made a note on his paper. Beth wrote briefly on hers. Bruce finished writing something and they all handed the sheets to Charlie, who added them to the growing stack.

"Anyone else?" When no one spoke, he asked Jake, "Why didn't you witness for Gary?"

"By then I'd begun to get a feeling about the magnitude of his accomplishment in Smart House and I wanted to talk to him, but seriously, not with the game in the way. I thought we were heading for a talk, but at the door to the television room, he said something like 'Gotcha' when he saw Bruce. I realized I'd be witness, and, frankly, I decided not to help Gary win the game if I could help it. I ducked out."

"Where did you go?"

"To the garden for a nightcap, then up to my room with my drink."

"You didn't see him again that night?"

Jake shook his head.

Charlie turned to Bruce again. "Where did you go?"

"I was going to go to the kitchen for a snack, but he kept following me, yelling, and I got on the elevator instead and went up to my room and stayed. I think he turned and went on into the kitchen."

Charlie frowned at the printout he had opened on the table. He tapped his eraser on it absently and said, "According to the official printout, Gary went into his room on the second floor at ten-ten Friday night and never came out again. And he went into the kitchen at one-twenty-five and never came out of it again, either. Maybe the rules he had were different from the ones the rest of you were using."

"How about when he got that damn dagger?" Bruce demanded and got up to look at the printout over Charlie's shoulder.

Charlie shook his head. "Nothing." He looked at Alexander thoughtfully. "Could he have programmed the computer to erase selected activities and still allow him to open doors?"

Miserably Alexander said yes.

"All right. Could he have programmed it not to record his movements when he was with another person? Jake here, for example."

Alexander nodded.

"I doubt that," Jake protested. "I mean, even if he'd been able to do it, why? It was a game, for God's sake! You just don't understand about him and games! What in God's name would be the point in programming a game like that and then cheating?"

"Don't know," Charlie said. "Could someone else have programmed in the same instructions, Alexander?"

The young man blanched, then flushed brightly. "I could have done it, or Rich. No one else knew the system yet. No one here, anyway. There were a couple of others back in Palo Alto who worked on it and could have done it."

"Okay," Charlie said then in his most pleasant voice, the voice that sometimes gave Constance a chill. What had he just learned? she wondered. "So you're all safely inside your rooms now. We don't know where Gary was. What came next?"

"Are you really going to make us go through every minute?" Laura asked in disbelief. "This is crazy. What possible difference can it make?"

"Don't know that either," Charlie said easily. "You get the picture of what I'm doing, you could shorten all this by trying to fill in the time before we drag it out second by second. When and where you got killed, who you killed, and who witnessed it; then backtrack, and go forward. If there wasn't any more activity that night, let's move on. Now, it's morning."

Minute by minute, encounter by encounter, he took them through the day. Now and then he stopped someone to ask a question, but for most of it, he simply listened. When Beth mentioned the blueprints she had seen at Rich Schoen's elbow on Saturday, he stopped her.

"I guess Rich carried the foam club rolled up in them," she said. "That's the weapon he used on Gary later."

"Where are the blueprints now?"

They all glanced at each other, and then Milton

Sweetwater shrugged. "In one of the offices, presumably."

"Rich brought them up from the Palo Alto office," Alexander said. "He was going to show them at the meeting on Monday. Usually they'd be down there, not in Smart House any longer. I don't know where they are."

Charlie nodded and let them continue describing the afternoon.

He stopped them again later. "So far no one has reported an encounter with Gary. Would that have been normal? It's nearly three in the afternoon."

Beth nodded. "He stayed up most of the night and never got up before twelve or one, and he liked being alone then for breakfast. I didn't give it a thought not to see him around."

"That's why we eat dinner at seven," Laura said with a malicious smile. "Gary wanted it over and done with by nine so he could go to work."

They went on recounting their adventures as killers and victims up to the time they gathered for cocktails, when Charlie stopped them.

"Let's call it a day," he said. "Papers, please, if you have any notes of times, observations, anything else. We'll finish this tomorrow." It was nearly midnight.

9

BETH stared at him in dismay. Leave it now? She looked around at the others. Jake and Milton were in a huddle whispering. Bruce hovered nearby as Charlie gathered up the loose sheets of paper. Laura had started to go out, apparently realized that no one else was leaving, and was now standing near Harry at the sideboard. Harry looked so tightly wound that a touch would make him explode; Laura did not get close enough to touch him.

Charlie glanced at them all and shuffled papers. Constance had not moved from her chair.

Abruptly Jake and Milton finished their dialogue and approached Charlie. Milton spoke in a commanding voice. "Charlie, it's obvious, to me at least, that you've decided murder was committed; those two deaths weren't accidental." No one else moved. "If you're up to continuing tonight, I strongly urge that we do so. If anything is going to come out of all this, it would be better to have it out tonight. If we have a murderer here, and if anyone did see him do anything suspicious, that person may be in danger. I, for one, intend to secure my door somehow tonight."

"I agree absolutely," Jake said. "You've managed to scare some of us to death," he said levelly. "I'm not willing to leave it here."

Charlie held up his hands. "Fine with me. Objections anyone?" No one moved. "Let's take a break, say twenty minutes. We could use some fresh coffee, maybe some sandwiches. During the break maybe you could all just jot down the next game killings, who the victim was, the weapon, witness, the next victim, time, whatever is appropriate. It will save time. And meanwhile, Alexander, would you mind showing us where Rich Schoen worked here? Did he have his own office?"

Alexander jumped up, evidently relieved to be able to do something. Before he could speak, Harry said, "We all know damn well that Rich wouldn't have let himself be suffocated in that elevator. And this surprise that one of us might be a murderer, bullshit! We've known that too. We've always known it," he said harshly, "and we chose to pretend not to." He scowled at Jake with bitterness. "But there is a place where the air can be exhausted in seconds. Those growing chambers in the greenhouse. They were designed airtight, with an exhaust system, a gas-pumping system."

"I thought of that," Jake said with disgust. "It's the same problem. Why would Rich stay there while someone went over and turned the knob, or punched keys in the computer, or any other damn thing? He designed it! He knew what it could do!"

"But if the killer had the hand-held computer, he could have controlled everything in the greenhouse, too. A push of a button would have done it," Harry said. "Remember, later that night a pesticide was released in there. Things got smashed up. I think the killer did that to cover his trail. Maybe Rich did struggle and something got broke earlier. No one could have known after things got so messed up."

Charlie turned to Alexander.

The young man nodded unhappily. "It could have

been programmed to do anything like that," he said, and then added almost pleadingly, "But it would take time. Time to learn the system, the language, the program for that function. It wouldn't be like turning a light on or off."

Softly Harry said, "For Gary it would have been exactly like that. Who had more time than he to program whatever he wanted into it? Who else would Rich have gone into the chamber for?"

"Oh, God!" Beth whispered. "Gary? Why?"

"I don't know why. But who else could have set things up in advance? Just one of those three, Rich, Gary, or Alexander."

Alexander looked helplessly from Harry to Charlie. His face crinkled as if he might burst into tears. He shook his head. "We didn't. Wreck our one dream? Ruin everything we planned for?" He shook his head harder.

"And then our heroic, athletic Gary picked up Rich and moved him to the house, down the hall, hoping all the time that no one noticed that he was carrying a hundred-ninety-pound dead man, of course," Jake said with heavy sarcasm. "He put him in the elevator, and went to the Jacuzzi and threw himself in out of remorse, and conveniently covered it so the sight would not be offensive to anyone. And somewhere along the way, he disposed of the little computers, just to muddy the issue." He started to move toward the door. "I volunteer to make coffee and sandwiches, but I want a witness, to make sure I don't add arsenic to the sugar bowl."

"That's not funny!" Laura screamed at him. "Do you have a better idea of what happened? At least Harry's trying."

Harry didn't even look at her when he snapped, "Just shut the fuck up!"

Charlie motioned toward the door and Constance got up and walked out with him and Alexander.

"This is awful," Alexander said glumly. "Worse than I thought it could get."

"You think so?" Charlie asked in surprise. "I thought it was going pretty well myself." He was grinning.

Alexander looked at him in shocked disapproval. So young, Constance thought. So bright and so ignorant.

"I'll help with coffee," Beth said. "If we can find it."

"I'll go, too," Laura said. "I know where it is."

"I think you know too much about Smart House," Bruce said suddenly. "You did last spring, too. You'd been here before, hadn't you? You finally got around to Gary, didn't you?"

The look Laura gave him was venomous. Before she could respond, Milton took her arm, not very gently, and turned her away from Bruce. "I want a word with you," he said.

Beth found herself studying Harry; he looked metallic. Even his eyes. He did that where Laura was concerned, she thought with a chill. Somehow he made himself absent; he became iron or some other cold dark metal that reflected nothing of what he was feeling. Bruce glared at Laura and Milton, swung around as if seeking a new target for his anger, and Harry turned his granite face toward him. Bruce stopped all movements and, after a moment, stalked silently from the living room. Again Beth examined Harry and knew that if he looked at her with that expression she would flee also. It wasn't even that he looked particularly threatening, she thought; it was worse than that. He looked inhuman.

Beth realized in surprise that she felt sorry for Harry. She had never liked him—he had always seemed too brusque, too singleminded—but now she sympathized. No one should be forced into inhumanity. She found herself wondering what he was like when he was happy, when he was nearing the peak of a new mountain, maybe, and knew he had won. She never had seen that side of him.

Then Jake touched her arm, and she went out with him.

"A lot of unpleasant things are going to be brought up the next day or so," Jake said in a low voice as they drew near the kitchen. "I understand the necessity, and it has to be, I suppose, but I'm sorry that came out like that."

She shook her head. "It's all right. I knew." She had known, just not the details, like when it started or how long it lasted. But she had known. Then she said, "You're right, though. Things will come out now. We'll all remember things we'd forgotten, see them in a new light. Charlie is a bit scary, isn't he?"

"Smart. He knows what he's doing."

They had stopped outside the kitchen door. She glanced at him and said almost apologetically, "While we were recalling the game, I remembered how angry with you I was, not that you killed me, but that you were enjoying the game."

He looked somber and troubled now. "You were right about it. You, Maddie, even Harry. That night, when we met in the upstairs hall and went down together, I was as tongue-tied as a junior-high school boy. I thought you were still sore with me, and I was full to bursting with excitement about the house, having fun with the game."

She smiled faintly, also remembering how stilted and awkward that brief encounter had been, how relieved she had been when he left her in the wide corridor near the television room.

"And then Gary laughed," he said in a harsher voice. "Come on, let's get coffee and stuff."

"Talk about Rich," Charlie had said to Alexander on the way to Rich's office. It had been painful, but eventually Alexander told them a little, in stumbling, halting, even agonized phrases. He told them about the team within a team that Gary had started to assemble more than five years ago. Constance glanced at him sharply and he shrugged. "I was still in school," he said. "Anyway, Gary had this vision of Smart House, an integrated system using both kinds of computers—"

"No more computer talk," Charlie interrupted. "He put together a team. Go on."

"Okay. But that's the basic idea . . . Okay. Rich was a leading developer of a particular CAD—a computer-assisted drawing and drafting program for architects," he added hastily. "He was written up in the journals. So Gary gave him a call and they met and talked, and Rich joined the team. Gary even gave him a percentage of his shares because he knew the money would get tight down the road, and he wanted to make certain Rich was in to stay if things got rough. That wasn't even necessary, but Gary did things like that. He gave me shares when I came in. He told me it was because when the others knew what he was up to, they might try to oust us, the team, and this way they really couldn't."

"Right. So now the house was about finished, Rich's work about done. What was he going to do next?"

Alexander's pain increased. His voice dropped to a near mumble. "That was a problem." He led them through the basement, past the garish arcade games, the pool table, toys. His hand trailed over the glossy surfaces as he passed them, but he did not give any of them a glance. "At first the plan was to build Smart House and start showing it to hotel people, resort people, developers, building management people. They could buy the whole system, or just a part of it. Rich was going to manage all that, package the separate programs, or integrate them, whatever. But Gary kept changing things. He hated the idea of having groups come for demonstrations. He decided Beth could be the hostess for demonstrations, when it came to that. He hated people he didn't know, and didn't want any part of that aspect. But he liked working here with his own projects. He seemed to think he could keep doing that and just avoid everyone."

"And you? You were after the artificial intelligence aspect of it, too, weren't you?"

"Yeah. Gary and me." He waved toward a door. "That's where Rich had his office."

They went inside. It was another spacious room complete with several computers, drawing tables, deep shelves for blueprints, vertical bins for drafting materials. One of the biggest printers Constance had ever seen was hooked up to one of the computers. Everything was scrupulously neat, as if it had not been touched in months, as was probably the case, Constance thought, surveying it. There was nothing of Rich's visible, nothing human visible. It might be a display room itself, the perfect work place for an architect. She glanced at Charlie. "I'll start over there," she said, indicating the right wall covered with many shelves of neatly stacked graph paper.

Alexander looked bewildered for a moment, then nodded. "You're looking for the blueprints?"

"You got it," Charlie said.

"I don't think they're in here."

"Neither do I. But why don't you?"

"A lawyer came for his things. You know, to settle

the estate. If the blueprints had been in here, I would
have found them. They would have got sent back to
Palo Alto, the main office where the other blueprints
are kept. We didn't find them. Of course, we weren't
looking for them specifically. I never gave them a
thought. I mean, who needs blueprints after the
house is built? Besides, there must be a dozen
copies."

"Good point," Charlie said, and took Alexander's
arm, steered him back to the door. "Thanks again for
guiding us, and now you go on back up. Okay? We'll
be up in a few minutes." He did not actually say "run
along now," but the inflection was there. Alexander
flushed and left quickly. As soon as the door was
closed after him, Charlie took Constance into his
arms and nuzzled her fragrant hair. "Missed you," he
said. "Get anything out of Mom?"

She laughed softly and pushed him away. "Dirty,
scheming old man. I thought that was a show of af-
fection."

He drew her to him again and kissed her. "Who
said love and business don't mix? He lied. Tell me."

She grinned. "As we say in the trade, right."

When they got back to the living room, there was a
platter of sandwiches on a low table, the coffee urn
filled again. Charlie surveyed the various guests of
Smart House. Maddie had returned. She was pale,
her face scrubbed, but she was composed and watchful. Most of the others were helping themselves to
the food, coffee, or booze. He waited until they were
settled once more.

His voice was brisk when he spoke. "Okay. It's
cocktail time Saturday evening. What next?" No one
volunteered. He said, "Safety in numbers. Right. So
on through dinner. Then what?"

Bruce cleared his throat. He looked more disheveled than he had earlier, as if he had purposely tousled his curly hair to make it stand out wildly; his sweater sleeves were stretched out at the cuffs, one pulled above his elbow, the other down to his finger-tips. His mouth was pouty. "I was probably next," he muttered. "Rich got me with a poison snake in the ice bucket in the garden bar. Milton was the witness."

"Time?"

"About ten," Milton said. "We recorded it, and I went on to the library."

Charlie turned to Bruce. "You stayed there with Rich?"

"For a few minutes. Then he left, I assumed to go to his room to check out his next victim, and then get another weapon. I finished my drink, went down to talk to Alexander in the basement awhile, and then went to the kitchen."

"Next," Charlie said.

"Me, I suppose," Milton said after a brief pause. "I took the elevator to the basement to get a weapon at ten after ten. I heard Rich and Jake, and the door to Gary's office closed when I got near it. I went on past the door to the showroom, and when I went back out, Rich was at the elevator door. I looked in to make sure no one else was there, and we went up to-gether."

Charlie looked at Jake. "And where did you go then?"

Jake glanced at the notes he had made, then spoke briskly. "I waited until they were both on their way up, and then I left and went up the stairs to my room. I realized that Milton must have been getting a weapon and I didn't even know who my next victim was supposed to be." He spread his hands expres-sively and said, "It turned out to be Rich."

"How did Rich open the office door? Wasn't it computer-locked the way the others were?"

Jake looked puzzled and slowly shook his head. "I didn't give it a thought. Maybe it was, and it was programmed to open for him."

Alexander said hurriedly. "It wasn't. Gary said he was the only one who could go in. The program was being run by the computer in there. I couldn't even get in."

Jake looked more puzzled and shrugged. "I don't know. He just opened it."

Charlie nodded. "Okay." He turned to Bruce, and said mildly, "You left Rich and went to the basement to talk to Alexander. Right?"

"Yeah," Bruce said sullenly. "I wanted information. With Gary keeping out of sight, I thought he might be running things from his office, not the computer doing it all." He turned his venomous glare toward Alexander, who squirmed unhappily.

"Gary warned me that Bruce would try to quiz me," Alexander said in a rush. "He told me not to tell him anything. I was just doing what Gary told me."

"He didn't even want me in his fucking lab," Bruce said furiously. "They were telling the others everything, but me they didn't even want in the offices! He kept trying to hustle me out the door, down the hall. He even walked to the stairs with me, looking for Gary or Rich or someone to save him. It was ten to eleven and I knew Gary would be making his damn popcorn pretty soon, so I went on up to the kitchen to wait for him, but he was in there already getting the stuff together, the popcorn maker, popcorn, salt. He said how did I like his playhouse, and was I having fun, and stuff like that, and when I told him what I thought, he laughed and took the popcorn maker and stuff out, laughing."

Charlie held up his hand. "You were in the basement at ten to eleven? And you used the stairs? Say another minute went by. How long did you and Gary talk?"

"Two minutes, three. We didn't talk. He laughed at me, mocked me. That's not talking. He was having the time of his life, a real birthday party."

"What door did he leave by?"

"What the fuck difference does it make?" he yelled. He glanced at the others watching him stonily.

"It'd be nice to understand why no one else saw him that night," Charlie mused. "That main hallway is like a fishbowl."

"I got between him and the door to the main hall, and he laughed harder and walked out the other door to the back hall. He walked on his own two feet, under his own power!" With a visible effort he controlled himself and went on. "I decided to see what else my money had bought and I was looking around the kitchen when Mom came in to raise hell with me. By then I'd about had enough of the bullshit and I just left her there yelling, out the door to the back hall, to the elevator. I was ready to go to bed, but the fucking elevator didn't come, and I went to the john by the dressing room, got a drink in the garden bar, and then . . ." He rubbed his eyes and shook his head. "I don't know. The breakfast room. The library. Harry came in right after me. I didn't want to talk and left again. TV room. Gary was laughing in the garden, and it went right through me. I said something to Beth and she ran out, and I couldn't stand the stupid movie. The Beatles. I went back to the library. Milton was there, and Jake came in." For the first time he looked at the sheet of paper covered with childish-looking handwriting, ran his finger down the page, and then tossed it down on the floor. "That's it."

Charlie nodded. "Thanks."

Alexander was folding and refolding his sheet of paper, as if trying to see how small a package he could make of it. "Bruce came down," he said, "and later on Harry came down, and I didn't see anyone else and I didn't go upstairs all night. I had too much work to do. I was in my lab all that night."

"All night?" Charlie murmured. "But you went to the stairs with Bruce, didn't you?"

"Yes, but I didn't go up. We stayed at the bottom of the stairs a few minutes. He wouldn't go away and leave me alone. I had to go with him that far or he wasn't going to get out of my lab. Then I went back and stayed there." His paper had been reduced to the size of a flattened straw. In a few minutes he would start shredding it, Charlie thought, and turned his attention to Jake.

"Let's back up. How long did you stay in the office after Rich left?"

Jake held up his paper. It had a single line of neat script. "It didn't exactly overwork my brain to recall," he said dryly. "I waited until the elevator door closed and I knew no one was around, a minute, maybe. I wasn't paying much attention to the time. I went to my room for a while. I consulted the computer and learned that my new victim was Rich, and I decided to go hunting. I was just leaving my room when Beth came out of hers, and we went down the stairs together. She went to the television room and I headed for the library. When I heard Gary laughing, I figured Rich would be around somewhere, too, and the library was as good a place as any to start looking. I sat where I could keep an eye on the door figuring that he'd either come in or pass by eventually. He didn't. I was still there when Maddie found his body."

"Did you notice the time you went to the library?"

Jake nodded. "Eleven-fifteen. I looked at my watch

and thought I'd give him until midnight and then go
to bed if he didn't show up."

"Good," Charlie said. "Nice and succinct. Milton,
you took the elevator up with Rich on your way to
find Laura. Right?"

Milton looked very much the somber attorney considering a worthy client. "Exactly right. I knew she
had been watching the movies, and I went there to
wait for her. It was ten-forty-five when I got her, and
Rich was the witness. We retired to the library to record the kill. Rich left immediately afterward. I had
the impression that he was in a hurry. Laura and I
talked for a few seconds." He cleared his throat and
looked at Laura and said quietly, "We agreed to meet
on the roof at eleven. I remained in the library until it
was time to go up, and then used the stairs and met
her going up. We talked on the roof for about ten
minutes. The elevator was in use then and we
walked back down. She went back to the television
room and I returned to the library and remained
there the rest of the evening."

Laura looked incredibly bored. Harry watched her
broodingly.

"Laura?" Charlie said.

She swept a contemptuous glance over him and
shrugged. "I haven't the slightest idea. Here and
there all evening. I wasn't paying much attention."

Charlie regarded her without expression for another moment, then turned to Harry with raised eyebrows.

Harry unfolded the sheet of paper he had written
on and read from it. "In our bedroom. Down the elevator to breakfast room. Couldn't work. Maddie and
Bruce fighting. Downstairs to Alexander's lab, five
minutes. Stairs to first floor, to garden for drink.
Started back up to our room, saw Laura going up,
and went to library instead. When Milton returned, I

left, looked in TV room, then upstairs to our room and stayed."

"Did you notice any times?"

"No."

"How did you go up the last time, elevator? Stairs?"

"The elevator was tied up. I used the stairs." His voice was so toneless it sounded mechanical.

"Did you hear Gary laughing?"

"No."

If Charlie was disappointed by his dry account, he gave no sign of it; he turned to Beth, but before he could ask her to begin, Harry spoke again.

"I forgot. I was ready to come down when Beth came up. I pulled the door closed for a minute, and when I opened it again and actually went out, she had gone into her room." He shrugged. "If it helps."

Charlie nodded gravely. "Everything might help. Beth?"

"That's who it was," she said in a soft voice. "Charlie, you just don't realize what it was like that night. Everyone ducking out of sight, doors opening and closing, people vanishing."

"I'm beginning to get the picture," he said. "You were in the TV room, and then what?"

She glanced at her paper; the words were scrawled so badly she could hardly read them. She recounted her night, watching the movies, up to her room, back down. She finished: "I was in the television room when Bruce came in and then we heard Gary laughing and smelled the popcorn and chlorine. I went to the kitchen for a drink of water and then back to the movies."

Charlie looked around at the others. "Anyone else smell popcorn or chlorine in the television room, or the library? Anywhere?"

"You could smell it throughout the hall outside the

atrium. You know how the odor of popcorn carries," Jake said with an edge to his voice. "He made popcorn every night."

"Milton, did you smell it?" Charlie asked.

"Yes. He left the door open to the garden, apparently. If it's open even a minute the smell of chlorine drifts out, and that night it was mixed with popcorn." He sounded a touch impatient, but then straightened in his chair. "It was after eleven—ten, fifteen after at least. I was back down in the library by then." He looked at Charlie shrewdly. "That didn't come out before."

Charlie had already turned to Maddie. "You're the last one," he said kindly, "and then we can all get some rest."

She shook her head. "Not until you find my son's murderer. Then we can rest." She had drawn herself up very straight and looked almost regal. "I won't take long. I was lying down in my room for half an hour or so, and then went down on the elevator. I talked to Bruce in the kitchen. We certainly were not fighting or making loud noises." She looked at Harry severely.

"I heard what he was calling you," Harry said with a touch of anger. "Want me to repeat the conversation I caught before I got disgusted and left?"

She held her head a bit higher. "My mother said you cannot believe a word an eavesdropper reports. We were not fighting." To Charlie, she said, "From the kitchen I returned to the television room to watch the movie. I became fatigued and decided to go to bed. And you know what I found when I summoned the elevator."

"Yes, I do," he said. Then very briskly he started to gather up papers. "Thank you all, and please let me have your notes. You may find that this discussion stimulates memories of other things you simply haven't thought of before. If you do, please tell me. I'll want to talk to you all again, of course, but singly from now on."

10

THEY straggled out, not talking to each other now, avoiding each other's eyes. Alexander vanished swiftly. Harry and Laura went up the stairs together, not speaking, not touching. No one took the elevator.

On the second floor, Charlie and Constance stopped to look down again at the atrium where the soft lights were glowing, the trees and blooming plants Edenlike, the pool glimmering with underwater lights in pale blue. The waterfall made a geyser, gleaming spray rising, flashing, settling without end. Milton appeared and vanished in the shadows behind the pool; in a moment the pool lights went off; he reappeared, glanced around, and left the atrium. Here and there dim lights remained on; the shadows deepened, but the room took on a new dimension, seemed to expand, to become what they called it—a garden. Charlie made a low noise in his throat and took Constance by the arm. They went on to their room.

Constance kicked off her shoes as Charlie added his papers to the ones he had already stacked on the desk. He frowned at the messy pile.

"Charlie?"

"Hm?"

"Why would anyone bother to steal one set of blue-prints when there are so many of them altogether?"

"Don't know."

"Not fingerprints. Anyone might have handled them and left prints. A bloodstain or something like that?"

"Two bloodless deaths," he said morosely. He picked up a chair and crossed the room with it, wedged it under the doorknob, and stepped back to regard it with an unhappy expression. "Know what I hate? Hotel rooms without locks on the doors."

"I don't like Smart House," Constance said. She went to the sliding glass door to the balcony and made certain it was latched. There wasn't a lock on it, but she knew that if anyone tried to force the latch, both she and Charlie would hear it in this abnormally quiet house. The building was so solidly constructed that no sound of the sea penetrated, and beyond the balcony the fog was so deep that nothing showed, no lights, nothing. She shivered, and turned to find Charlie at her side. He put his arm around her and drew her close.

"I'm still wide awake. How about you?"

She nodded. "What are you up to?"

"A little prowling. Let's give them fifteen minutes to get settled first."

During the next few minutes he sorted through the papers he was accumulating, studied the floor plans for several minutes, then gathered up most of the papers and put them in one of the suitcases. He locked it and returned it to the closet. Constance had put her shoes back on and found a penlight. Charlie arranged the remaining papers, most of them in a heap, a few scattered, and regarded them for a moment. With a sigh he turned to Constance and she meekly bowed her head. He plucked a single hair and went back to the desk with it and lifted the top sheet of paper, placed the pale hair on the next one, where it seemed to disappear, and covered it again with the top piece.

"Did you know polar bears have hollow hairs?" he asked then. "Transparent."

"You should work with a polar bear," she said agreeably.

He shook his head. "Too bad-tempered. And they can't cook."

He took the chair away from the door, flicked off the lights, and they stepped out into the wide hallway that curved away from them in both directions. Ahead, the glass wall of the atrium gleamed. He took her hand and positioned her next to the glass.

"I want to find out just how visible people are coming and going in there," he said softly, nodding toward the pool, the atrium in general. "You watch while I prowl a little. Okay?"

He brushed her cheek with his lips and left her. He vanished around the curved hallway in a few steps, and then appeared again on the other side of the glass wall. He had entered the second level of the atrium. Almost instantly he was out of sight again.

Charlie ducked behind some kind of plant and then another. He could still see Constance, but from the way she was looking around, he could tell that she had lost him. He kept behind plants and trees and made his way down the broad stairs that looked like natural terracing. At the first level he paused again and no longer could see her through the glass wall. He went on to the bar and tables. The illusion of being in a jungle was nearly complete now. The dim lights were like moonlight filtered through a hazy cloud cover. He stepped behind another planter containing a banana plant with eight-foot-long leaves; he did not linger, but made his way to the pool, around it to the corridor that led to the Jacuzzi and the dressing rooms. The light control box was on the wall here. He turned on the pool lights, crossed to the Jacuzzi room and looked inside, recrossed the hall to glance inside the dressing room, then stepped out to walk around the pool to the exit nearest the elevator. He felt very exposed and vulnerable, bathed in the pale blue light that seemed brighter than he remembered. At the door he stopped and waved to her, motioned for her to join him. He could not be certain he was visible to her; he could see nothing through the glass wall.

Constance watched him appear and vanish, then appear again after the pool lights came on. When he waved to her to come down, she drew in a long breath and only then realized that she had been breathing guardedly, unwilling to make a sound. She left her place at the window and started down the hallway. When she reached the stairs she turned to descend without even considering the elevator at the far end of the hall.

Something, she was thinking. There was something . . .

Charlie walked toward her in the hall and she said under her breath, "Of course!"

When he reached her, he put his arms around her shoulders and could not account for the feeling of relief that washed through him. "Well?" he asked.

"Wait a minute. How did it seem to you?"

"Like you were watching my every movement. How much did you see?"

"That's how they all felt during the game. As if every movement was being watched. And not just during the game. It's this damn house," she said, and waved her hand. "Right now, I feel as if a thousand eyes are on me."

"Honey," he said patiently, steering her into the

kitchen, "tell me." A dim light had been left on here. He found the switch and turned on brighter lights.

"Oh, that. Not much. I saw you at the bar, and again after the lights came on, when you walked along the edge of the pool and went to the door. But, Charlie, there's something else . . ." Her thoughts raced as he pulled out chairs at the long oak work-table and seated her, then himself very close to her. He did not nudge, did not ask anything else. He waited, his gaze fixed on her.

"It has to do with Gary," she said at last, her voice very low. "Even now, knowing the computer is off, listen to me," she said with a wry smile. "There's nearly an irresistible urge to whisper, to look around to make sure no one's watching, listening. It's this house. How big? Ten thousand square feet, more? And wide open. No privacy anywhere. You feel as if it's watching you every minute, as if all the others can see everything you do. It's all that glass, the ar-rangement of the rooms, everything about it. A giant fishbowl. And Gary was emotionally childlike. That's what they all keep telling us, he was like a small boy with secrets, loving games and surprises and secrets. Charlie, he had the money to play with, he would have had a secret way to move around without being seen. I know he would!"

"The missing blueprints," he breathed. He looked at her with an expression that was close to awe. "You've hit on it."

"It might not have anything to do with the mur-ders," she said thoughtfully. "If he saw Rich carrying them around, he could have hidden them himself, to keep his secret until he was ready to reveal it."

Charlie nodded. He was reconstructing Gary's bed-room suite and his office. His mental maps were very accurate. Some people called it uncanny, his ability to reproduce drawings of buildings, rooms, halls, staircases, closets, electrical systems, everything about them, but he knew it was simply training. Exacting, painstaking training as a fireman had forced him to develop this skill, and he had used it for many years as an arson investigator in New York, before he quit that department to become a police detective. Now he was placing light fixtures and plumbing in Gary's rooms, and he knew where the extra space had to be. He stood up.

"Let's go have a look," he said, his voice as soft as hers.

A few minutes later Constance stood out of the way while Charlie examined the walk-in closet in the room that had been Gary Elringer's. A large sliding door opened to the closet, which was paneled with fragrant cedar; it was bare now, with only a few wooden hangers on one of the rods. There were shelves and drawers on one wall, two clothes rods, a ceiling light. Charlie was feeling the wood along the end wall. He finished inside, and examined the wall on the bedroom side just as minutely. He stepped back finally and nodded.

"Three by three," he said, still speaking very softly. "Either a ladder or an elevator. My money's on another elevator, side by side with the big one on the other side of that wall."

"Can you open it?"

"Nope. I can't even find the damn door, but it's there. Probably computer-operated." He took her arm. "Let's trace it all the way. His office next."

"Fruit cellar," he murmured in Gary's office, pacing off the space. Behind the wall was the refrigerator room, the bins for long storage of fruits and vegetables, and then the dumbwaiter. He measured it off and was left with three feet unaccounted for. He was humming under his breath. Again nothing showed to indicate a door; the office was paneled in a golden-hued wood, expensive wood, exotic. Although Charlie could not identify it, he nodded at it approvingly. "Onward," he said at last. "First floor, pantry. We'll save the roof for daylight." He was very cheerful.

The dumbwaiter was next to a freezer in the pantry, and there was the same three feet of space tucked away between them and the big elevator. The paneling hid the door in the office; the sliding closet door masked it in the bedroom. On the first floor that wall had wainscoting, white and dark wood, perfect disguise again. He turned off the hall light and was ready now to find a snack and then go on to bed. Good night's work, he thought; suddenly Constance's fingers dug into his arm.

"*Shh,*" she whispered, and turned toward the atrium. The swimming pool lights illuminated this end of the area, leaving the rest in murky darkness with small pale spots here and there. Someone was there, moving about.

They froze in place, trying to see past the glass wall, past the pools of pale light. Cautiously, after a moment, Charlie edged closer to the main hallway. Too many exits from the atrium, he was thinking. Four or six on this level, at least four on the bedroom level. A shadow passed between him and one of the light spots.

"Keep an eye out for him," he whispered. "And stay here."

He raced back down the hall to the kitchen, through it to the dining room, and out into the main corridor again, this time at the foot of the wide stairs. He ran up the stairs and stopped at the top, hugging the wall. Here, too, a few lights had been left on, dim, unevenly spaced. He waited a moment to catch his breath, and then edged out into the hall, ducked in order not to eclipse a wall light, and stopped to peer down into the atrium, knowing no one there would be able to see him. At the same moment he caught a motion across the expanse of the atrium, on the far side of the upstairs hall, and he cursed under his breath. The other prowler had beat him upstairs. He trotted down the curved hall; empty. But someone had been there, probably had entered one of the two last rooms, or had gone down the front stairs. He kneeled at the door of the second to last room and put his ear against the door, listening. Nothing. He passed the front stairs to the foyer and listened at the last door just as futilely. He had one hand on the carpet in front of the door and slowly he raised it, examined his fingers, and then the carpet. Dirt. Potting soil. Soundlessly he drew out his wallet and extracted a stiff credit card and used it to scrape the soil together and lift it. There wasn't much, a teaspoonful, moist, crumbly, with bits of grainy stuff, little pellets of planting medium. And now he could smell chlorine.

He found the door to the second floor of the atrium and slipped through, pulled the sliding door shut, and made his way down the broad stairs. He could not see Constance, and he thought she probably could not see him either. The cover of greenery was dense.

When Charlie emerged on the first level of the garden, approaching her, Constance left her position and joined him in the hall. "Did you get a glimpse of him?"

"Nope. You?"

"Just a glimpse. About halfway up. Not enough to tell anything. What do you have?"

"Dirt. Let's see if we can find a plastic bag or something in the kitchen. And a couple of spoons maybe."

They returned to the kitchen where Constance

found the drawer that held plastic wrap, aluminum foil, plastic bags. Together they gazed at the soil before Charlie carefully slid it off the card into a bag and secured it with a fastener. He replaced his card and put the bag in his pocket. "Spoons," he said.

Constance looked doubtful. "There are an awful lot of plants in containers in there."

"I know," he said unhappily. "If we don't find something in a couple of minutes, we'll let it go until tomorrow and have the gardener do his stuff. Let's give it a try now, though."

At the door to the garden, Constance paused again. "You know where the lights are for the whole place?"

He did. He went behind the pool to the light panel in the hallway and tried several switches before he found the one that turned on every light in the garden. It was like sunrise. His unhappiness increased. It was a damn jungle. There were pots and containers of every conceivable size and shape—some long troughs, some like half barrels, some simple round pots. Sphagnum moss was everywhere, in between the containers, piled on top the soil in them. At first he had thought it would be simple to find where the prowler had been digging, just by looking at the tops of the things, but he realized now that such was not the case.

"Well," he said, "he dropped dirt upstairs, maybe he did it more than once."

She nodded, surveying the pots through narrowed eyes. "He must have been putting something in, not taking it out, and depending on the size of the object, there could be dirt left over."

"Why not digging something out?"

"Just wouldn't make much sense. These are all portable, repotted often, I imagine, moved around. The gardener would have found anything left in them more than a few days, I imagine. The big ones are on casters. I expect they all spend part of the time in a greenhouse, maybe get rotated on a regular basis. They do better in a greenhouse," she added, almost absently, not moving yet, considering the task before them.

Charlie began to mount the stone stairs, studying each one before he put his foot on it, searching for more loose dirt. Each riser was on a slant, not really noticeable unless he examined them closely, and there were drainage channels along the rear of each one, and, he cursed, even an automatic watering system, the kind people installed in lawns, with pipes that would emerge and spray water and then sink back out of sight. He was not quite certain why it infuriated him, but it did. Then he knew. If they didn't find the right pot, the system might come on at dawn and wash away every trace, just as the little vacuum cleaners would pop out of the wall and clean up any dirt in the carpet.

He mounted another step, then another. A heavy perfume was cloying; white flowers and pink, then a bigger pot with a climbing vine, and a palm tree. . . . He grunted softly and squatted. Dirt.

Constance joined him and they looked at the scattering of dirt, then turned their attention to the pots. The gardenias were in bloom, with many buds that had not opened yet. Verbenas crowded them, and a dainty trailing lobelia covered with blue flowers. Charlie began to move the sphagnum moss out of the way. The soil in the first pots he uncovered looked untouched. But the dirt came from somewhere, he thought morosely, and reached out to take away more moss.

"Wait a second," Constance said. She picked up a pot of gardenias and grasped the plant, tilted the pot, and was holding the plant, roots in a tight ball. She replaced it and lifted the next one. Charlie stared. He never had seen a pot-bound plant, she realized. "They like to fill the pot before they make buds," she said, and turned the next pot over. And the next. He moved ahead of her to uncover the big pot that held the palm tree. That at least had room to dig in, he was thinking, when he heard her soft exclamation. "Charlie! Look."

She was holding a plant in one hand, the pot in the other, and when he looked inside it he saw an object that might have been a calculator, but that he knew was the hand-held computer control. He lifted it out carefully, holding it by the narrow edge.

"What the fuck are you doing?"

They both looked up to see Bruce and Jake coming down the wide stone stairs. Jake was in his robe and slippers, Bruce in the disarray of clothing he had been wearing all night, the misshapen sweater, untied sneakers, jeans.

"Is this the gadget you were talking about before?" Charlie asked pleasantly, as he watched them both walk through the dirt on the stairs to join him and Constance.

Jake whistled and nodded. Bruce reached for it, but that, Charlie thought, was going too far. He drew it back. Now Jake looked down at the pots, the sphagnum moss that had been tossed out of the way. He frowned. "It was in the plants? How did you find it?"

"Wild guess. Let's go to the kitchen. I can use a wash."

"Is there just one? Maybe . . ." Jake looked over the nearby pots, then gazed around the room, and finally shrugged. "If there are more, they could be anywhere," he said.

"If so, they'll keep until tomorrow," Charlie said. He waited until Constance returned the gardenia to its pot, and then led the way down and out of the garden.

In the kitchen Constance got another plastic bag out and they all watched Charlie put the computer control in it and fasten it.

"Shit!" Bruce cried. "Just like in the movies! You're actually going to look for fingerprints? Don't you think a smart killer would have wiped them all off?"

"What makes you think he's smart?" Charlie asked as if he were really interested in a new and strange idea. He slipped the second bag into his pocket and went to the sink where Constance had already started to wash her hands.

"Up until today, everyone in this house was smart," Bruce said.

Charlie nodded and grinned. "You both just happened to be up guarding the pool room?"

"I wasn't up," Jake said, and he yawned. "I heard someone on the balcony. I looked, of course, but didn't see anything. I was good and awake by then, so I decided a drink was in order. Met him up in the hall. He was watching you and Constance."

"That's a damn lie!" Bruce yelled. "You can't hear anything on the balcony from inside. I was on my way down to get something to eat. I thought we had burglars. You're lucky I didn't go back and get a gun."

Jake nearly choked. "My God!" he said incredulously. "*You* have a gun?" A shudder passed over him and he averted his face.

"Yeah! And I'm a damn good shot! So just be careful, you asshole!"

Jake faced round again, and it became apparent that he was laughing. He shook his head. "I'm getting that drink I came down for. There must be something in the kitchen. I certainly don't intend to go to the bar in the garden, not until someone makes a search anyway." He began to open cabinets, grinning widely now. He found a bottle of bourbon. "Charlie? Constance?"

Bruce began to rummage in the refrigerator. Jake poured drinks for Charlie and Constance and himself and went to the door with his. He raised it in a semi-salute, "Cheers. See you tomorrow. And, Bruce, you do know which end shoots, I hope." He left.

Bruce's mouth was more pouty than ever when he took out a plastic-wrapped platter of sliced ham and started to make a sandwich. Charlie joined him and picked up a piece of the meat. It was very good.

"Did you handle the computer control when your brother showed it to you?" he asked.

"No. No way would he let me get my hands on it. Mustard," he said, and returned to the refrigerator.

"I'm just trying to get an idea of what it could do," Charlie said. "Did he demonstrate it?"

Bruce looked at him with contempt. "You don't know a goddamn thing about computers, do you?"

"Nope." Charlie was being inhumanly cheerful and pleasant. Constance sat at the table and watched them both.

"Okay. Okay. Look, the main computer has the program, and the control is really like a radio signal that it can pick up. You looked at it? There's a keyboard, and numbers. Say you program it to turn on lights when you press *A*. A signal goes to the main computer and it takes the command and carries it out. You don't really program the little one to do anything except send a signal." His voice had lost its petulance; there was the same underlying patience that Charlie himself could assume when he explained something to a naive student. "What that means," Bruce went on, "is that you can use all the letters, the numbers, any combination of them to make it send the right signal, up to the limit of the main computer's memory, anyway. So it can do whatever the main computer can do, if you programmed it in in advance."

"Seems kind of risky," Charlie said thoughtfully. "What if you touched the A accidentally?"

Bruce took a bite of his sandwich and shook his head. "You'd activate it first, some sequence of letters to tell the main computer you were going on line with it." He talked with his mouth full; the words came out muffled.

Charlie reached for another piece of ham. "How long would it take to reprogram something once it was in the computer?"

Bruce shrugged. "Depends. The whole thing, a couple of minutes. One or two commands, seconds, if you knew the program to start with. None of us did, remember. That would make it a little longer."

Charlie looked surprised. "You mean you could do it even though you didn't know the program, the language, whatever?"

"You can't keep a good hacker out of any program. Look, you know anything about music?"

"I can tell Wagner from Verdi," Charlie said cautiously. "Why?" But from the blank expression on Bruce's face, he knew the names were the wrong ones.

"Let's pretend you know music," Bruce said. "Like you recognize the style if it's Springsteen. Or Simon. Or anyone. The good ones have a style you hear; you know who's playing. Right? Same with programmers. The good ones have a style you get to recognize. They do the same things over and over. Maybe one's succinct, someone else is wordy, someone else uses shortcuts that get familiar. Alexander's maybe the best. And he's got style that stands out. And he was the group leader for programming, see. So someone who knows his style knows what to look for, what he's likely to do next. Anyone here with computer smarts could crack his software, anyone. And, like I said, until today everyone in this house was pretty damn smart."

Charlie nodded absently. "I wonder," he said, "why no one's mentioned that before."

Bruce shrugged and took more ham.

"If it was that easy, I wonder why your brother didn't reprogram the computer to take your mother out of the game."

Bruce wiped his hands on his jeans.

"Or if he didn't do that, why he thought he could get her to confirm his killing you, if she had said she wouldn't play." He glanced at Bruce who had become very still; his mouth was sullen again, his eyes narrowed.

"What does that mean?" he demanded. "What are you getting at?"

"Damned if I know. Didn't you think it was curious at the time that he'd make such a big thing of it when he knew she wasn't in the game?"

"He was an asshole."

"Did he rig the game to get you for his first victim?"

"Probably. It would have been like him."

"But then you knew he had your name, even if the first attempt wasn't recorded, didn't you? Seems you might have tried to avoid him after that try. When did he show you the control computer?"

Bruce's face went slack, then it wrinkled, like the face of a child about to throw a tantrum. Charlie remembered how he had treated his daughter Jessica when she was small and her face changed that way. "Storm front moving south," he would say then, and she always had turned suspicious eyes on him, scowled, and most often refused to weep simply because it was expected. The memory was very sharp. How like Constance she was, more so every day. He blinked and focused on Bruce.

"He didn't tell me," Bruce muttered. "I overheard him telling someone else."

Charlie raised both eyebrows and said nothing.

"I thought he was going around telling everyone but me. That's why I . . . Anyway I thought everyone else knew. I was looking over the stuff in the basement, the automatic pool stuff, the vacuum systems, all that. I went behind the elevator to look at the vacuum intake and exhaust, and I heard him. On the elevator, I thought. Must have been for me to have heard him. Anyway, I don't know who was with him. I didn't see them, and the other one didn't say anything. Gary laughed and said, 'Don't be stupid. Of course, I have a safety backup system. In my pocket. Look.' And I knew what it had to be, and about how big it was. Nothing else made any sense. And it would have been stupid not to have a control."

Charlie nodded. "Then?"

"Then nothing. They stopped talking, or the elevator went up, or they left it. I went up the back stairs, the ones that go to the Jacuzzi area, the outside door."

"That's the space where all the pipes are, the wires, tubing to the greenhouse and the cold-storage room?"

Bruce shrugged. "You'd need access to all that stuff. I figured that out and went back there to examine the system."

"What time did you hear them?"

"How the fuck do I know? Sometime in the afternoon. If I'd known it was going to be a federal case, I'd have made notes! I'm going to bed."

He stamped out of the kitchen, and now Constance left the table and joined Charlie at the counter where he was picking at the ham absently. She moved it out of reach. "You'll have nightmares."

"Probably. What do you make of him?"

"Being eaten alive by jealousy. If it's this bad now with his brother dead, what must it have been when he was still alive? That poor man."

"Remember, that 'poor man' has a gun, and he's something of a nut."

She looked at him in surprise. "You believed it about the gun?"

"You didn't?"

"Of course not. It was a typical, my father's-bigger-than-your-father kind of little-boy threat. It never occurred to me to take it as literal truth."

And it had not occurred to him, Charlie thought darkly, not to accept it as true. "Where are you taking that?"

Constance had picked up the platter of ham. "To the refrigerator. And then I'm taking you to bed. You know, the more of all these other men I see, the better you keep looking."

"And you," he said, "are a proper sort of wife."

11

THE next morning the fog swirled outside the window wall, was lifted by the offshore breeze, dissipated, then formed again. Charlie watched it broodingly as he and Constance waited for their breakfast.

"Problems?" Constance asked.

He nodded. "Time problems. Not enough at the right time. Look, let's place people and set them in time as if they were cherries being plopped in whipped cream. First, we know Rich was alive at ten-forty-five, and we can assume he was alive at eleven when Maddie used the elevator. And Gary was alive at eleven-ten or eleven-fifteen. But by then everyone's pretty much accounted for. We have to make another assumption, that Rich died first, simply because the others were all together from eleven-fifteen on. See what I mean by not enough time at the right time?"

Constance raised her eyebrows questioningly, but he was gazing at the restless fog. "Around eleven," he said unhappily, "Harry hears Bruce and Maddie fighting in the kitchen, and the elevator is clear. Rich must be alive somewhere. Harry goes to chat with Alexander. Milton and Laura take off for the roof.

Maddie and Beth watch the movie until Beth goes to her room. Bruce is alone, wandering about. Then at ten after eleven, Milton and Laura rejoin others either in the television room, or the library. Beth and Jake come downstairs together. Bruce is with others in the TV room when they all hear Gary laugh, and smell popcorn. Meanwhile Harry has gone upstairs. So he's free now, but he wasn't free earlier. So it seems that almost anyone could have found time to get Rich, but not Gary. He's a problem."

She said in a low voice, "Alexander was alone from the time Harry left him until after the body was found in the elevator."

"Yeah," he said gloomily. "And he's probably the only one who really needed to keep Gary and Rich, and the project, alive and well and funded."

"And," Constance added thoughtfully, "we really only have Harry's word for it that he looked in on the people watching the movie before he went upstairs after talking with Alexander. It's possible that he was free from then on, too."

"Milton saw him," Charlie said. He sounded disgusted. "He didn't mention it, but it's in his notes of his own movements. Harry looked in seconds after Milton got down from the roof rendezvous. It's not the sort of thing he would be likely to want to talk about, I guess, but he did make a note of it."

"But that still left him time . . ."

Charlie was shaking his head. "There's the problem of Rich, though. And damn, I don't want to think about two killers, a conspiracy—" He stopped when Mrs. Ramos entered with the breakfast tray.

While she was placing soft-boiled eggs before Constance, and then pancakes and eggs for him, he asked, "When Gary made popcorn at night, what did he use? An automatic gadget, a pan, what?"

She raised her eyebrows a fraction of an inch; her idea of a surprised expression, he assumed.

"A popper. Automatic."

"Did he have a special bowl he used?"

"Yes. A stainless steel bowl."

"And the day after his death, after the police had gone, where did you find the bowl?"

She finished serving them and paused thoughtfully. "In the cupboard where we always keep it. But the popcorn popper was in the garden, the pool room."

"Had it been used?"

She studied Charlie for a lengthy moment, then nodded. "It was filled with popped corn."

He asked her about the blueprints and the hand-held computers and drew a blank. Then Laura and Harry Westerman joined them and Mrs. Ramos left.

Laura's gaze swept over Constance; she nodded slightly and inspected Charlie more leisurely with a hint of a smile, as if they shared a secret. Reflex, he thought; was she even aware of it? He grinned at her and Harry. He was wearing a sweat shirt and pants. "You've been running?"

"Yes." Harry poured coffee for himself. Laura poured her own, and neither of them looked at the other. He tasted his, set his cup down hard, and asked bluntly, "What the hell is going on in the garden?"

Charlie shrugged, but did not explain. He had caught Mrs. Ramos before seven, had spoken with her husband a few minutes later, and now Ramos and a helper were searching pots. It didn't surprise him, he reflected, that Harry had been out running. He didn't keep that muscular physique sitting all day in an office adding up columns of figures. Ignoring the question, he commented, "I noticed, during the recital of killers and victims last night, you weren't a very active player."

Harry drank his coffee. When he spoke again, his

voice was frigid, "You noticed right. Damn stupid game. I did not participate."

"Oh? But you took a weapon, and you were witness to two murders. What weapon did you choose, by the way?"

"A water gun. A plastic water gun. And the day after the deaths, the real deaths, I went to the edge of the point out there and I heaved it as far as I could into the ocean. I never even put water in it."

"Why did you take it if you didn't intend to play?"

Harry finished his coffee, poured more, and did not answer.

"We didn't have much choice," Laura said. "Gary had it in his head that we'd play the game, and we had to go along, or risk having him in a tantrum all weekend. He could have done that, stormed around for days, you know. Others were doing it too, going along with him just to keep him happy. Taking weapons, tossing them. We were talking about it last night while you were out with Alexander. Bruce found a pea shooter at the bar in the garden, Milton picked up a water gun on the roof when we were up there, I found two balloons in the television room. We had to take them but we didn't have to use them."

"And you thought Gary would be able to check up on all of you? Cheat?"

She tilted her head and her smile deepened. "Wouldn't you have thought so? I mean, he made the rules, provided the weapons, programmed it all in; of course, we assumed he'd supervise."

Charlie nodded. "What weapon did you take?"

"The garrote. A pretty blue ribbon with Velcro on the ends."

"And did you toss your weapon out into the ocean, too?"

"I don't have an idea about what happened to it. I never gave it another thought," she said with elaborate disinterest.

Charlie turned back to her husband, aware suddenly of the amusement in Constance's eyes that to anyone else might simply look bright with interest. "Can you tell me exactly what happened when Rich Schoen killed Gary? In the game, of course."

Mrs. Ramos appeared with their breakfasts before Harry could speak. She put half a grapefruit down for Laura, and a bowl of what looked like straw before Harry. Charlie stared at it. Shredded wheat, he thought in astonishment. He had not seen shredded wheat in more than twenty years.

After Mrs. Ramos was gone again, Harry said, "I was talking to Rich, about Smart House, of course. That's what we were all doing, finding out as much about it as possible. He spotted Gary and motioned for me to go with him. In the garden, by the bar, he unrolled the blueprints he was carrying and pulled out a foam bat of some sort and touched Gary with it. It counted as a kill. We went to the computer around the bar and recorded it and had it confirmed. Rich left, and I followed him. I didn't want to hang around with Gary mad, and he was mad. He was not a good loser."

Charlie held up his hand. "Slower. What about the bat? The blueprints?"

He munched on his straw, frowning. "I don't know. He put the blueprints down on one of those tables in there. Maybe he put the bat on the counter at the bar. I didn't pay any attention. Beth came up while we were recording the kill. Ask her."

"Okay. You left with Rich, but then you went back, and this time you witnessed Jake murdering Beth. Why'd you go back?"

Harry sighed in an exaggerated manner. "Look, try to get the picture of that goddamn weekend. We were not happy, none of us. It was a stupid game, and we had serious business. Okay, the house is a miracle of innovations, but it's a black hole, too. And

Gary was being childish. No one knew when he'd blow hot or cold. I was fed up with him, with the goddamn game, with his tantrums, just about the whole damn show. Even this hideaway. Stuck out here for a whole weekend. He never gave a thought to how inconvenient it would be for us, for prospective clients, for staff, everyone. I sure as hell wasn't planning out every step, keeping track of every minute. Most of us were simply trying to learn what we could, and keep out of Gary's path. I didn't have a reason to go back. I just did it."

"Why did he build the house here? Why not down in California?" Charlie asked when Harry paused.

"Because he was a goddamn maniac!"

Laura said coldly, "Because he knew the industry was full of spies. He told me the reason. He had a contract with a private airline to bring him and his crew up here, and actually it's only a couple of hours out of Palo Alto. And he knew no spy could get in."

Charlie nodded. "Did you fly up when you came to visit?"

If he had wanted to shake her, he did not succeed. She shrugged. "A couple of times."

He turned back to Harry. "The day of the game, when you went back to the garden, was Jake already there?"

"Jesus Christ!" He rubbed his hand over his eyes. "Yeah, I think so. I just wandered in. He motioned for me to come with him. Beth was standing by the bar. We weren't even trying to keep quiet, just walking, and she didn't notice. She'd been fighting with Gary, obviously. She spent the whole weekend in a rage. She wanted a divorce; that's all that was on her mind apparently, and he, for God knows what reason, wasn't letting go. Ego, I guess."

"Not just that," Laura said coldly. "He was going to make use of her, let her be his hostess in this place. He liked to use people he knew."

"Everyone seems to be aware that she wanted a divorce even before she had made up her mind about it," Charlie said. "Did Gary mention it to you two?"

"He told me," Laura said, and suddenly her voice was hard and bitter, her face strained.

Harry looked at her with surprise, then deliberately stared at his cereal again.

"You were Rich's last victim, weren't you?" Charlie asked.

"I don't know," Harry replied. "The rules stated that no one tell anyone things like that. How the hell would I know?"

"Oh yes. I forgot. But if Bruce had your name, and he did, and if Rich killed him, then Rich inherited you."

"You've got a good memory," Harry said in a tight voice.

"Just fair to middling," Charlie said modestly.

"Well, remember this. Whoever had that goddamn hand-held computer could get a weapon any time he wanted one. That's one of the things it could have done without any trouble at all."

Charlie glanced at Constance. She appeared to be so placid, so removed and distant, that she might have been off in her own reverie. She felt the look and came back, and her own glance at him said *wait a second*.

She looked at Harry and said, "You knew Gary for a long time, didn't you? Why do you think he insisted on a game like this at that particular time?"

Harry put his spoon down and poured coffee, watching his own motions, as if considering if he would even bother to answer, or considering what kind of answer would satisfy—or, she thought, perhaps he had not asked himself the question until this moment.

Finally he said, "I think he intended to keep us apart as much as possible, and still make us switch our position, those of us opposed to sinking more money into this project. He and Rich were working on Jake, getting his support, most of Saturday. If they had lived, I would have been next to be won over. I think every single move had been planned in advance."

"Were you won over by the house itself?"

"No. Remember, I'm the company treasurer. I knew better than anyone what it was costing, what it would continue to cost." His voice had gone very flat again. He picked up his spoon, but did not use it; this time he examined it. "Sterling," he said in that flat hard voice, and tossed it down.

"I see," Constance said thoughtfully. "I can understand why a tall man like Jake would choose a garrote for a shorter woman like Beth. Did you see the ribbon?" she asked Harry, who was regarding her with dislike, possibly even contempt. Charlie blinked at the sudden change of direction.

"No. He had it palmed, and then her hands went up to it the way people would do if they're being strangled."

"Oh, of course. That's a reflex, isn't it?"

Charlie was watching her closely. God help the guy who tries to strangle her, he thought. She was a black belt in aikido, had given demonstrations for years. Her hands would go to places and do things a would-be killer would not like.

"Did you learn who your victims were before you picked weapons?" Constance asked.

Laura and Harry exchanged irritated glances. Laura looked at her watch and said, "Either way. I don't know about the others, but I did. What are you getting at?"

"Just curious," Constance said brightly. "A garrote is such a strange weapon for a woman to pick when her victim is so much larger than she is. You're what, five seven, five eight? And Jake is six one at least, isn't he? I just wondered if you tried to use the weapon and failed, if you gave him the idea of using it on Beth later."

"I couldn't even find him all day!" Laura said furiously. "He kept himself holed up with Rich or Gary or Alexander all day long."

Harry jerked his chair away from the table. "If you two are finished," he said roughly, "I have some work to take care of." He stalked from the room.

Constance turned back to Laura, who was glaring at her.

"I planned to sneak up on him when he was sitting down. I never had a chance to get behind him."

"How long have you and Harry been married?"

Charlie blinked again, and Laura flushed an angry red; her lips tightened.

"That's none of your damn business!"

"Of course not," Constance said pleasantly. She held Laura's gaze with her own clear-eyed, cool look, the unanswered question hanging between them until Laura jumped up and ran out of the room.

"What the hell was that all about?" Charlie said softly, impressed that she had been able to rattle Laura's cage so effectively. His own attempts had been water on the proverbial duck.

"Just curious. I wondered if they were sleeping together. They aren't."

"How do you know?" He peered at her through narrowed eyes.

"I just do," she said. "I guess he's impotent. No pheromones at all."

"Good Christ!"

"Now, Charlie," she said kindly. "All the signs are there, you know. The way he talks about Beth, looks at her, the way he looks at me, the way he treats Laura. I thought at first maybe homosexual, but I don't think so. Asexual is more like it. She plays the field and he knows it and doesn't do anything about it. She rather taunts him with it, like bringing up again the fact that she and Milton met up on the roof, and deliberately choosing a weapon that meant close physical contact with Jake. If he tried to get rid of her, the threat is that she'll tell and he'd rather die than have it known. All those mountains, you know." She sighed. "Poor Harry. And she might have flown up in the company plane, but Gary ended their little affair, not her."

Charlie sputtered on his coffee, and she looked surprised. "Well, it's obvious. He held people by giving them shares of stock, didn't he? And he never gave her any. And she's rather mean-spirited about the way Gary treated her, considering her own actions, I mean. I believe he told her there was a divorce in the works soon, and then he told her of his plans to use Beth for his hostess, a role ideally suited for Laura but never for Beth. Oh, she's angry. And of course she wouldn't try to sneak up on a man from behind. She would have gone up to Jake openly, put her arms around his neck, and then said, 'Gotcha!' Don't you think so?"

"You said no pheromones," he said darkly. "Literally? How do you know?"

"You know, the green cloud of buzzes that most people carry around with them, a little shock here, there, a tingle in your toes when you get near them. Some are pink, of course, or blue, but green is common, too. His are missing. Laura's cloud is puce, and very dense."

Charlie had been listening seriously, intently. He began to laugh, his face crinkling the way it did, taking off many years. "That'll teach her to give me the glad eye in front of you."

Constance looked innocent.

* * *

The air was almost too cool when they walked out on their way to the greenhouse. Mist was still snagged in the tops of trees, still hid the horizon and lingered on the hills behind the house. The grass sparkled with droplets; even as they walked among them the rhododendrons seemed to shrug away the last of their burden of overnight moisture and straighten up for a new day.

"Nice," Constance murmured. The rumble of ocean, the crash of an occasional breaker, the sharp sea air, it was all very nice, a perfect morning.

Mr. Ramos met them at the open doors of the greenhouse, a building large enough and with enough plants to pass for a commercial enterprise. Charlie whistled softly. No wonder the shareholders were griping about money down the tube, he thought. Gary had done things in a big way indeed.

Mr. Ramos was wiry and sharp-faced. His muscles and sinews and bones all were of a piece, all alike, sharp. He was in his fifties, his hair gray, his eyes nearly black and too small. When he smiled, his teeth gleamed white, with gold inlays that flashed. He smiled at Charlie's awe.

"Good greenhouse," he said. "You want to see it?"

"Sure do. You finish going through the plants?"

"All that's been inside. Nothing. They haven't been bothered. This here's an experimental special environment room." He pointed to one of the small glass-enclosed rooms within the big glass structure. There were six of the small rooms altogether, each with an assortment of plants, many in flower or fruiting. "We can keep different temperatures in them," Ramos said. "And mix different air for them, more carbon dioxide, or not so much, things like that. Some like more oxygen than others. That's the propagating room back there."

They walked through the building with him as he explained the various areas. When he got to a maze of pipes, Charlie stopped him. The pesticides were stored in a separate room on the end of the garage; the carbon dioxide came through a pipe from the house. Water and fertilizer came through other pipes, and the whole could be run by the computer. "Except for now," Ramos added, flashing his gold-edged smile. "Now we just do it the old-fashioned way, by guess and by God."

"And the night of the deaths, insecticide was released in here," Charlie murmured. "I'd think you'd be pretty happy to have the computer out of the picture."

"Told the police, and I tell you now. Computer didn't do it. Took a hand to open that valve, not a computer giving orders."

"Show me," Charlie said.

Ramos led them to the end of the wall with the spaghetti tangle of pipes. "See that one," he said, pointing to a narrow steel pipe. "Goes to the malathion in the storage shed. From the unit it goes to a mixer and then gets mixed with water and pressurized and comes out like a spray. I turned it off early that day because we were out of malathion and had to install a new unit. Didn't need the stuff right away and never got around to opening the valve again. Told the police that, too. They chose not to believe me, I guess. Thought I might have forgotten."

"Which valve opens and closes that pipe?"

Ramos pointed again. One valve among dozens. "The idea is that they stay open all the time and the computer regulates what goes through them. But when something runs out, I'm in charge. Me or one of the boys. Bring in more fungicide and set it up, or more pesticide, fertilizer. And when we run out, we shut the valve, or it messes up the readings, pressure, that sort of thing. Stuff might be forced through the wrong way, or not enough of whatever would get sprayed. I don't forget stuff like that."

"Who would have known about it?" Charlie asked, trying to follow the network of tubing that spread throughout the large greenhouse. It was futile; he couldn't do it.

"Mr. Schoen or Dr. McDowd, the horticulturist. He's a consultant, comes in two, three times a week now. Me. One of my men. He wasn't here that weekend, though."

"Gary Elringer?"

"Not to my knowledge. Not his department. Didn't care to know what went on in here."

"How did you get rid of the poison once it was in the air?"

"We can exhaust the air in here in four minutes flat. Just about all of it. Takes just a couple of seconds for the experimental rooms. That's what the police wanted to hear about, not the valve."

Charlie studied him curiously. "They thought Rich Schoen might have been suffocated in here and moved?"

"Course, they didn't tell me what they thought, but they sure looked over the experimental rooms and asked questions about how we could exhaust the atmosphere in them."

"Was any other valve turned the wrong way? Off or on?"

"Nope, not that I could see. The alarm went off and some damn idiot broke the glass to let the air out. By the time I got here and got things organized, the exhaust system working, there was glass everywhere, and they broke the water pipe somehow, so there was water underfoot. A mess! They sure made a mess."

"They all trooped out here?"

Ramos looked toward the big house and shrugged. "They must have had a dozen or more cops up there. The computer flashed the alert about poison, and Alexander and Bruce Elringer led the whole pack out here. Bruce, I guess, was the one who began banging away on the glass with a spade."

They continued the tour, Charlie feeling more and more frustrated. Too many ways it could have been done, he thought grumpily. The cold-storage room, in here, the vacuum system in the elevator, God alone knew what else. They paused when a tractor with a grader blade started up. It was moving a pile of bark mulch; two men shoveled the stuff into big plastic bags.

"Buy it by the truckload," Ramos said over the noise of the machine. "Some of the plants don't like sphagnum. We dress them up with bark mulch." He looked at Charlie shrewdly then. "The police wanted to see the wheelbarrows, the garden cart."

Almost helplessly, Charlie nodded. "I might as well see whatever interested them."

Two wheelbarrows, one large-wheeled cart that was piled with sphagnum moss in burlap sacks. Charlie regarded them, feeling nothing but blank, and then took Constance by the arm. "Thank you, Mr. Ramos. You've been helpful."

"Be damned if I have," Ramos said.

12

LOOKING for Alexander they found Beth instead. She was pale and nearly in tears. "I just can't stand much more," she said wearily. "They're all driving me batty." She had a sweat shirt over her arm, and was dressed in jeans, a plaid shirt, and sneakers. "I'm going down to the beach."

"What happened?" Constance asked.

At the concern in her voice, Beth nearly wept. She shook her head dumbly.

"Have you eaten anything yet? Come on, let's get something in you before you go out. It's pretty cool, and everything's still wet from the fog. I'll catch up with you, Charlie."

He watched her lead the young woman into the breakfast room, and continued on his way to find Alexander. Whatever was bugging Beth, Constance would learn within five minutes, he thought, and he would have bet on it if there had been anyone around to steal money from.

Charlie had turned toward the basement stairs when he saw Harry and Bruce in the wide corridor outside the library door. They seemed to be arguing. Abruptly Harry took Bruce's arm and steered him to the nearest garden door and they entered. Charlie changed his goal and trotted up the stairs to the hall, on around the curve, and entered the garden on the upper level, moving quietly now. He knew that no one below could see through the greenery to this area. It's a jungle out there, he thought, and began to make his way around the garden cautiously, ducking when he had to keep out of sight in case one of them happened to look up.

He had gone two-thirds of the way around before their voices floated up to him. They were at the bar, one on each side of it. Now he could see the tops of their heads. Moving with even more caution, he edged his way down the steps closest to the bar until the blur of their voices cleared enough to catch the words, and then he stopped moving altogether. A luxuriant banana plant screened him from them. A large red protuberance indicated that the plant was going to bear fruit. It looked strangely obscene. He listened.

Bruce had been cursing steadily for nearly a minute already, a monotone of filthy words; Harry hit the bar top with a hard slap.

"Just stow it for Christ's sake, and listen. There's no time for that now. Can you get her in line?"

"I told you already. Sure. I'll get Mom on it. Don't worry."

"Don't worry! Right. I'll remember that. Look, we need to float a rumor. I want the word out that BOS and BOS Two make UNIX look like a child's game. And that we'll announce in the fall and show in the spring. That's all."

"Fuck you! We never went for vapor ware before!"

"Will you shut up! Grollier would be good to start the leak. Who can we get to spill it?"

"Not Beth, even if we had her already. She knows too much to spill, and Grollier knows that. One of Alexander's team?"

"No. Same reason."

"But why vapor ware? Why now? What the fuck are you digging in that shit for?"

"Christ!" Harry moaned in a despairing voice. "Use your head! We need cash, lots of it, and we need it soon. Or it's bottom's up for us. We can't go for DOD money, but what if they come to us? Our terms? They all know what Gary was working on. Good Christ, the whole world knows what he was after. Now a rumor that says he did it. They come to us. You have to keep Beth in line, keep her trap shut, don't rock the boat for the next three, four months at least. That'll give us time for the rumor to come back home to roost. And then, fuck her!"

"It's too vague," Bruce said after a pause. "BOS they know, but they'll see BOS Two as a series boost, no more than that."

"Wrong," Harry said. "We want this leak phrased very carefully; that's why it has to be someone who isn't aware of the significance. That's why Beth wouldn't do. BOS 3.7 and BOS Two 2.4, say. That should do it, don't you think?"

There was a longer pause and then Bruce spoke again, his voice more guarded now. "It wouldn't have to be Grollier. There are a couple of others who'd work out just as well. Sal Vinton, for example. Laura could do it, Harry. With Sal Vinton Laura would do great."

Charlie had been content just to hear the voices; now he wished he could see the two men as well. He moved the branch in front of his face slightly, and caught another movement from the corner of his eye. He looked harder and saw Jake eavesdropping exactly as he was, from the upper level, hidden by foliage. Jake obviously had been aware of Charlie for some time. He nodded slightly and made no other motion, made no sound.

"The next item is when," Harry said finally, without a change in his voice at all. "As soon as possible. This weekend will be a bust, naturally. Monday she can get it started. Two weeks, three should be time enough . . ."

Jake was moving now, easing himself back up the steps. He made his way to the nearest sliding door and pushed it open, then stepped before it, as if he had only then entered the atrium. He called out, "Beth, are you in here?"

Charlie watched the two heads below as Bruce and Harry quickly left the bar, and then the garden altogether. He turned to Jake. "Thanks. I was getting a lesson in computer ethics, I think."

"If we wanted to save souls, we'd have joined the ministry," Jake said sharply; he turned and went through the doorway.

Beth had felt too awkward to ask Mrs. Ramos for breakfast, and too much in the way to go to the kitchen and make something for herself. Now she admired how matter-of-factly Constance asked for scrambled eggs, toast, and fresh coffee for her. "It's the idea of so much money," she said suddenly, and felt as if she had only then learned something important. But that was it. The money was turning everyone into a stranger, and she was a stranger to herself. "I just blew up at Maddie," she said in a small voice. "Funny. All the years I was with Gary, all the times when I might have found excuses to blow up at her, I never did, but now . . ."

"What does she want you to do?"

"Be nicer to Bruce, for one thing," she said bitterly. "It's like saying be nice to a rattlesnake."

Mrs. Ramos brought in dishes and coffee and left again without a sound. Constance poured for them both, although she felt afloat in coffee already. Somehow, she thought, sharing coffee, sharing food made conversation easier. Made self-revelation easier, she corrected herself.

"She's treading awfully close to hysteria," Constance said when Beth seemed disinclined to continue. "People in that state do and say things they might not ordinarily."

"I suppose. We never had money before. My family never did. My father worked for the state government; my mother was a nurse for a time and quit as soon as we were in college. My brother and me, I mean. We had scholarships, but he dropped out. Too rough financially for him, and he wanted to get married. Even when Gary began making money, we didn't really have money. You know what I mean? He would get a check for a thousand dollars and spend it on something that cost two thousand, instantly. Then the company came along and everyone was on salary, and we still didn't have money. Always a bigger or better something to be bought, more work space to rent, more help to be hired. On and on. It was just starting to get better when I went back to school. I really thought all the scrimping was over with by then. I think they all thought so. None of them had real money, either. Ideas, schemes, dreams, hopes, but no cash. Except Milton, I guess. But not the rest of us."

All this was beside the point, Constance realized. This was not what Beth and Maddie had fought about. She waited. When the door handle started to move, she got up and very pleasantly took the tray from Mrs. Ramos, murmured something, and returned to the table with it. Beth was still gazing out the window, oblivious.

"She's saying if I had been nicer to Gary, if I hadn't walked out on him, none of this would have happened. He turned mean because of me. And now everyone's being so terrible to Bruce that he'll be hurt, he'll turn mean or something. She wants me to be nicer to him, tell him I don't want any money for the shares of stock, that I'll wait until it's convenient, until the trouble here blows over."

"Eat your breakfast," Constance said when she fell silent again.

Beth took a bite, then another, without looking at the food. Then she put her fork down and drank

more coffee. "She said Bruce agreed to awful settlement terms with his wife. His ex-wife. Because he
thought there would be money. If I'd been with Gary
he wouldn't have thought of that stupid game. Grown
men skulking around with balloons, water guns,
brother against brother. All my fault! If I'd stayed
with him and we'd had children, he wouldn't have
got involved with Smart House!" Her chin was
quivering again, and her eyes were glassy with un-
shed tears.

Constance put her hand on Beth's arm and said
firmly, "Beth, she's very frightened, you know. Why
is she so frightened?"

"Her world's ending. Gary dead. Bruce a . . . She
thinks Bruce killed his brother, I suppose. Gary was
the sun, Bruce is the moon, and that's all she ever
had. It scares her to death."

Charlie and Alexander were in Gary's suite. Charlie
was in the chair before the computer, hating it
fiercely; Alexander was in a second chair at his side.

"You don't have to know how I know," Charlie said
murderously. "He had a separate set of commands, or
something, that he could get to through this damn
machine. Take my word for it. You knew him. Put
yourself in his head. If you had a secret room, for
instance, how would you open and close the door?"

Alexander chewed his fingers and looked here and
there nervously and refused to put himself in Gary's
head for even a second. "Anything. He could have
programmed in anything he wanted. How should I
know?"

Charlie sucked in his breath. "Okay. Okay. Let's
play a game. We can talk to the main computer
through this machine. Right?"

Alexander nodded warily.

"Let's pretend I want to lock that door and I don't
want to get up to do it. What could I do instead?"

"Go through security. It's a separate program. Under *security*. Just type it in."

"Good. He'd use regular words like that? No secret codes or anything?"

"It depends on what he was doing."

Charlie muttered a curse under his breath and faced the young man. "Would he have a record of a secret code, if that's what he used?"

"I don't know."

"You do know!" Charlie yelled at him. Alexander looked as if he might bolt for the door, and Charlie got up and grabbed his arm, pulled him to the chair before the keyboard. "You know, and you're going to find it for me. Not security. Anyone could find it in the main computer that way. A different program? A signal? An access code or command? What would it have been?"

Alexander looked terrified. He shook his head.

"You're not getting up until you give it to me. You hear that?"

Miserably Alexander tapped the keys. He was a two-finger typist. He watched the monitor as text began to scroll. He did something to clear it, and typed again, and then again, and again. He looked up with hope a few minutes later when there was a knock on the door.

"Don't you move!" Charlie opened the door a few inches, saw Constance, and admitted her.

She looked past him to Alexander, back to Charlie with questions in her eyes. He was scowling ferociously.

"Alexander is searching for the code Gary used," he said darkly.

"It's no use," Alexander said, appealing now to Constance. "He can't make me tell something I don't even know."

"What about the directory?" she asked.

"I know all the items on it. He thinks there's something in addition to those things."

Constance nodded. If Charlie thought so, there probably was. "Maybe not in addition to, but buried in one of the files you know about?"

"That's what I'm trying to check out," he said miserably.

Constance watched him for several seconds and then said, "What was he least interested in? The greenhouse? Kitchen? Something out of the house? The garage?"

Alexander shot a fearful glance at Charlie and keyed in a new command. Another. He was scrolling inventories of various rooms, the music room, library, and had just touched the key for kitchen, when suddenly he started at the sound of Charlie's voice, this time as soft and low and soothing as a fond parent's. "That's enough, Alexander. You may go now. I know you have work of your own to do."

He glanced from Charlie to Constance and then jumped up and nearly ran from the room.

"Did you see?" Charlie asked. She nodded, and he sat down at the keyboard and typed in: *TV Room.* A whole new screen appeared, with subcategories of furnishings, and then video cassettes. This list had caught his eye, and hers also. The first item listed was *Sesame.* Charlie moved the cursor to it and pressed Enter. Constance made a low noise, and they both turned and watched as a piece of the wall moved to reveal a door.

"I knew the son of a bitch could do it," Charlie muttered. Constance grinned.

He began to hum, a low droning sound that was more like a cat's purr than a human noise. He did not touch the door, but leaned forward to examine it, and then returned to the desk and picked up a pencil. He pressed the eraser against the first of three dots on the door facing. The door opened. They were looking at another elevator, this one no more than three feet by three, and on the floor there was a roll of blue-prints and two of the hand-held computer controls, exactly like the one they had recovered from the gar-denia pot.

"Well, well," Charlie said softly, very pleased. "Now, how about that!"

Beth stood at the top of the long trail that led to the beach two hundred feet down. The day was calm now, and even warm, a rarity for the Oregon coast. In the distance she could see tide pools left by the re-ceding tide; no one else was in sight. She started down. The trail had been carved into the rock in places, paved in some places with a black topping, stairs added where the trail was too steep for safety, a railing here and there. Going down was simple, she had learned the last time she had been here; coming up again was not. Ever since talking to Constance in the breakfast room she had felt curiously blank, empty, and what thoughts had come had fled again too fast to consider. Yet she knew she had to think through the various things Maddie had babbled about that morning. It wasn't fair, she found herself thinking again and again, and this time she seized the thought and went forward and back with it. If she agreed to a deferred payment for her share of stock, she would stay broke for months, years even, and that certainly wasn't fair. But if she demanded her rights now, they would have to sell the company at less than market value, and that wasn't fair either. And she had left Gary's bed and board because of what he had become; he hadn't become that because she'd walked away. It wasn't fair! Bruce wasn't her responsibility. Nor Maddie.

What she really wanted, she thought then, was to

collect some of the money the company owed her. Owed her, she repeated. Invest in Margaret Long's small press, go back to editing the kinds of books no commercial publisher would touch. No one even considered that she had her own dreams, her own ambitions, she thought miserably.

She slipped and grabbed the railing. There was a shady area of the path that was wet; a trickle of water crept across it, vanished in the tough dune grasses that went down to the high-water mark. The tide was lower than it had been the other time she had come down; the beach was wider than she had realized it would get. To the north another headland made one boundary, and the cliff that held Smart House made the other, but today she could get over the rocks in either direction, keep going for hours. She thought again: It isn't fair, and bit her lip in exasperation. Then she made the last turn off the trail and waded through sand to the hard-packed beach where walking was easier.

In the tide pools there were pink and purple starfish, and multicolored anemones that closed when she touched them, bubbling angrily, she thought. Small pink crabs scurried in their unreasonable sideways motion. She sat on the edge of a rock and stirred the water in a tide pool and watched the frightened creatures until she became ashamed of herself, and then she walked again.

At the northern boundary as she clambered over the newly exposed basalt prominence she stopped to gaze at the next crescent beach, as deserted as this one, with another rocky barrier at the far end. She turned and went back the way she had come. It wasn't fair. Going back, she did not pause at the many tide pools, some already brimming over with the incoming tide; she strode briskly, trying to think, trying to define what her responsibility actually was.

She reached the southern prominence and stopped again. This cliff rose almost straight up and was broken into massive blocks and boulders only for the bottom twenty feet or so. From above one could look straight down into crashing surf when the tide was high. Now it was possible to climb over the tumble at the base of the cliff and go on, and on, and on. To California? To Mexico? Forever.

She started to climb over the fragmented rocks, and stopped again, this time frozen, mouth open, but no scream issuing. She was too frightened, too stunned to scream.

Wedged in the rocks was the body of a man in a dark suit coat, one hand hanging almost to the surface of a pool captured ten feet above sea level. He wore a gold watch. She could see the back of his head, the upper part of his back, his shoulders, one arm and hand. Hung out to dry, she thought, draped over the rocks because he was wet. The gold watch gleamed in the sunlight. His other hand and arm were not visible. Broken off when he fell, she thought clearly, and suddenly she vomited.

She had no memory of scrambling back up the trail, or of getting back to Smart House, but once inside, it seemed they were all there, and suddenly Charlie was giving orders in a crisp and even reassuring way. It was good he was there to take charge, she thought, because Milton was dead. Then she wept.

Charlie sent Constance and Bruce to the cliff top overlooking the headland. "No one's to go near it," he said. "Alexander, call the sheriff and the special investigator from the attorney general's office. Tell them we won't touch him if he's dead, unless the tide starts to move in too fast. I want the sheriff's homicide crew as fast as they can make it. Jake, Harry, come with me."

"You're assuming he's dead?" Jake asked as they trotted to the beginning of the trail.

"I don't know. But that damn tide has turned and I want a crew here before it reaches him. If he's alive, we'll call back." They would haul him to high ground if he were alive, but Charlie knew he wasn't. Beth knew it, too.

On the beach, Charlie and Jake watched Harry climb up the face of the black basalt to the level of the pool, the rock that had broken Milton Sweetwater's fall into the sea. Harry climbed carefully and very surely. He skirted the pool and reached out to touch Milton, to feel for a pulse in his neck. He yanked his hand back fast, and now he hesitated, clinging to the rocks. He began to work his way back down.

"Jesus," Jake said in a low voice and turned away to gaze out at the ocean. He was hunched, his hands thrust deep into his pockets, as if he were very cold.

Charlie was remembering that the last time he had seen Milton Sweetwater he had been going around turning off lights. When Harry rejoined them, his face was gray. He shook his head.

"Someone has to stay here and make sure he doesn't get swept away by the tide," Charlie said brusquely. "Both of you. Don't go up there again, and don't let anyone else go up, either. If the water gets to him, give a yell and we'll get him off that rock."

He did not wait for agreement or questions, but left Jake and Harry on the beach and started back up the trail. The sheriff would be there soon, and he had a few things he wanted to do before that. The first thing was to have a look at the top of the cliff.

He sent Bruce back to the house, and as soon as he was gone, he turned to Constance. "Anything?"

"No. He wanted to go closer, but I stopped him. I wanted to get closer, too. Doubt that it means anything. He's dead?"

"Yeah." Charlie looked at the immense house against the cliff. The greenhouse was visible from here, and two cottages, the servants' quarters. The red tile terrace circled the house, then down a couple of steps to the landscaped grounds, paths surfaced with bark mulch, some with tiles or bricks. Nothing high grew between the house and the edge of the cliff, nothing to obstruct the view; he and Constance would be perfectly visible to anyone looking out. He turned his back on the house and studied the ground. Here the lawn had yielded to the basalt, and the basalt ended in a cliff. No fence, no guardrail. But why would there be? This was not a family residence; it was a showcase for business people who presumably would have enough sense not to fall off the cliff.

He walked toward the edge slowly, looking for anything. He stopped and got down on one knee to examine brown spots, dull against the basalt that had a surface shine. He looked until he found three more of the brown spots, skirted them carefully, and moved on.

"Is it blood?" Constance asked, keeping back.

"Probably." Two small areas, four spots, about a foot from the edge of the cliff. He took one step closer to the dropoff and felt a catch in his stomach, a tremor of fear in his bowels, the way he always did when he first approached a high place with no rail. It passed, and he looked down. Almost straight down here, to the jumble of broken rocks where the land and sea were slugging it out. Harry and Jake were standing where he had left them, both of them turned to face the sea. No one else was in sight, except Milton Sweetwater.

"He could have fallen," Constance said.

"Or jumped."

"But you don't think so."

"Do you?"

"No."

He put his arm around her shoulders. "We might as well go in with the others. I just wanted a look."

The sheriff arrived soon after they reentered the house. He took two deputies down to the beach, with Charlie tagging along behind them. No one spoke to him. The three investigators surveyed the body, consulted, and two of them went back up the trail. Jake, Harry, and Charlie followed. The sheriff was in his fifties, weathered with deep furrows in his face, his skin shiny and hard. He looked like a farmer, or a fisherman, Charlie thought, watching him work. He went straight to the telephone, still not speaking to anyone in the house, and he called for a helicopter, the Coast Guard rescue team. Then he hung up and regarded Charlie with unhappy eyes.

"There's what looks like blood on the edge of the cliff out there," Charlie said.

"I'm not on this case," the sheriff said. "State investigator is. But the tide's moving in pretty fast. If it wasn't, I'd just post a guard and wait it out." He looked beyond Charlie at the others, who had spaced themselves as far as they could get from each other and still be in the same room. The sheriff surveyed them with disgust. "No one's to go anywhere until Dwight gets here." He stalked from the room.

And that solved his own dilemma, Charlie decided. He didn't have to tell the sheriff about the little elevator. The question before had been when to tell him, and the answer was never. Dwight, he thought, Dwight Ericson, the state attorney general's man. He sat down to wait for him.

13

FOR the next hour they waited. Now and then someone got up to go to the bathroom, or to get a drink or get coffee, and was accompanied by a sheriff's deputy, right to the door, anyway. They spoke in monosyllables when they spoke at all. Maddie picked up a book and put it down repeatedly. Bruce paced, sat, got up, and paced again. Alexander twitched and fidgeted. Laura sketched, flipped pages, and sketched again. Harry and Jake were both quiet, subdued, and each one seemed wound so tightly that no spring could hold such tension.

Charlie played solitaire and watched them all. They were staying as far apart as the room allowed, as if each recognized that a touch, a look, might be enough to set off an explosion. The helicopter had come, and they all had watched from the wide windows as it circled, hovered, then dipped down out of sight in a crescendo of noise, and departed again. Now they waited for the special investigator. One of the deputies stood at the window, looking out. And no one had had a chance to ask Charlie if he intended to talk about the game. He gathered up the cards and shuffled, dealt again.

Finally there was a soft rustling in the room, al-

most like a collective sigh of relief, and two state police officers in uniform entered with a third man not
in uniform. He wore a khaki jacket over a tee shirt,
and denim jeans. Harry and Jake both got up, and
were silenced by his icy survey of the various mem-
bers of the group. His gaze lingered on Constance
and lingered longer on Charlie, who had leaned back
in his chair to watch.

"You know the rest of us," Jake said then. "This is
Charles Meiklejohn and his wife Constance Leidl.
They're . . . consultants. Captain Dwight Ericson,"
he finished.

Looking at the newcomer, Constance realized that
Dwight Ericson could well have played the part of
the younger brother she never had. How pleased her
father would have been with such a son. Her father
had never even hinted at disappointment over not
having a son, but he had taught his tall daughters to
ski and shoot, ride horses and milk cows, and had
insisted on college and professional careers for them.
He would have liked a son who turned out like
Dwight Ericson. He was not yet forty, large—over six
feet tall—and broad in the chest, narrow through the
hips. His hair was as blond as Constance's, his eyes
the same shade of pale blue. She sat and watched as
he and Charlie sniffed and circled like two stray dogs
even though neither of them moved; she suppressed
a smile.

"A consultant?" Ericson said, not quite voicing his
utter disbelief.

Charlie nodded. "You're a special investigator?"
His tone said Dwight Ericson was too green, too
young, too naive for his position. He stood up lazily.
"You know all about the fun and games that went on
here last spring, no doubt. No point in going into all
that again. But now there's a third body to consider.
Shot?"

Ericson's eyes narrowed and he nodded.

"I think we'd better talk," Charlie said.

Ericson hesitated only a second, then turned and led the way out, into the library. One of the state policemen stayed behind, one went with him. The sheriff's deputy left. Charlie and Constance followed Ericson. Constance knew every eye in the room was on Charlie; everyone wanted to ask how much he would tell of the stupid game of murder they had agreed to months ago. There was no way to reassure them that he had decided not to talk about it; he had told them already, if they had just been listening.

In the library Ericson stopped at a long table and seemed to be considering it. Then he turned and looked at Charlie and Constance more closely. "Meiklejohn. You were in on that Ashland murder case, weren't you?"

Charlie nodded.

"They brought you in to look into those other two deaths in May?"

"To be precise, Milton Sweetwater came to see us and brought us in." He pulled a chair closer to the table for Constance and another one for himself. "Ericson, we can work together, or I can poke around on my own, but one way or the other, I'm afraid I'm in."

Dwight Ericson sat down and rubbed his eyes. "I'm not fighting you. You know the population of the state of Oregon? About three million. And it covers an awful lot of territory. And I'm *the* special investigator. I'm it. Frankly, Mr. Meiklejohn, if you can help, believe me, I'll accept it."

Charlie's nod was sympathetic. "Doesn't matter, three million, thirty million, you're always short-handed. I can show you how Gary Elringer, and maybe others, moved around this damn house on the night of the other murders without being seen."

"They lied about the computer keeping track of their movements?" He looked offended, like a little boy who had just been told the tooth fairy was a myth.

"To a point. At least some of them have lied."

"What about the shooting? How did you know Sweetwater was shot?"

"Didn't," Charlie admitted. "But it was a logical guess. I told the sheriff about the blood on top the cliff. And I sure didn't see a weapon of any kind. He was a vigorous man, in good shape. Didn't seem reasonable to assume someone just pushed him off, or that he fell or jumped. The blood didn't fit those scenarios. Not much left except a gun."

"Right. Okay, how did they get around without the computer tracking them?"

"Best way to see our find," Charlie said then, "is from Gary's office, I think. It was Constance's idea. She figured out that Gary Elringer would have had a private way to get in and out." They went down the stairs to the basement.

"See," Charlie said in Gary's office a few seconds later. "You call up the television room directory on the computer, and use the secret code and watch!" Ericson made a soft noise in his throat. "We just got here yesterday," Charlie said, almost apologetically, without a trace of mockery. "Haven't really had time yet to start digging, but this seems a pretty good beginning." He pushed the open button with the eraser as he had done before and they gazed into the small elevator with the blueprints and the computers on the floor.

Ericson stepped closer, then snapped, "Have you touched anything yet?"

"Nope. We just found it when Beth came in after spotting Milton Sweetwater's body. Didn't really have much time to investigate. But there's a back door," he added softly, "and the only place you can use it is on the first floor, exit behind the big walk-in freezer, into the small hallway behind the john and the dressing room. From there it's a straight shot to the Jacuzzi, or outside through a door in that hall."

Ericson motioned to the uniformed officer. "I want prints, fast. Everything in there."

He turned back to Charlie and Constance, and now he paid as much attention to her as to Charlie. "You just figured this out? Or did someone tell you?"

"I think most of them will be surprised by this," she said thoughtfully.

They moved aside as a second officer came in and the two men went to work on the elevator.

"No one knows yet that we found it," Charlie said. "I told you we had something for you. There's this, too. You might want to look for prints." He took the third computer from his pocket, handling it carefully by the top of the plastic bag. He described finding it and explained what the hand-held computers could do.

Suddenly Ericson grinned, and he looked many years younger. "Okay. What else?"

"Your turn," Charlie said gravely. "Was either man moved, dragged, dumped? You know what I mean."

They were playing a game they both understood, Constance knew, neither of them yielding an inch yet, still feeling each other out, gauging how far to go.

"No," Ericson said.

"Can you be certain?" she asked.

"Oh yes. You look for scuff marks, disarranged clothing, marks on the floor or carpet, shoe polish, bits of thread, things like that." He glanced at Charlie, but did not go on. "We thought of that, naturally."

Charlie nodded. "Naturally."

"And you just figured out how that gizmo works, too?" Ericson asked, pointing to the computer in the plastic bag.

"They talked about it last night," Charlie said. "Bruce Elringer assumed everyone else knew about it, and they pretty much admitted that they did know, or should have known, but it slipped their minds."

Ericson made a rasping sound in his throat, as much like an animal growl as a person could make. "What happened last night?"

"I asked questions. They answered some of them. Then everyone split to go to bed. Constance and I could have been the last ones who saw Milton Sweetwater. We watched him turn off the lights. I doubt you'll get much more than that from any of them. No point in driving too hard until we have a time of death, is there?"

It was a question, but also a suggestion, very nearly an order. Dwight Ericson considered him another moment, then shrugged. "We'll do what we can." He started for the door, paused again. "You want to sit in on it?"

Charlie shook his head. "Thanks. Rain check? What I bet they'll tell you now is that they went to sleep, those we didn't meet again anyway, and no one heard or saw a thing."

"Yeah. Bruce Elringer and Jake Kluge were up and prowling. And Bruce claimed he had a gun." Ericson took a breath and started to leave again. "Bet it's missing."

Charlie grinned. "Mind if I do a little prowling of my own?"

"Help yourself. When I'm done upstairs, maybe we can sit down somewhere and have a cup of coffee? See you later."

Charlie chuckled. Not quite a question, more like a suggestion or even an order. He decided Dwight Ericson was okay. He took Constance by the arm. "Let's go to the roof for a breath of air."

They left the office and walked to the main elevator at the end of the corridor, eighteen feet, twenty feet away, but side by side with the secret one. The arrangement on the second floor was like the basement setup: Gary's suite with the elevator door in the closet was as far from the main elevator as it was here. And on the roof, they were right next to each other, he knew. He wanted to look at the two doors, at the concealment provided there. He had not yet examined that. The housing was a redwood structure on the roof. Charlie walked around it slowly, then entered the storage section. There was the pile of outdoor furniture, several small tables, lounges. From the inside it was not at all obvious that a second elevator had been provided for. From outside, the little elevator was just as invisible, the door perfectly hidden in the redwood siding.

"Are you looking for something in particular?" Constance asked after a moment. Charlie was on his knees examining the wood.

"Damned if I know," he muttered. "We'll have to wait for Ericson's men to finish with it, I guess. Are you getting hungry?"

"Yes. It's after two."

"How about we continue this search in the kitchen."

Mrs. Ramos was heaping turkey and ham and cheeses on platters under the supervision of another uniformed officer. Her composure wavered momentarily when Charlie and Constance entered.

"Wonderful!" Charlie said. "What we'll do, Mrs. Ramos, is make up a few sandwiches and take them into the breakfast room. If that's okay with you."

"Or even if it isn't," she said and went on arranging a tray with onion rings, pickles and lettuce.

Charlie nodded pleasantly and began to make sandwiches. Silently Mrs. Ramos brought a tray for him, and napkins, coffee cups. She filled a small pot with coffee from an urn and put it on the tray, then went back to the big one she had been working on. In a few moments Charlie was satisfied; he picked up the tray and started out.

"Will you tell the captain I have a sandwich for him in the breakfast room?" he asked the officer who was eyeing the tray hungrily. In a low voice he added, "She can't stand to see anyone go hungry. Go sniff the ham a time or two." The officer was already moving toward the worktable before Charlie reached the small hall that separated the kitchen from the breakfast room.

They were just finishing their sandwiches when Dwight Ericson joined them and sat down with a grunt. He stared out the wide glass expanse at the sea where fog was forming again in the distance. Closer, the ocean sparkled.

"Nothing?" Charlie asked, and there was the note of sympathy in his voice that had been there earlier.

Dwight Ericson shrugged. "I wasn't pushing too hard yet. Not until we get the time of death and the weapon." He faced Charlie and grinned slightly. "Bruce Elringer says he never owned a gun in his life. His mother backs him up, naturally. Harry Westerman says that Milton Sweetwater always took a gun with him on trips. A thirty-eight. We haven't found it."

Charlie glanced at Constance who very definitely did not say I told you so.

She said, "We could probably find a thirty-eight and shoot it over there and see how much sound carries to the bedrooms. But it would be better to wait for the fog to move in, don't you think?"

Dwight Ericson looked from her to Charlie who raised one eyebrow and said in a kind voice, "You should have something to eat." He stopped there, although he might have added, "She does that, you see,

picks the words out of your mind and says them before you quite get around to it. And puts others in
your mind." But he didn't say any of this, not with
the captain looking at her so warily.

Ericson picked up a sandwich. "It was pretty much
the way you called it. Jake Kluge says he was in bed,
almost asleep when he heard a noise, he thought, on
the balcony. A door closing hard, something falling;
he can't say. He couldn't go to sleep then and eventually got up and wandered down in time to see Bruce
watching you. After he got his drink, he went back
up and to bed and fell asleep right away. Period.
Bruce says he was up working and got hungry and
saw you two in the garden area and stopped to see
what you were up to. Period. He didn't hear anything.
No one else heard anything, and no one else was up
wandering around. All sound asleep."

"But those two both managed to get some of that
dirt on their feet while I watched," Charlie said. He
picked up another half sandwich. "That end room is
Bruce's."

"Yes. I didn't tell him you found dirt outside his
door before he walked through it in front of you."

"Where are they all now?" Constance asked. The
house was eerily quiet again. She very decidedly did
not like Smart House.

"I asked them to stay in the dining room until
we've made a search for the gun. They aren't happy,
but they're staying put for the moment. All hell's
going to break loose when the reporters start popping
in."

"Right. You sure as God don't have to be clair-
voyant to see the headlines: Smart House Claims
Third Victim." Charlie finished his coffee and leaned
back to brood at the sparkly ocean and the approaching fog.

"Did your people find any fingerprints on the little

computers or the blueprints?" Constance asked, but without hope. The people in Smart House were also smart, too smart to leave prints. She felt something that refused to be more than a stir of uneasiness.

"Clean as a whistle," Ericson said.

"And that means that neither Gary nor Rich put them there, more than likely," she murmured, wishing the stir would come back with some definition the next time. Dwight Ericson was looking at her with a question in his eyes and she added, "Either of them had a reason to handle the blueprints and the computers, but the killer didn't, so he had to get rid of all prints in order to be able to deny he knew about the secret way to get around, or about the way to erase his record from the main computer."

"If your guys are finished with the little elevator, I'd like to have a look at it," Charlie said.

Ericson nodded, drank his coffee too fast, and stood up. "Me too."

In Gary's office a young officer saluted snappily and stepped aside for Charlie and Dwight Ericson to approach the elevator.

"I made measurements, sir," he said, looking at Charlie. He sounded like an adolescent at summer camp. "Two and a half by two and a half and seven feet high. But there's ventilation holes in the roof, and the doors don't really make a seal—the inside doors don't. I figured he might have suffocated in there and got moved, but it's too big, and too ventilated. . . , sir," he added and blushed furiously. He set his face deadpan and looked past Ericson who regarded him sourly for a moment, then continued on to the elevator.

"Thank you, Howie," Ericson said. "Go get a sandwich in the kitchen."

The young officer nearly raced from the room. Ericson glanced at Charlie and said, "We've all heard of you, apparently."

But Charlie was paying no attention. He stood in the elevator and looked at it, turning slowly to examine each wall; they looked like quilted aluminum. Both doors were made of the same material, to keep the weight down, he imagined. He reached out to touch the wall and nodded. Cold. The fruit cellar/refrigerator room was on the other side. This wall was backed up by the dumbwaiter, and the second door that was still closed was on the wall in the fruit cellar, the space where the carts were stored. Satisfied, he nodded again, and turned to examine the open door more closely. The young officer had been right; it did not make a seal at the bottom, nor did the other one. There was a crack less than an eighth of an inch, but there it was. He sighed and looked upward. The ventilation holes were very small, but there was a ventilation fan in the light fixture. But, he reminded himself, Rich had died in the big elevator, so it didn't matter. He sighed more deeply.

A small handle on each door, the control buttons, up, down, open door, close door, none of it held him much longer. The second door did not budge when he tried the handle. Locked because there was no rear exit on this floor. He moved out and let Ericson enter and stood with his hands in his pockets scowling at the elevator that had become nothing more than the repository for the hand-held computers and the blueprints.

"Let's try one more thing," he said when Ericson finished his examination of the space. "How does the light come on? And the fan?"

"The computer's turned off," Ericson said. "Maybe it won't work without it."

"The computer opened it," Charlie reminded him. "But what are the buttons for if you can't run it manually?"

"Go ahead," Ericson said.

Charlie tried the buttons without effect until he

closed the door, and then the ceiling light came on. On the other side of the door Constance gasped when the wall slid back into place and the elevator vanished. Ericson stifled a curse and moved in to examine the wall that appeared completely intact. There was a slight noise from behind it, and then it started to move again, and in a moment the door was visible and then swung open. Charlie looked strained.

"Claustrophobic," he said. "The fan must come on when it's in motion."

"My turn," Ericson said. "Meet you on the first floor, back door."

This time Charlie watched the wall slide into place silently, and just as silently he led the way from the office, down the corridor to the main elevator, and entered with Constance at his side. They listened for a sound from the small elevator next to this one, but there was nothing. On the first floor they hurried around to the back of the house; when they got to the rear of the main elevator, Ericson was already there, the elevator door opened behind him. Here they were in the narrow hallway that ended at the back of the large walk-in freezer in the pantry.

"The front door doesn't open on this floor," Ericson said. "I'll get back in and let you see how the wall works, and then I'll watch it."

Now Constance said, "You can both watch. I'll push buttons this time. And then what, on up to the bedroom suite?"

"Might as well," Charlie said glumly.

As soon as she closed the door, she wished she had not volunteered. The elevator was cold and she shivered, but also she had a feeling she did not identify, uneasy. Claustrophobia? Perhaps. The ride was very smooth, starting and stopping without a bump, the fan operating without a sound, and the feeling intensified until she could identify it. Dread. As soon as the motion ceased, she hit the button to open the door; when nothing happened, the dread threatened to become panic. She remembered that on this floor the other door opened and she quickly turned and hit the button on that side. The door opened as silently as all the other mechanisms. She left the cage exactly as Dwight Ericson had done on the first floor, unwilling to spend even a second in there that was not necessary.

It took Charlie and Dwight at least a minute to reach the bedroom. By then she was breathing normally. Obligingly she stepped back inside once more and closed the door to let them see it work here, and then went to the roof. By the time she left the cage and breathed in the good cool sea air, she knew she would never willingly ride in that thing again. This time she had to wait a bit longer for Charlie and Dwight Ericson to catch up with her.

Charlie looked as strained as he had when he had been the one inside, and she thought, of course; if she was uneasy, so was he. It just worked out that way.

"Try one more thing?" he asked her, his arm around her shoulders.

"Or a dozen," she said, managing a light tone, wanting to ease that tightness in his face now.

"Just one," he said. "Promise. I'd like to know if you can hear people talk if they're inside. Dwight?"

The captain nodded and Charlie and Constance stepped inside one more time. It was a tight squeeze. He closed the door and put his arms around her, kissed her, and then drew back and said in a normal conversational tone, "You are my good and true friend. Let's get the hell out of here."

She laughed and opened the door and they faced Dwight, who was shaking his head. "Nothing. Not a single sound."

"Now to see how you close it when no one's inside," Charlie said then and surveyed the open door, the redwood siding that had moved out of the way. "Here goes." He pushed the door to and felt it click into place, and at the same moment the siding began to move. It was so well constructed that by the time it was restored there was no sign that a section could move.

Dwight was looking sour again. "It blows to smithereens the alibis the computer record gave them," he said. "Whoever knew about that could go anywhere he wanted a damn sight faster than anyone on the main elevator or stairs and not leave a trace." He glanced at his watch and got in the big elevator. "Enough fun and games; back to searches and missing guns and noises in the night."

14

CHARLIE and Constance walked the grounds, the garden area behind the house, where the stone wall rose straight up like a fortress. Charlie regarded it with brooding eyes. "Maddie thinks a burglar scaled the wall to gain entrance," he muttered. "Fat chance."

"She doesn't really think it," Constance reminded him. "She'll probably make up a story about how Milton was out for a stroll and came across the same burglar, with a gun this time. It's comforting to her."

"I know." He linked arms with her and they continued to walk among the rhododendrons. The back garden was too shaded, with the house wall on the west and the cliff on the east, for much sunlight to penetrate. It was pleasantly cool and moist. The paths were bark mulch.

"You couldn't get a cart through here and into the house without some of it clinging to the wheels, leaving tracks," Constance said, finishing the thought he had abandoned. "Of course, if they both died where they were found, it wouldn't matter anyway." She paused and he looked at her expectantly. "I want one of those garden carts," she said with a nod, thinking of their apple harvest. "You can haul really heavy stuff in them easily."

He took her arm in a firm grasp and steered her around the front of the house. The vista there was of tennis courts, and a formal flower garden with masses of roses and lilies and flowers he never had seen before. Men were searching among them. The fog had moved in closer, lower, truncating the cliffs to the north and south; the sun looked pale and deformed already. Soon it would be completely obscured and this would become another foggy, misty day on the coast.

"Let's take a walk on the beach," Charlie said, and they veered seaward, only to stop again at the top of the cliff where Dwight Ericson joined them. Several men were gathered above the high-water mark, waiting for the tide to run out all the way. Two men were clinging to the basalt formation where Milton's body had come to rest.

At Charlie's questioning look, Dwight shrugged. "Nothing. They're using metal detectors on the potted plants in the house. But it's a big ocean. A good toss can get rid of a lot of stuff out there. Especially heavy stuff."

They watched in silence as one of the men searching among the rocks slipped and caught himself and did not move again for a time. When he did, Constance exhaled.

"You're sure Harry Westerman didn't have a chance to pick it up?" Dwight asked.

"Sure. Or put anything down, either. I was watching."

"Yeah. Well, I'm holding them here as material witnesses until we get a prelim on the death and time, through the rest of today, at least. But I can't keep holding them longer than that."

One of his men appeared and spoke quietly to him. He nodded. "Maybe that's the preliminary report on Sweetwater. See you later."

Neither Constance nor Charlie mentioned the walk

on the beach now, as they continued to watch the men on the treacherous rocks below. Even in retreat the ocean hissed and crashed; the men were getting soaked. The fog had completely covered the sky, the temperature dropped, and Charlie shivered and found himself thinking longingly of the hot sunshine at home. Jake and Beth appeared then.

Beth looked very tired and pale, and Jake was still too tight, too tense.

"They said we can go anywhere we want as long as we don't leave the grounds, or go down on the beach, or into the atrium, or—" Beth stopped as her voice became shrill. She looked down at the men on the rocks, then let her gaze go beyond them to the visible ocean, all gray and foamy white. "They're still looking for the gun? They'll never find it."

"You're probably right," Charlie agreed unhappily. He glanced at Jake, who was watching the men below. "How smart is Bruce, would you say?"

Jake appeared startled by the question. "Plenty damn smart," he said after a moment. "I know he hasn't been showing it, but he was a hair's breadth behind Gary, that's all." Beth started to say something; he took her hand and held it. "Wait a minute. This needs saying. Gary made mental or emotional cripples out of everyone he came in contact with." Beth pulled her hand but he continued to hold it. "I observed you with him all those years," he said. "I'm not blind. He turned Maddie into a slavering idiot. Maddie's smart, too, you know. Her husband worked on ENIAC years ago, and she worked with him. She's kept up, but Gary turned her into a *Saturday Evening Post* mom with flour on her cheeks and apple pie in the oven. That was the mother he wanted; that's what she became for him. Rich, Alexander? They worked on Smart House *for* Gary, not really with him. We all worked for him. And we're all pretty much okay, but, Charlie, he was a genius, a bona fide genius, and we all knew it. We stayed."

Beth had been tugging at her hand. Jake turned to look at her directly, and the expression on his face was no longer tight and frozen in tension, but rather puzzled, even hurt; a muscle twitched in his cheek. "Why didn't you leave him? Really leave him, divorce him?"

Abruptly she stopped trying to free her hand. Confusion crossed her face as she stared back at him. He released her and jammed his hands into his pockets.

"Sorry," he said. "That was uncalled for." He glanced at Charlie and then turned to look out over the ocean. "The point is that I did know what was going on, we all did, and no one left. No one could leave. One way or another he held each of us. Sometimes, being with him was like being caught in a blizzard of ideas, a white-out of ideas. Not pie-in-the-sky spitballing, but things that would work, that you could see happening, and you knew that never in a million years would you have thought of them. That was the attraction for some of us. He was stimulating and challenging and he made us be more than we are, more than we thought we could be. But no matter how good we were, he was so far out in front, we knew we'd never catch up—and that was the attraction, just knowing we were in the same circle, that big things were happening, bigger things would happen. He made us do the impossible, and by God, that was the attraction! And if he wrecked our lives along the way, we let him."

His words had started out measured and calm but they began to tumble and his voice became low with intensity. He was nearly whispering now. "If I ever met another man like him, I'd run like hell away from him. If Gary came back to life today, knowing the dreams he had, the plans he had, the ideas he hadn't even started to work out—" He was facing out to sea, his face bleak and haggard when he stopped talking abruptly. "We'd all be exactly where we were before," he finished in a flat voice.

"Right back in the dream," Beth whispered.

He shook himself and looked at her, then nodded. "Right back in the dream, and loving and hating every minute of it. Let's take that walk."

She nodded, and silently, without glancing again at Constance or Charlie, they walked away, side by side but not touching.

"Well, well," Charlie said, then fell silent as a uniformed officer approached them. It was Howie, the one who had reported to Charlie in the office earlier.

He started to salute, blushed, and stopped the motion before it was completed. "The captain said I should tell you we're going to shoot in a couple of minutes and see if anyone inside can hear the noise." Almost unwillingly, he finished, "sir."

Charlie nodded gravely, and Constance suppressed her smile, and hand in hand they walked back to Smart House.

"What I thought we might do," Dwight Ericson said when they entered, "is have people in several different rooms and see what happens. With the draperies closed, doors closed, as much like last night as possible. Okay?" He did not wait for an okay. "I already told them what we'll be doing. They were supposed to leave their doors open."

Charlie ended up in Laura and Harry's room. He glanced inside the bathroom; it was almost identical to the one he and Constance had, but the bedroom was quite different. There were the two beds, and a desk, and comfortable chairs, but also a bookcase with very nice books inside, and crystal bookends. A crystal ashtray held paperclips and two cigarette butts. Laura's, he knew; Harry wouldn't risk his health that way. The usual clutter of hairbrushes and toilet articles, and two fine crystal-based lamps, were on the dressing table. It looked rich. His and Constance's room had articles in cloisonné, a bird, an ashtray, lamps. Each room had been decorated with care, with handsome accessories, apparently all different. Black hole, he thought. The term was taking on more and more meaning. He checked the sliding glass door, pulled the drapes together the final inch or so, and waited for the sound of a gunshot. A minute later he heard a tap on the door and when Constance entered, they both shook their heads.

She glanced about the room, nodded her approval, and they went out to the corridor to wait for Dwight Ericson. He looked disgusted when he joined them.

"Anything taken from Milton's room yet?" Charlie asked.

"No. Want a look?" He led the way down the corridor to the room numbered three, beside Beth's room, which was next to the stairs. On the other side of the stairs was Gary's suite. They entered the room; a uniformed officer rose from a straight chair and looked at Dwight Ericson for orders. Dwight waved him back down. This room was different again, the walls ivory, rich dark mahogany touches here and there, forest green carpeting, paler green bedspreads on the two beds. The accessories were gleaming copper. One bed had been turned down; white silk pajamas and a matching dressing gown were precisely arranged at the foot of it. The white fabric gleamed against the green spread. A briefcase was on the other bed, and papers were on the table. In the midst of them sat a copper ashtray with a half-smoked cigar and ashes in it. A glass with half an inch of what looked like water was also on the table, and an assortment of pens and pencils. Some papers were in neat stacks, others spread out as if Milton had been going back and forth among them. An almost military neatness was displayed by two brushes and a comb carefully lined up on the dressing table; the same neatness was repeated in the bathroom, the closet. A fastidious, precise man who had treated his possessions with respect, who liked order, smoked little, drank little, looked like a movie star and knew it, and died too young. Charlie sighed.

"How I felt when I was done with it," Dwight said with a last glance around. "Exactly nothing. He hadn't gone to bed yet, was working, and went outside to get himself shot and tossed into the ocean. Someone must have tapped on his door, or maybe someone was taken by surprise on the cliff by his late-night walk, or maybe he had a date out there. But why the edge of the cliff?"

"How did you get in? He said he intended to secure his door. I used a chair in our room."

"Never got around to it, I guess. We just walked in. You're assuming he went out through the balcony door?"

"At this moment, I don't think I'm assuming a damn thing," Charlie muttered. He could feel Constance's invisible fingers between his shoulder blades, and he looked at her. She was standing at the door, out of reach, but that didn't matter; he had felt her touch.

She shook her head slightly, bothered as he was by something not quite right but not immediately identifiable either. "Have you taken fingerprints in here?" she asked slowly.

"What for?" Dwight Ericson asked. "Even if we found prints, what would that mean? They could have trooped in and out of each other's rooms all day."

"Things look too clean," Constance said. "Cleaner even than our room. Would he have been likely to go around and shine things? What if there aren't any fingerprints at all?"

Dwight motioned to the officer stationed in the room. "Get Petey up here." As soon as the man was gone, he asked Constance, "What makes you think there might not be any?" He glared at the room as if it offended him.

"I don't know," Constance said. "It just looks obsessively neat, and I didn't think Milton Sweetwater was an obsessive man. I could be altogether wrong, of course. About the room. About him."

Half an hour later Dwight was regarding Constance with something like awe, and Charlie with resignation. "That couldn't have been just a guess," Dwight said.

No fingerprints had been found on the desk or the dressing table, on the lamps or light switch or any of the shiny copper accessories. The glass had yielded good prints, as had various surfaces in the bathroom.

"Get pictures first and then strip it," Dwight said to the technicians at work searching for fingerprints. "Everything portable to the lab. You can leave the furniture here. Come on," he said to Charlie and Constance.

In the wide hall outside the room, Charlie held up his hand. "I don't know about anyone else, but I intend to head for the bar and get a drink."

"Wish I could," Dwight said in a growly way. "Later."

"Speaking of later," Charlie said, "are you going back to Portland when you wrap it up here?"

"My office is there, but I'm setting up shop for a couple of days in Coos Bay. Why?"

"Dinner. We pump you. You pump us. The company pays. Deal?"

"Sure sounds like it might beat MacDonald's." He glanced at his watch and grimaced. "Seven-thirty? I'll pick you up."

Apparently the police had finished their search of the atrium garden. When Charlie and Constance entered, Bruce waved at them from the bar, and Maddie nodded. A tray of cheese, tiny sausages, and crackers was on the bar. Charlie headed for the bar and motioned Constance to the table.

"I'll be waiter," he said cheerfully. "What'll it be, lady?"

"Wine, please. Are they letting people down on the beach yet?" she asked Maddie, who held a martini but seemed not to be drinking it; she merely touched the glass to her lips and put it down again.

"I think so." Maddie's voice was that of a very old woman, throaty, rough, quavering. "They didn't find anything, according to Harry. I think they're still on the grounds somewhere."

Charlie brought the wine and a plate of snacks, took a sausage, and returned to the bar. Constance helped herself to cheese, a very good creamy Brie that she spread on a wheat cracker. "Good," she said, and to her surprise she found herself thinking of one of their cats, Brutus. He had come in off the streets in New York City and was a street-smart beast. His favorite food was Brie, or any other cheese that Charlie had. For years she had tried to break Charlie of the habit of leaving a plate of cheese in the living room. In New York it was an invitation to untold millions of uninvited guests, and she had got in the habit of picking up his plate and taking it to the kitchen herself. Then Brutus came into their lives and within a week Charlie was retrained.

It was the damnable house, she realized, making her want to go home, back to the heat, the awful cats, everything that meant home, and no chlorine smell permeating everything all the time, no cloying gardenias and orange trees . . .

"Well, this must be where the party is," Laura said then in a too loud voice. She walked to the bar. "If there's a way to turn on some music, I'll furnish the quarter."

"And we," Charlie said, "are heading for the beach. I've been trying to get in a walk since morning. Maybe now." He held up his glass and surveyed the contents. "This goes with me. Ready?" He stood up and extended his hand for Constance.

"Yes indeed." She glanced at Maddie. "We won't be here for dinner, by the way. I guess we'd better stop by the kitchen and tell Mrs. Ramos."

"I'll tell her," Maddie said in her new old voice.

"You'll need sweaters," Laura called after them as they left the atrium. "Oregon summer! Hah!"

When they left the trail down to the beach they saw Beth and Jake walking toward them slowly. Beth's head was bowed, her hands in her pockets; Jake was several feet from her on the ocean side, kicking at froth and ocean detritus as he moved. He looked up and waved first, and then Beth waved and picked up her pace a bit.

"Relax," Charlie said as they drew near. "We're out for a walk, nothing more exciting than that." He looked around approvingly. "Nice down here." They all pretended not to notice that two men were still searching the jumbled rocks as the retreating tide uncovered them more and more.

Jake nodded. "About a mile to the next rock pile. Run up there and back and you've put in your two miles, a good workout for the day."

"I should hope so," Charlie said with a slight shudder. "I think we'll dawdle and poke." He had the firm conviction that an adult should run away from a menace, or run to a treasure, and walk in between. Children ran simply because they could.

"We've been finding agates," Beth said almost awkwardly. "But there aren't that many in the summer. It's best after a winter storm." She looked embarrassed, and said briskly, "Well, I need a shower. I'm gritty all over."

She and Jake started to walk again, then he stopped to say, "If you go past the rocks, keep an eye on the tide or you could be stranded. It comes in pretty fast."

"Thanks," Constance said. "We'll be careful. See you later." She and Charlie headed on up the coast.

"A mile," he said dubiously. "Doesn't look that far, does it?"

The cove was a perfect crescent between the two rocky arms that stretched into the sea and ended in twin jumbles of broken rock fingers. Now, with the tide still running out, the beach was two or even three hundred feet wide at the center of the curve, but the high-water mark indicated that most of it vanished when the tide was high. Against the mass of the cliff there were piles and heaps of water-borne, water-discarded logs, some of them over seventy feet long, three or four feet thick. Charlie regarded them with respect. A log that size tumbling in the surf would be a killer. An entire tree, skeleton-white, rose from the sand with the root mass higher than the branches that remained. The spread of the roots was twelve feet high, each root ending in a water-sharpened daggerlike tip.

They walked slowly and stopped now and again to pick up something for closer examination, then return it to the sand. More and more tide pools came into existence, each with its busy inhabitants, each needing study—purple starfish, gaudy anemones that closed with a disapproving snap at their approach, darting fish, and mixed-up crabs scurrying through life sideways. They covered the mile quickly after all and clambered up on the rocky outcrop to survey the next cove, identical to this one, just as isolated, just as protected. The rocks continued out to sea with waves breaking over them, foaming, crashing with eruptions of spray, like miniature rainstorms. They did not go farther.

There were the cliffs, sandstone with black basalt exposed like the substructure of the earth itself, the pale sand that looked silver in the fog shroud, the ocean silver and gray and foaming white. On top of the cliff was a black fringe of trees, and nowhere another person. Charlie slipped his arm about Constance's waist as they walked back; her arm slipped around him and they matched their steps.

"Know what I'd change about my life, if I could do it over?" he said after a few moments.

"Tell me."

"I'd marry you earlier. Think of all those years we weren't married. Wasted. Just wasted."

"Charlie, we were practically children when we got married, just out of school!"

"You might have been too young," he said judiciously, "but I was a mature, responsible, horny male." He ignored her chuckle and added, "Beth and Jake look good together, don't they? Something going on there?"

"If there is, they haven't got used to the idea yet. They looked like kids caught in a back seat." She tightened her arm about his waist and asked in a lower voice, "What's wrong? What did you hear or see or do or think?"

He stopped walking and stood still, facing the ocean, and told her about the conversation between Bruce and Harry that both he and Jake had overheard in the garden.

A shiver ran through her, and this time his arm tightened. Finally she said, "Harry sent Laura here to find out what Gary was up to, didn't he? Now this . . ."

"Doubt that either of them would admit it," he said, "but I'd bet on it. They're playing real-life chess, using each other, mating . . ."

She nodded. "That explains something else. She was so bitter, remember, because Gary talked about divorce and then so obviously sent her packing. He must have known what she was up to; he was playing their game, too."

"I think it's a miracle that he lived to reach his thirtieth birthday," Charlie said. They started to walk again. After a moment, he said aggrievedly, "You know, when they talk computers, I don't understand a thing they're saying. And they're not even really talking nuts and bolts computers, but the business end, the wheeling and dealing part, and even that is like a foreign language. I take it they're planning to get the government to force them to accept development money. Damn, I should have made notes so I can get in the money line myself someday."

When they got back to their room, Constance said she was gritty and salty and went into the shower, where Charlie joined her. She pointed out that there was time for two showers, and he pointed out that he had other things on his mind, and by the time Dwight Ericson arrived to pick them up, they were both fragrant and moist and shiny eyed.

The restaurant Dwight took them to was too elegant Charlie decided after they were seated and the waiter confided that his name was George and implied that he had been born to serve them and make their dinner a happy occasion. Charlie sighed and looked at Constance, who was studiously absorbed in the elaborate menu, her mouth twitching with either hunger or amusement. He looked over the menu and thought with regret of the buckets of steamed clams he and Constance had shared the last time they had been on the Oregon coast. Here the food was overpriced, overwhelmed with sauces, and served by George.

When the drinks came, perfectly composed, perfectly chilled, he felt considerably more cheerful. They ordered their dinners, and then Charlie looked severely at the young waiter.

"George," he said, "I am a cranky old man, very, very set in my ways. In exactly twenty minutes, I want another Gibson exactly like this one to appear on this table, unaccompanied by conversation. And she will have another daiquiri at that time, and he will have another Scotch and water. And meanwhile I do not want any food to appear, nothing. No salads. No bread. Nothing. Got that?"

George looked more frightened than offended; he ducked his head and scurried away. Charlie sipped his drink appreciatively, then said to Dwight, "We may have twenty minutes of peace and quiet. Anything?"

"Something," Dwight said, and leaned forward. "And it makes about as much sense as anything else in this cockeyed affair. The preliminary report has it that Sweetwater was killed by the fall. He was plenty smashed up, cause of death a head injury. Also he was shot in the head, but the wound didn't bleed. He was already dead. Charlie, it looks like someone followed him down to the rocks and shot him after he took the tumble. Or else, someone hit him with a rock or something and then shot him and pushed him over the cliff. It doesn't make any sense either way."

"Good Christ!" Charlie drank the rest of his Gibson and thought he had been premature in saying the next one should appear after such a long time.

"Yeah," Dwight said with a bit too much satisfaction. "The only way I can make it work is that he was out there with someone and they argued. The other person picked up a rock and let him have it, one of those smooth, decorator rocks up there, and then he took Sweetwater's gun and shot him, thinking, I guess, that he might not be dead yet. That explains why there's so little blood on the cliff. Sometimes the good old-fashioned blunt instrument does the job without a lot of blood being spilled. Then the killer rolled him over the edge and threw the gun out as far as he could. Low tide's at six-forty in the morning. I have a couple of divers lined up to search for that damn gun. What do you think?"

"I think it's a goddamn mess," Charlie said glumly.

"But the tide was in," Constance said then. "It really doesn't make any sense. He was dead, but even if the killer didn't know that for certain, he was surely not moving, obviously unconscious. There couldn't have been any doubt about that part. Why not just roll him off the cliff and let the ocean finish it? It might even have passed for an accidental death that way. A man walking in the fog slips, falls into the surf among those dangerous rocks. At least, no one could have proved murder in that situation."

"I know," Dwight said with a deep sigh. "I know."

No one spoke for the next few minutes. George appeared with a new tray of drinks and timidly removed glasses, replaced them, stole away again without a sound. Dwight lifted his and stared into it.

"I'll tell you what else I think," he said with a touch of anger. "They're all lying in their teeth, protecting each other, protecting Bruce Elringer, protecting the company. Sweetwater finally came to his senses, brought you in, threatened to blow the whistle—that's why he had to be taken care of. And now they think they can close ranks again the way they did before."

"Bruce?" Charlie murmured thoughtfully.

"Bruce." His face was grim now. "I've known since spring that he killed his brother and Rich Schoen, and I couldn't put together a shred of proof because they're all lying up and down the line. If there's any way to tie him to that gun, I've got him this time."

15

THEIR food arrived and as they ate, Dwight talked. "The key for me was Rich Schoen," he said. "Why kill him? I can see why they'd all want to get Gary off their backs. From all indications he was a real monster, controlled his family and everyone at work with some kind of insane power that they all bowed to. Everyone who knew him must have had a motive to kill Gary Elringer at one time or another, while that bunch up there hardly even knew Rich Schoen. But who had the *most* cause to commit murder? Bruce Elringer. His brother had made life hell for him apparently, and he's in debt that makes the federal deficit look reasonable. His ex-wife took him to the cleaners, and it's been downhill since. So he had a real motive. Now *he* controls the women in the family, and they control the stock and the money, and he makes out okay. And who else had a real motive? Rich Schoen."

George sneaked up to the table and asked hesitantly if everything was all right. Dwight looked down at his plate as if he had to remind himself and then said, "Fine, fine." Charlie nodded. "Fine, just not clams." Constance laughed and coughed at the same time and had to drink wine to keep from choking. Dwight looked from her to Charlie in bewilderment and she said, "Never mind. Go on." George tiptoed away again.

"Okay. You know about the setup at the house, Smart House? It's some kind of miracle, to hear them tell it. And Rich Schoen's job was finished. He wanted to start showing it, to be the head honcho of the next step, raking in the dough. And Gary wanted to play genius inventor or something. They were split down the middle about it, I guess. And the company was going broke. So Rich and Bruce huddle and decide to get Gary out of the picture. Maybe it was Bruce's idea, maybe Rich's. Maybe Bruce will tell us one of these days. Anyway, it would take two to get Gary to the Jacuzzi, hold him under long enough to drown. We looked for bruises, anything to indicate he went in unconscious, that he was slugged first, or doped, and nothing. Hardly enough alcohol to measure. Nothing else. It's not easy to hold a grown man under water if he's conscious. He fights. I think they both were in the Jacuzzi, stripped, and got him in and held him, and when it was done, they got out and dressed, covered the pool, turned up the heat to confuse the picture, and got the hell out of there."

"That's pretty damn impressive," Charlie said when Dwight paused. "I never thought of that."

"I've been on it a long time," Dwight said, pleased. He took several more bites while they considered his scenario.

Finally Charlie asked, "And you figured out how he killed Rich in the elevator?"

"Yeah. You know there was a big to-do in the greenhouse, poison released, things smashed, water and dirt everywhere. I kept coming back to that. What in hell was that all about? Then I saw those big plastic bags the gardeners use to shovel bark mulch in, dirt for the atrium plants, all kinds of things. And

I realized that that kind of bag would work just like a thin plastic film bag, better even. Bruce could get hold of one without any trouble—folded up they don't take much room, and there are three different sizes they use in the greenhouse. So he gets Rich in the elevator and pulls the plastic bag down over his head. It wouldn't take long, Charlie," he said soberly. "And the reflexive reaction would be to grab at the bag, not the one holding it. Too tough for him to break, or even scrape his fingernails in and leave a trace. A couple of minutes and he's out cold, another minute or two and he's dead. Bruce probably put the mesh bag on him to hide any possible mark he left. There were a couple of very small bruises on one cheek, actually. Then he had to get rid of the plastic bag he had used, so he staged the mayhem in the greenhouse and ditched it when everyone was milling about." He stopped and leaned back in his chair watching Charlie.

Charlie was deep in thought as he finished his dinner and then was surprised to find everything gone. "Not bad," he said almost grudgingly. "Coffee?" He didn't have to raise his finger to get George, who appeared and deftly began to clear the table without a word.

"Coffee for three," Charlie said absently. "And please bring a pot."

George looked startled, but he said, "Yes sir," and was quickly gone again. It seemed only seconds until he was back with a coffee pot and cups, poured for them all, and retreated once more.

Now Charlie regarded Dwight and nodded. "You've covered the bases. Why didn't you go after him?"

"That goddamn computer security printout," Dwight said with poorly concealed fury. "They snowed me, all of them. Alexander demonstrated it and we tried to get around it and couldn't. It tracked every step and kept a record, and no one peeped about the hand-held controls, or about the little elevator that let him get around without anyone seeing him. Not a single peep."

"And you think the others would lie to protect Bruce?"

Dwight shook his head. "They hate him, maybe even more than they hated Gary. But they'd sure lie to protect that company. And when that didn't work, and the company kept on the slippery slide, they decided they had to end it, even if it meant Bruce's skin. Sweetwater must have realized it, being a lawyer you'd think he'd have known it from the start, but anyway, eventually he did. Maybe he even had the proof and confronted Bruce with it last night. Plead insanity, something like that probably would have been his pitch. Get the company off the hook, let them go back to making money, but by then Bruce was off on his own course. He wants the company for himself. Charlie, that company is big bucks, really big bucks. Multimillion neighborhood."

Charlie poured more coffee for them all.

"Dwight," Constance asked, "isn't there a test you can make to see if anyone has fired a gun recently?"

"We did it. Nothing. But we found a pair of gardener's gloves tossed in the shrubbery under the balcony. Under Bruce's window, in fact. We're running the test on them. Want to make a bet he wore them when he shot Sweetwater?"

"I never bet," she said. "But that makes it more complicated, doesn't it? I mean, he either planned it and took the gloves with him and knew the gun would be on Milton, or else he hit him with the rock and went back for the gun and gloves, and that is truly insane. Isn't it?"

"Maybe he's a nut," Dwight said slowly. "That might be his best plea. And if they all decide to go along, they'll provide anecdotal evidence to support such a plea. So could I," he added, "because he is a nut."

Constance looked at Charlie who raised his eyebrows and shook his head. "Could be," he said. "I sure as hell can't come up with anything better."

There was another long pause, then Charlie said, "It's circumstantial as hell. I don't think you can tie him to the first two in a way that'll satisfy a jury."

"I don't need to. If I get him for Milton Sweetwater, I'll be satisfied. One murder, or three, he'll be out of circulation a long time." His voice flattened and his face hardened as he added, "I'm afraid you'll have to appear as material witness."

Charlie sighed. "I thought you were being pretty free with information. Let's see. The gadget in the flower pot. What else?"

"You heard him admit he knew about the gadgets in the first place, while everyone else was still denying any knowledge of them. And he's the one who brought up the subject of a gun. It was on his mind, obviously. The dirt outside his door, before he had a chance to get it on his shoes in front of a witness. I may think of another question or two before we're done here. Tomorrow we use divers and see if we can't locate that damn gun."

"What if you don't find it?" Constance asked.

"It's there someplace, if not in the water, then on the grounds. No one's taken it anywhere. We'll hold them all until it turns up."

"It's a big beach," Charlie said thoughtfully, remembering the heaps and piles of mammoth driftwood, all the crannies and crevices among the logs, the arm of rocks at the northern end of the beach, with more beach north and south, on and on and on. He shook his head. "I don't envy you the search."

"I don't think we have to pay much attention to the

beach," Dwight said with a touch of triumph. "I thought of that, and had the guys look over the various bedrooms, the clothes in the closets, to see who had tracked in sand. You know you can't go to the beach and not track in sand, no matter how careful you are. Even if you take off your shoes, sand seems to cling to you somewhere, to your clothes. Most of them were down there, but not him. Not Maddie Elringer, either, but somehow I just can't see her committing murder."

Constance was looking at him with admiration. "You've been very thorough. I'm really impressed. If the gun doesn't turn up, maybe you should consider the possibility that he got one of the others to hide it up the beach for him. I mean, if he got Rich to help get rid of Gary, that's possible, isn't it?"

"Well," Dwight said dubiously, "considering how they all feel about him, I don't think it's likely."

As he continued to explain why he did not accept that theory, Constance watched him in rapt attention, and Charlie ducked his head and began to fumble among his credit cards. When they left the restaurant a minute or two later, Dwight was in the lead looking pleased, Constance in the middle, and Charlie last. Charlie pinched his wife, who jumped, but did not look back at him, and George watched them all from a distance.

Back at Smart House, they stood on the verandah as the lights of Dwight's car turned into a hazy red glow, and then a patch of pink in the fog, and then vanished. "Dinner was very good," Constance said.

"And that was a mean trick you pulled on the poor guy."

She laughed softly.

"Don't giggle about it. It was mean."

"Charlie, he was trying so hard to impress you I

felt sorry for him. One of us had to be impressed. And I don't giggle."

He opened the door and they entered. "You giggled very distinctly. I heard you. Want to bet the gun doesn't turn up under the cliff?"

"How much and which side do you want?"

"It's my bet. I say it won't turn up. Ten bucks."

"That's the side I'd want, that is if I gambled at all."

They were in the spacious foyer where they could hear Bruce's braying laughter from one of the closer rooms. Charlie scowled and motioned toward the stairs, and they went up and to their own room.

"Paperwork," Charlie said in a disgruntled way. "I've barely even skimmed the stuff Milton put together for us. Okay?"

She nodded. "I want to make a timetable of sorts before I lose it all."

Together they cleared the table and pulled chairs closer to it, then seated themselves, Charlie to start reading the material that made a considerable stack by now, and Constance to try to decipher the various notes people had made about their movements the night Gary Elringer and Rich Schoen had been murdered.

When Charlie looked up again, she was staring at nothing in particular, a slight frown on her face. "What?" he asked.

She slid the sheet of paper she had been working on in his direction. "The timetable," she said with a sigh. "They keep turning up together all evening. But also, at least four of them tried to use the elevator after Maddie went down at about eleven, and it was busy each time. Or locked in place somewhere."

"That's one of my good questions," he said, scanning her timetable. "Why didn't it come when it was called?"

"Ghost or no ghost," she murmured.

Charlie groaned. "Rich could have been aboard, dead, or alive and chatting with a killer, or a chair could have propped it open, or a computer glitch could have done the same. Or they're all lying and alibiing each other like crazy."

"But if they aren't all lying, and if those men were both killed after eleven-fifteen, there are only two real suspects in this group, or else an outsider got in somehow," she added slowly.

"Right. Tell me something. Harry says he tossed his water gun out into the ocean, and Laura says that Milton picked up a water gun on the roof that night. What the hell does that mean? Would she try to implicate Harry on purpose?"

Constance looked troubled; slowly she shook her head. "I really don't think so. It's a relationship that most people would reject, but in a way they are mutually dependent. Each protects the other. There's real need in a relationship like theirs. If it was his water gun that Milton found, what difference does it make? Oh, he would have been lying about going to the roof that night." She paused, and asked again, "But what difference does *that* make?"

He shrugged. "I wish I knew. Let's go to bed. I feel like suddenly I'm on West Coast time and it's bedtime." It kept coming back to the same problem, he thought grumpily. At least two of them had the opportunity, and probably all of them the motive. But how the devil had anyone managed to kill two vigorous, strong men without a hell of a fight?

She began to stack the papers again as he got up and stretched, then pulled the bedspread off the bed and tossed it on a chair. He was unbuttoning his shirt when she whispered, "That's it!"

"That's what?"

She was eyeing the bed narrowly. "I knew there

was something else wrong in Milton's room, more than just all that shiny copper stuff. Look at what you just did." She pointed to the spread. "That's the normal way to get a bed ready for use. Pull the spread off, or fold it down and take it off if you're fairly neat. But Milton's spread was still in place, turned down with the blanket and sheet. Remember how white his pajamas looked against the spread? Why were they even there? How do you get ready for bed?"

He blinked. "I give up."

"Your robe is still in the closet and even if you had got it out, you wouldn't lay it out neatly on top of the bedspread because that has to come off. Maybe in the winter in a really cold room you would leave the spread on, but not in this house, not in summer, not with a blanket on the bed. It would be stifling. And Milton was too neat, too orderly to have left his pajamas and robe out on the bed all day. I don't think he would have got them out until he was ready to put them on, and, remember, he didn't put a chair under his doorknob, or secure the door in any way. He must not have had time. The killer must have gone to his room, or he must have left it almost instantly. I don't think he would have turned down the bed with the spread in place. I think he would have folded it very neatly and put it on the chair, if he had had time to do it at all. Charlie, someone else turned down that bed, not Milton."

"And then wiped off fingerprints from everything in the bedroom. Laura?"

"Why would she? She didn't seem to care who knew what she did before."

"Harry, to protect her? Maybe. Beth? Her room is next to his and she says she didn't hear a sound. Beth?"

She had no answer. A few minutes later, he watched her fold down the bedspread on the second twin bed and remove it in a neat bundle, the way she did every night.

16

From the top of the cliff Charlie watched the men below swarming over the rocks, and Dwight Ericson prowling at the edge of the black jumble, where erratic waves now and again splashed on him. The tide was lower than Charlie had yet seen it. The morning was cool and still; the sun in the east had not cleared the cliff behind Smart House.

Jake Kluge appeared on the trail, coming up from the beach, wearing running shorts and a sleeveless shirt. He was very muscular and fit, and his loose-jointedness seemed appropriate now. He was not breathing hard after his run and the climb up from the beach. He waved but continued on to the house. Only a moment ago, Harry had gone down to start his morning run.

Charlie thought about how much he disliked men who showed off muscular legs in shorts, who made a ritual of running at dawn. At last he turned to the house again and saw Constance on the wide verandah waiting for him. He walked to her with dignified, sedate moderation as befitting his position in life, and they entered to have breakfast.

Bruce was standing at the door of the breakfast room glowering at Alexander. He yelled, "I don't give a fuck about that! I want that list! I have a right!"

"I'll make another copy for you," Alexander said. "I'll make copies for everyone. After breakfast."

"Be sure you do!" Bruce stamped out and slammed the door.

Alexander began to inch toward the door after him; he looked terrified, more of Charlie than of Bruce.

"Well, the boy's in a snit this morning," Charlie said cheerfully and drew out a chair for Constance, another for himself. "Sit down, Alexander."

Miserably he perched on the edge of a chair.

"This thing you will copy for him, what is it?"

"It's nothing, really. A list of things the police took from Milton's room, that's all. But Bruce is trying to make an inventory of the house, the contents. Afraid someone's stealing stuff."

If he looked any guiltier, they'd haul him away and hang him, Charlie thought.

Constance said, "I'll copy it for him." Alexander hesitated in confusion; she held out her hand and said firmly, "I'm sure you have more important things to do."

His indecision, while brief, was painful to watch. Finally he drew a sheet of paper from his pocket and handed it to her. He looked instantly relieved. "How long will they keep all of us? What are they waiting for?"

Charlie shrugged. "They're looking for the gun. As soon as they find it, they'll probably release everyone."

"If they don't let us go soon. . . ," Alexander started, then shook his head. "They have to let us go. They don't realize the strain, the tension, tempers. We all have work to do. They don't understand."

"Oh, I think they do," Charlie said dryly. "I'm sure they do."

"Alexander, how well do you people know each other? Off the job, I mean?" Constance asked idly.

"Some more than others," he mumbled. "I don't know."

"Does anyone here know any of the martial arts, do you suppose?"

He stared at her as if she had uttered an obscenity, or was speaking Swahili. Charlie found that his patience with this skittish young man was wearing very thin. Alexander shook his head and mumbled something inaudible; he got up and sidled toward the door. Neither of them tried to stop him this time, and, close to the door, he turned from them and darted out.

"We can probably find out," Charlie said thoughtfully, "but why?"

"I was thinking of Gary. I could put someone in that whirlpool, winded, without a bruise. I wonder if anyone else here could."

Upstairs at that moment Beth was leaning against the frame of the sliding glass door in Maddie's room. She felt heavy, leaden all over, even her brain; she could not seem to comprehend what it was that Maddie was suggesting. All night she had twisted and turned and stared into darkness, and twice had started upright, holding her breath, listening. Finally she had turned on the light in her bathroom and left the door open a crack, and then she had been able to doze off, but fitfully.

Maddie had started out by asking if the detective intended to drag them all through the mud over the stupid game, but she had left that very quickly, and what she was saying now made no sense to Beth.

Maddie's eyes were red, her lids swollen, her face puffy. She kept looking past Beth, out the glass at the sea below, lifting and putting down her cup repeatedly without drinking from it. Her breakfast was on the table before her, untouched.

"You owe us something," she said. "You could have prevented all of it. All of it. He needed you always, and you knew that. You destroyed him and now you'll wreck Bruce's life, too, and mine."

"I don't know what you're talking about!"

"You do. You do. You drove him to that woman! He despised her. He told me over and over, and you drove him to her. And now you'll have the money and Bruce will be ruined. You owe us something!"

"What do you want from me?" Beth demanded, determined not to cry, not to scream at this woman who appeared insane to her now.

"You come home with me. Bruce is coming with me, too. We'll be a family again, the three of us. Bruce needs someone he can trust, someone to help him now. There will be enough money; you don't need it all, no one does. Not the money Gary made out of nothing. You owe us . . ."

"Stop it! Just stop it! I don't owe you anything! Not you, not Bruce. My God, he would have me hanged if he could!"

Maddie apparently had not even heard her. "He wanted a family. I know he did, a real family with you, children, a real home. He would have been happy then, contented. You took that away from him, from me. How can you be so heartless now? There's enough money. You don't have to destroy Bruce, too. How can you do it? Be nicer to us, Beth. Please don't hurt us any more."

Beth jammed her hands over her ears. "I won't listen to this! Maddie, you know what it was like, living with Gary. You do know, goddamn it!"

"How he worked," Maddie said, and started to weep again. "All his life, just work, and you. The only two things—"

With an inarticulate cry, Beth ran to the door and out, to stand shaking in the wide corridor. She was startled by the sound of Jake's voice calling her.

"Are you all right?" he asked, approaching her with a worried expression.

"Fine," she said. "I've been talking to Maddie. Before breakfast yet. That's a mistake."

"I knocked on your door," he said, and suddenly he sounded awkward. "I thought we might have breakfast together. But after yesterday, maybe you'd rather not. Beth, I'm sorry. I shouldn't have dumped on you. Me yesterday, now Maddie."

"But you didn't," she said. "I mean, it wasn't what I'd call dumping." And now, she realized, she sounded just as awkward as he did. She took a deep breath and attempted a smile. "Anyway, I'm glad you talked to me a little."

"A little! Just my life history."

They walked to the stairs where he stopped her with his hand on her arm, and now he looked at her steadily. "Listen, Beth, you let everyone take advantage of you. Me included. Now Maddie. Whatever it is she wants, she isn't your worry. She doesn't need to tie you in knots. Any more than I do. Last night, a bad night," he added grimly, "I kept thinking how I went on about Gary yesterday, and about my hopes, my plans, my concerns, and I realized all at once that that's how we all treat you and always have. I used to come over to your place, yours and Gary's, and watch you now and then and wonder how and why you put up with him and his pettiness, his constant demands, and last night I realized that I had put you in exactly that same position. I'm sorry." Suddenly he grinned and took her arm, started to propel her down the stairs. "There. I was sure I wouldn't be able to get through that, and I rehearsed it over and over when I was running this morning."

As Constance and Charlie ate ham and eggs and biscuits, Constance glanced over the list of items the police had taken for laboratory examination. She started to speak, then handed the list over instead, pointing to one of the items. "That's strange."

He read the line: 3 *sheets*, 2 *blankets*, 2 *bed-spreads*. The door started to open and hastily he folded the paper and put it in his pocket. Beth and Jake entered the breakfast room.

Beth looked from Charlie to Constance and blurted, "Have you talked to the police yet about— you know?"

"No, I don't," Charlie said.

And Constance said, "Oh, you mean the game?"

"Yes. Have you? Maddie thinks you have, and I was sure you wouldn't, not without telling us. Have you?"

"Why does she think we have?"

"Something Bruce said to her. The police accused him of keeping something back, lying to them. That captain practically accused all of us of lying."

"We haven't mentioned it, Beth," Charlie said. "But, Jesus, he has a point. All of you have been lying to him."

She bit her lip and looked down at the coffee cup at her place, moved the cup around on the saucer until it scritched like fingernails on a blackboard. Jake took her hand from it. "I told Maddie I'd try to find out for her. We should tell them, shouldn't we?" she whispered, not yet looking up. "Maybe it would help their investigation if we tell them."

"Has it helped you, Charlie?" Jake asked.

"Don't know yet. But, Beth, if it seems necessary to tell them, I will. You do understand that, don't you?"

She nodded.

"How stable is Maddie right now?" Charlie asked.

"She's not going to pieces, but she's close," Beth said. She glanced at Jake, who nodded. "I think she's had just about all she can handle. Why?"

"What would it do to her if they accuse Bruce of murder? Could she handle that?"

"Oh, God! Are they going to?"

"I think they might. In any case—" He stopped when Mrs. Ramos appeared with a tray and watched her until she finished and went back through the doorway. Suddenly he stood up. "Excuse me. Right back." He followed Mrs. Ramos to the kitchen.

Beth stared after him, then turned bewildered eyes to Constance, who shrugged. Slowly Beth started to eat, but after only a bite she put her fork down again. "She'll take it really hard," she said soberly. "She thinks she failed Bruce over the years, and he knows it and reinforces that feeling every chance he gets. Last night, it was just awful. He kept laughing the way Gary always did, and she kept shaking. It was awful."

"Did he always try to mimic his brother?"

"Not really. I think this is part of the reversed Turing test they were playing with several years ago. He's perfected his imitation since then."

Constance shook her head, smiling. "Would you mind backing up a bit? What's a reversed Turning test?"

"Turing," Jake said. "After the mathematician. He came up with the original test. The subject sits at a computer terminal and types in questions and tries to determine which answers come from a computer, which from a person in another room. It's a forerunner of the research going on now with artificial intelligence. Gary's idea was to make voice prints and program the computer with them, plus pertinent data about each person being used, and then try to perfect it to the point where even a professional mimic couldn't fool the computer. So, a reversed Turing test, trying to fool the computer instead of a person." He added dryly, "The computer never misses any more."

"My goodness," Constance said softly. "People do all the time, don't they? You hear a voice and think it's someone you know and turn around to see a stranger. Can it pick out voices in a crowd? I'd think the intelligence services would be after it."

Suddenly the silence was strained as Beth and Jake exchanged glances. Constance felt as if she had stumbled onto forbidden territory.

"That's one of the reasons for the isolation of this place," Jake said after a moment. "Gary wanted complete secrecy until he was ready to disclose the entire package he was developing. I wormed that much out of Alexander finally."

"Good heavens," Constance said then. "If it was tracking people by voice the night Gary and Rich were killed, it must have overheard the killer with them." She realized with a chill that she was talking about it as if it were a person.

"It wasn't a tape recorder," Jake protested.

"But it was," Beth said quickly. "Remember the first program Bruce wrote that was successful? It was a music program," she explained to Constance. "He could synthesize music, any instrument, and play back a complete symphony, every instrument with its own part, every instrument unique. That's how they could work with voices, any number of voices treated as instruments, to be played back."

And that explained Bruce's appreciation of Alexander's accomplishments as a programmer, Constance thought suddenly; Bruce would recognize exactly what it was that Alexander was doing, what it meant.

"Bruce. . . ," Beth whispered then. "If Maddie thinks she's likely to lose him—"

Jake took her hand. "Beth," he said firmly, "remember what we were saying? They aren't your problem, none of them." He was gazing at her steadily, with concentration, as if trying to force her away from her thoughts. He did not relax until she finally nodded and lifted her fork again. "After breakfast, let's take a walk and then drop in on Maddie and see how she's doing. She likes to play bridge. We'll get Laura to play, too. Maybe it would help all of us to play cards for a while today."

Constance watched him with great interest. He could have gone into counseling, or the ministry, or anything having to do with an intense dialogue. He had the gift of focusing that was one of the requirements. She felt that during this short interlude he had forgotten her altogether. Now that the moment had passed, he once again could include her, and, in fact, did include her, invited her to play bridge with them in a polite way that meant her refusal was taken for granted. She refused.

When Charlie returned only a minute or two later, Constance was surprised that neither Beth nor Jake reacted to the new charge in the air. She could feel it almost like an electric current. She pushed her plate back slightly and stood up. "I think it's time for our walk," she said. He nodded and she joined him at the door. "See you later," she said over her shoulder and went out with Charlie.

"What did you find?" she asked as soon as they were in the hall.

"*Shh*. Outside."

On the verandah she tried again. "What are you up to?"

"I want Dwight Ericson to get his ass up here and get his men to work for me."

"Charlie."

"I looked at the popcorn popper. It's exactly like our old one that Jessica stole when she went to school."

He had never forgotten that their daughter had taken the popcorn maker away with her when she left for college. Having a new one come into their house had done nothing to dim the memory, the feeling of being suddenly bereft that he had complained bitterly about. Constance dug him in the ribs with her elbow. "Charlie!"

"And I found out that Mrs. Ramos had two sheets on every single bed in that house. She thought I was insane to ask."

"Ah. Well. You should have known."

He chuckled and put his arm about her shoulders and steered her toward the cliff. They went down the trail to meet Dwight at the bottom. He looked disgusted and tired. Seeing him next to Charlie gave Constance a little jolt as she realized that this was how she and Charlie must appear to others: one tall and lean and very, very blond, the other chunkier and shorter and very dark. She liked the way it presented itself to her mind's eye.

"Nothing," Dwight said, responding to Charlie's question.

"Not even a sheet?" When Charlie sounded that innocent, Constance always feared that someone might hit him.

"What now?" Dwight asked.

Charlie told him. "So one missing sheet. Maybe the gun's wrapped up in it and they're both at the bottom of the ocean."

Dwight chewed his lip scowling at the horizon. "You think he was killed in his room?"

"Maybe. The bed was funny, prints wiped off too many things. Maybe."

"And was wrapped in a sheet and moved to the cliff? Jesus Christ!"

"Maybe. If I had a crew of men, I'd have them search for bloodstains, and a burn mark maybe."

"Burn?"

"Picture the ashtray," Charlie said dreamily. "Half-smoked cigar, and a smidgen of ash. Where was the rest of it? Suppose Milton was smoking it when he was gonged. It would fall, obviously. Not in wet grass or weeds, or it would have gone out, and in that fog just about everything was good and wet, but the cigar was still lighted when it was put down in the ashtray. You could see the dead ash on the end where it burned itself out. And that means it was still lighted when it was picked up and replaced there, and that could mean a burn mark. Or someone re-lighted it, and somehow that sounds too damn macabre even for this bunch."

"Damn it, Charlie, that's reaching too far. He could have partly smoked that cigar anytime, anyplace that evening and put it down to let it burn out."

"And when did someone wipe the prints off the ashtray? Picture it. You've got a half-smoked cigar, and you have to get your prints off the ashtray for God knows what reason. You put the cigar down on the edge of the table or something and clean the ashtray and put the cigar back and let it burn without disturbing it again. That's one scenario. Another one is that Milton got bashed somewhere other than in his room, dropped the cigar, and the killer tidily returned it to its proper resting place after wiping off fingerprints. So a little ash is in the ashtray and there's dead ash on the end of the thing. Undisturbed until the police move it."

"In that case, why mess around with the fingerprints?"

"I wish to God I knew."

Dwight was very gloomy now. "You know what's going on over in Jordan Valley? Three, four hundred miles away from here, near the Nevada border, a rancher got beaten to death last night. That's the sort of thing I usually get called in to see about. Round up his work crew, the foreman, ask a few questions, maybe start the search for a poacher, get it over with pretty damn fast. Sheriff could do it, but chances are he's got cousins or brothers or sons working for the rancher; might be biased, they say." He was watching his men scrambling out of the way of fast-moving waves; the tide was rushing in. "Well, this is a bust." He grimaced. "The last time I asked a few questions about the carts, the wheelbarrows, and then found out no body had been moved. This time I didn't bother. God almighty, what a mess."

They walked up the beach after Dwight and his men left. "Not bad," Constance said, patting Charlie's arm. She did not mean the scenery, as he well understood.

"They haven't proved anything yet," he said.

She waved her hand, dismissing that. "They will." She told him about the reversed Turing test and the voice prints. "I'm getting a better picture of what Gary was actually pulling off," she said slowly. "I think that computer must have been able to understand anything said to it and respond exactly the way a person might. It's scary."

"*Hmf,*" he said, the grunt more eloquent than anything else he might have thought of at the moment. "How about *I'm buffaloed*? Think it would get that?"

She nodded gravely. "Or *fly by night.*"

"*Chinese boat drill.*"

She laughed. "*Wolf in sheep's clothing.*"

"Wow!" he said, stopping. A particularly large wave crashed against the cliffs ahead of them. The rocks that reached into the sea at the northern end of the crescent were being covered rapidly by the encroaching tide. Waves smashed into them, sending spray and foam high into the air. "When the tide comes in here, it doesn't fool around," he muttered, and they started to walk again.

"It's damn hard to move a dead body," he said after

a moment. "That expression *deadweight* came from the real world. Why kill him and then push his body off the cliff? Why wipe the prints? It's true, anyone might have been in and out of that room earlier. The killer could have bluffed it out. Why shoot him in the head after he was a goner?"

"Maybe he wanted to make certain that no one even pretended to believe this one was an accidental death."

Charlie came to an abrupt stop, his fingers hard on her arm. "Jesus! That's it!"

Startled, she turned to see him staring fixedly at the waves smashing into the black rocks.

He came back. "Enough walking. Walking, running, bad for the joints, bad for the knees. Let's go."

They returned briskly; now and then Charlie muttered something under his breath, and in between he hummed almost inaudibly. They had a never-stated rule in their house that anyone was allowed to mutter without interruption. Sometimes, when it was not entirely clear if it was a mutter or merely conversation too low to catch, it was permissible to ask, "Are you muttering?" Constance recognized what he was doing now very definitely as a mutter; she did not interrupt.

They met Beth on the red tile verandah. "Hi," Constance said. "No bridge game yet?"

Beth shuffled her feet. "Maddie doesn't seem to care one way or the other, and I can't seem to concentrate on cards today. They're searching again. We can't even go to our rooms now. What are they doing?"

Before Constance could speak, Charlie's fingers tightened briefly on her arm, then withdrew. "I'll see if I can find out," he said. "Good-bye, ladies." He sauntered off.

"Of course it would be hard to concentrate now,"

Constance said. "I'll tell you a story. Once upon a time there was a beautiful princess whose parents both died quite suddenly and left her an orphan." She ignored Beth's incredulous stare and said with a smile, "Sorry, but that's how these stories always start: They get right down to the point without any shilly-shallying. So the princess's fairy godmother came to the grieving girl and said, 'You must go live with your eldest uncle until you come of age.' Thus it was that the girl went to live with her uncle."

As she continued the story, Constance appeared unaware of Beth's disbelief and even alarm, as if Beth was convinced that she was in the company of a madwoman.

"From the first day the uncle beat the girl if she was too noisy, or too quiet. If she wept, or did not weep for her parents. If she ate too much or too little. And gradually she came to know what he expected, and always did that before he could beat her. When her fairy godmother came to see how she was, she found the child cowering in a corner watching her uncle, trying to anticipate what might arouse his wrath next. And the fairy godmother spirited the child from that house and took her to the second eldest uncle instead. 'Here you must remain until you come of age,' she said, as before, and left her there.

"This uncle was married to a woman who said on seeing the child, 'Oh, you are so young and strong, and I am old and weak and soon I must die.' When the girl laughed, her aunt said, 'Oh, you are happy and gay, and I am careworn and sad and soon I must die.' When the girl ran, she said, 'Oh, you are straight and full of life, and I am tired and in pain and soon I must die.' This time when the fairy godmother returned, she found the girl with her hair tied in a tight knot, and wearing a voluminous gown that concealed her young limbs, walking with a bent, hunched position, rubbing her eyes often to make them red and watery. Of course, she removed her at once."

Beth found herself strolling the length of the verandah with Constance, listening to the silly story, strangely unwilling now to pull away and run inside.

"In the next house, her aunt wept bitterly when the girl erred. 'How you wound me who loves you with such complete love.' And in the next, her uncle found her so pleasing that he could not bear to be apart from her for even a moment, and when she walked, he walked also, and became red in the face and held his heart and drew in long, choking breaths, but never complained. And when she ate a sweet, he ate the same, and suffered spasms of the chest and stomach, but never complained.

"In the next house her aunt promised every day that if she did well, then tomorrow she might have this or that, and tomorrow was as long in coming as the sun on a gray winter day."

They had walked the length of the verandah two times when Beth stopped. "The story doesn't have an ending, does it?"

"Each listener determines when it should end," Constance said.

"You left out duty and shame and love and a few other things."

"Not left out, just not reached yet."

"It's a very good story. Thank you."

"You're welcome. I think I'll see if I can find out what Charlie's up to."

For another moment they faced each other gravely, and then Beth nodded. "A good story. I'll see you later." She walked away.

Charlie was at the table in the breakfast room watching Dwight Ericson take Bruce Elringer over the house inventory item by item. They had finished the dinnerware and were on pictures, statuary. Bruce was sullen and mean, his face flushed dark. Dwight was being extremely patient. And he might as well be, Charlie thought, since it was taking his men forever to make their new search. This was the part of police work he had hated when he was a New York cop, he remembered: detail work, searching, looking for one particular straw in a broom factory. He sympathized with Bruce when he considered the amounts of money that Gary had spent on Smart House: seventeen thousand for china, another three thousand for porcelain, nine thousand for silverware, on and on. Four dozen sheets at twenty bucks a piece. He shook his head and listened.

"Okay, okay," Dwight was saying. "The original inventory shows fifteen pictures, and there are still fifteen. Pass on. The statues in the foyer. None's missing, right?"

"Not yet," Bruce snapped.

"Okay, Mr. Elringer. You weren't able to update your inventory in the bedrooms, so I guess that about does it. I'd like a copy of what you have there."

Bruce clutched his notebook.

"Howie, go with Mr. Elringer to the basement office and get copies of what he has," Dwight said, still patient, but it was wearing thin.

"I'll make the copies," Bruce said quickly. "He can watch if he wants."

"He wants," Dwight said.

"Bruce," Charlie asked. "Exactly why did you start your own inventory? You did it last May, didn't you?"

"You know it. Because I don't trust the one Rich put together. Don't trust the people who've been free to come and go in this place. Five-hundred-dollar ashtrays, three-hundred-dollar lamps, thousand-dollar knickknacks! Someone's got to keep a list, keep track."

He stood up, still clutching his notebook. "You know how much has walked out already? Thousands! My money, and it just walks out the door!"

"Yes. So you said before. But exactly what walked out the door? I mean, was there something specific, or just a general suspicion?"

Bruce leaned forward and nearly spat the words. "A blue malachite whale, about this long." He held out his hands to indicate ten or twelve inches. "Seven hundred dollars! What the fuck for? Who needs stuff like that in bedrooms?"

"When was it gone?" Charlie asked. "How did you know it was missing already last May?"

Bruce glared at him, then at Dwight. "You fuckers, you'll try to pin that on me, too, won't you? It won't work! That's why I began the inventory, to prove that someone here has sticky fingers. It was in my room in May when we first came here, and I looked at it and looked at the price on the inventory and I knew the sucker would tempt someone. So I started the list. Every fucking room has something like that. Portable, pricey, tempting. What the fuck for?"

"When did you realize it was gone?" Charlie asked again, as patient as Dwight, but with an edge to his voice also.

"How the fuck do I know? June, July. When I came back in the summer sometime. It's gone, all right. Who the fuck knows what else is missing by now?"

"And did you update your inventory back then when you returned?"

"You bet your ass I did! And again this time!"

"Wonderful," Charlie murmured and relaxed back in his chair, finished.

One of Dwight Ericson's men entered the room as Bruce and Howie left. The newcomer was another of the earnest uniformed officers. He saluted, and

Dwight glanced at Charlie with a look of embarrassment.

"I think we might have found the burn mark," the young officer said, and Dwight and Charlie both stood up fast. "At least, there's a burn up on the balcony, and it might be fresh. No way of knowing, I guess."

"Oh, sweet fanny," Charlie breathed. "Don't let anyone touch it! Are they all still in the library or television room?"

The officer acted as if a stranger asked questions and gave orders routinely. Without hesitation he said they were.

"Make sure they stay there," Dwight said. "Let's go look."

The mark was hardly visible, a dark smudge against the redwood plank on the balcony. When Dwight started to get too close to it, Charlie automatically motioned him back.

"You're an expert on burns?" Dwight asked, irritated enough finally for sarcasm to overtake the patient voice he had been able to maintain before.

"Oh yes," Charlie said softly. "Oh my, yes." He surveyed the area, a foot in from the edge of the balcony, at the place where the floor was cut away for the stairs to the grounds below. The railing was waist high, with a middle bar; the balcony was fifteen feet wide, narrower at both ends where the stairs began. Ten feet here, five for the stairs. The closest window was to the suite that had been Gary Elringer's. Satisfied with the general survey, he now dropped to one knee and studied the burn mark more intently, and then he bent lower and sniffed it. He stood up and looked at Dwight.

"This is where he got bashed in the head and dropped his cigar. I think you'll be able to get enough ash from the wood to cinch it. There's a bit caught in the grain."

Dwight was regarding him with a very blank expression. "You are an expert on fires, aren't you? I read about that."

Charlie nodded. "For a lot of years. An awful lot of years." He turned away and gazed out at the ocean, the smell of rotten smoke in his nose, too many memories surging now, too many rotten fires blazing before his mind's eye. "Can your tech men deal with that?"

"Yeah. We'll cut out the section, but first we'll use a vacuum on it." He began to give orders to his men.

Gazing at the brilliant ocean, Charlie thought of the many smells of fire. The blazing fire without added water or chemicals, almost a clean smell, an autumnal smell; then the filthy odor of plastics and fibers and chemicals, wet wood and paint and insulation . . . A cold fire was worst. No more blazing, no more heat, but somehow smoldering still, emitting a poisonous vapor, that was the worst stink in the world. Then the builders came in and sealed it, and that was yet a different odor, almost corruption-sweet, and the glare of the sealant, a sickly blue-white with a high gloss . . .

"Let's have a look below," Dwight said at his elbow.

Charlie followed him down silently, thinking: They would find wheel marks that would now take on a significance they had not had this morning, and maybe a broken plant or two that had gone unnoticed before, with any luck a smear of blood. And so it was. They found the wheel marks and the broken plant, and even a very small smear that could have been blood. Lab tests would decide.

17

BEFORE Charlie left Dwight to oversee the removal of a section of the planking, he said, "The gun will turn up. I'd have them go through Maddie Elringer's room and car again." A glint of satisfaction showed for a moment in Dwight's pale eyes.

"Yeah. He could have moved it more than once. See you in a little while, Charlie."

Charlie walked slowly along the verandah to the sliding door where Constance was waiting for him. She took his hand when he entered.

"Coffee in the garden bar," she said. "With maybe a slug of something more potent than caffeine. Sound good?"

"Where are they all?"

"In the television room or the library. Seething. I stopped in and left again. Too turbulent for me."

"Garden bar," he said emphatically. He indicated the verandah. "You saw?"

"Enough to guess what I didn't see. But it's insane, isn't it?"

They went to the bar where she had coffee and cups waiting. She poured while Charlie scowled at the turquoise pool at the distant end. The waterfall splashed and glittered in the sunlight that came through the dome on the roof; the air smelled of gardenias and chlorine and felt too heavy. She rummaged among bottles and came up with Cognac, added a therapeutic dose and a spoon of sugar to Charlie's coffee, tasted it, and then slid it across the bar to him.

For many minutes they sat in silence until he grunted. "Milton's in his room shuffling papers, smoking his cigar. There's a tap on the window and he opens the door to admit the killer. Milton knows something, probably doesn't realize that he knows it. The killer talks to him a short time, then coughs on the smoke and suggests they step out on the balcony to continue their conversation. He picks up something heavy in the room and carries it out with him. He says how about we walk down away from the other doors. Beth's room is next door, she might hear us. They walk to the stairwell and he hits Milton over the head, kills him instantly. The cigar falls, but he doesn't notice it yet. He runs back and yanks a sheet off the bed, returns to the body and manages to get it wrapped more or less, and drags it off the balcony to the landing, out of sight. It's foggy; no one's likely to be out strolling, or if anyone does take a walk on the balcony, there's nothing to be seen. So far, so good."

He tasted his coffee for the first time and looked surprised. "You make a mean brew," he said with appreciation, and drank more of it. "So now he goes back up and sees the damn cigar and picks it up. He could just toss it, but he takes it back with him instead. He's staging a show, and this is one of the props." He paused, his eyes narrowed in thought, and sipped his coffee again. "We'll come back to that," he said finally. "So there he is, the bed a mess. He makes the bed, the one with a sheet missing now, and puts Milton's briefcase on it, and turns down the other one, and goofs. He leaves the spread on it, and you spot the mistake. That's okay, it works. The prints," he said. "The fingerprints. He shouldn't have left many, not on the lamps, the ashtray, all the copper stuff. Why clean all that stuff?" He became silent, finally exhaled softly, and said, "He had to wipe them because Milton's prints weren't there on any of that stuff."

He became silent again, this time immobile, staring blindly. Constance poured more coffee for them both and waited. There was no point in her asking anything yet, she knew; he was asking and answering questions in his mind, probably the same ones she would have asked.

At last he spoke again. "It was the ashtray," he said with conviction. "The murder weapon must have been the ashtray. Either he had already wrapped it with the body, or he carried it back and realized that it would be obvious that it had been used. Blood, or hair, something. Maybe he cracked it. That's why he had to get a different ashtray and wipe off his own prints, and that meant he had to switch the other stuff, too. Lamps, bookends, all that matching stuff, and not a piece of it with Milton's fingerprints. So, it wasn't to hide his prints, it was to hide the fact that none of that stuff belonged there. All right!" He smiled at her and finished his coffee, and then gazed about the mammoth atrium with pleasure. "Not bad," he said.

"Charlie, cut it out. Finish."

"Oh well," he said airily. "The rest is child's play. He gets the gun, then goes around to the greenhouse and gets the cart and parks it under the landing at the stairs. The landing's only four feet above the ground level; the cart bed is a couple feet high; no big deal to roll the body off the landing into the cart and trundle it down to the edge of the cliff, where he shoots Milton in the head and rolls him over the side." He paused again and added, "It wouldn't take a lot of strength, either, not with that garden cart we saw. It can carry a horse, make it possible for anyone to carry a horse."

"I'll roll you off that chair if you don't fill in the details. First of all, why? It would be no less a case of murder if Milton had been found on the balcony with his head smashed in."

"But he didn't dare fire the gun that close to the bedrooms. They would have heard, no matter how tight that house is."

Constance changed her position slightly, a change that was very subtle, but one that Charlie recognized. He had insisted that she study aikido in the beginning, had even urged her to show him personally what she was learning, but the time had come when she regarded him kindly and said that perhaps she should not demonstrate the new movements her class was studying.

Hastily he said, "Milton was not a small man. We all jumped to the same conclusion, remember? He would not have stood still for someone to push him off the cliff, but a shot? That's different. There weren't any powder burns, and that seemed to indicate some distance. Actually the killer was probably real close. When they find the sheet, they'll find the burns. But, most important, it had to be on the books as murder, and there has to be a weapon to implicate someone most decidedly, and then the rest of them will be out from under. Not another mysterious fatal accident, a possible fall from a balcony, or even from the cliff, but a deliberate murder with a gun."

She was still considering this when Dwight joined them, his lean face ridged and set. "We found the gun," he said. "Under Maddie Elringer's mattress. It wasn't there yesterday."

"Do you want coffee?" Constance asked.

He ignored her and continued to regard Charlie with hard eyes. They had become even paler, almost colorless. "I'm beginning to wonder if you don't know too much."

Charlie shrugged and looked lazy as he leaned back against the bar counter. "How's that, Dwight?"

"You're calling the shots, aren't you? Leading us where you want us to go, holding back until you get ready to give a little. What are you up to? You're working for that crowd all the way, aren't you?"

Charlie grinned mockingly. "Well, you know I'm not here on vacation, and the state of Oregon sure hasn't hired me."

"You knew damn well that gun would turn up in his mother's room!"

"Wrong. I didn't know it. Let's say I would have been surprised if it hadn't. He's being framed, Dwight." The captain flushed slightly, but before he could interrupt, Charlie went on meditatively, "Either that, or he's smart enough to mock up a frame-up." He raised his eyebrows at the wording he had produced.

Dwight turned to Constance. "Is it hot?"

"Oh yes." She poured out another cup of coffee.

He sat behind the bar and studied Charlie bitterly. "Okay. I'm the village idiot. The role fits. Explain."

"The problem is we're dealing with extremely clever people. They like puzzles and traps and counter-traps. That's how they earn their bread, solving puzzles. Computer puzzles, but the principle's the same. Anyway, suppose Bruce is our killer and he's smart enough to grasp early that he's the prime suspect, just because of who and what he is. Okay, he goes along with that and puts on his Gary act and generally makes an ass out of himself. Offensive, but not a hanging offense, you see. Then he goes further and plants evidence that is all clumsy and amateurish. Like the dirt outside his door." He glanced at Constance who had made a soft noise, an exhalation or a sigh, at his words.

"Ah," she said, "that's what I thought of when we found the computer in the flowerpot. Anyone smart enough to know how to uproot the plant and hide it there wouldn't have scattered dirt around to track to his door. It didn't make sense. Then I forgot it again. But the point is that when you examine plants that way, you don't usually scatter dirt at all. I didn't when I showed you how pot-bound the gardenia was."

"See?" Charlie said. "That's exactly the kind of thing I'm talking about. The gun was a cinch, either way. He hid it himself knowing a good lawyer would make mincemeat of your case, or else someone else is framing him. Mom hides murder weapon for killer son. Not very good. Clumsy. Interesting, either way."

"Charlie, you and I both know that pretty clever people do some god-awful dumb things when it comes to trying to beat a murder one. I say if it walks like a duck, and quacks like a duck, and swims like a duck, then by God it's time for the orange sauce."

"They won't even indict him if you can't tie him to the other two deaths in a more convincing way than you tried before. Can you?"

"No. Can you?"

"I'm working on it. No sheet yet?"

"No. Where do you suggest we go pick it up?"

Charlie smiled good humoredly. "It's a big beach, a lot of ocean. When's low tide again?"

"If it was in that damn rock pile, they would have found it."

"Maybe they've been looking in the wrong rock pile."

For a period that stretched into a long time Dwight

studied him bitterly. Abruptly he got up and headed out of the atrium.

When they were alone again, Constance said, "It was high tide when Milton was killed. The killer must have hidden the sheet somewhere until low tide and then tossed it, or it would have been exposed when the tide ran out. Down there in the driftwood? Who would spot it before he got back?"

"That's how I see it working," Charlie agreed. "He probably wrapped rocks in it to weight it down, maybe included the ashtray, and around dawn at low tide he could get out to the end of the rocks and give it a good toss." He sighed. "If he did, they might never find it, depending on currents, deep holes, how good an arm he had, a lot of things." He looked at his watch; it was after one. "Getting hungry? Let's see what plans Mrs. Ramos has for lunch."

Mrs. Ramos was busily preparing another buffet, hurrying back and forth between the kitchen and the dining room. Ten minutes, she told them brusquely.

"Enough time for another look at that cold-storage room," Charlie said, and led the way through the kitchen, out the back door into the narrow rear hall, and across it to the door of the room Gary had called the root cellar. Charlie opened the door and switched on the lights and they entered.

The air was cold and dank, oppressive; the lights were the fluorescent sort that turned lips purple and skin a sickly greenish-yellow. Constance shivered and hugged her arms about herself. It hadn't affected her this way the first time, she remembered, but now it seemed the very air carried a new menace. And that, she knew, was because the murderer was in this house now. Charlie quickened his pace down the stairs, across the room to the dumbwaiter, and she thought he must be feeling the oppression that she felt. He examined the door to the dumbwaiter, then opened it and examined the interior of the cage: a stainless steel cubicle without markings, revealing nothing. He dropped to his knee and felt the floor and wall joints, and then backed away from it, frowning.

"What are you looking for?" she asked, shivering.

"Not sure. If I send it up, the door locks automatically. I wonder . . ." He took out his pocketknife, opened it, and held it in the door frame with one hand, pushed the close button with the other. The door closed on the knife blade and he could not force it open again. He muttered under his breath and looked around. "Bring one of those carts over, will you? I think I've got the sensor here."

She brought the cart. He pressed the open button and the door swung open smoothly; he withdrew his knife blade. "Now, let's see if I can fool it," he said. He turned the cart on its side with the stainless steel handlebar along the edge of the door frame, then positioned himself on the side of it and pressed hard. "Try the close button and then send it up, if it'll go." He wedged himself firmly and held a steady pressure against the cart. The mechanism clicked, and then the dumbwaiter cage moved upward.

"All right," he muttered. "It might come down again when I let go. Let's see if we can let go and push the cart under the floor at the same time. At the count of three. One, two, three. Now." He let go and she gave the cart a strong push that sent it into the shaft. The cage did not start descending, and if it did come down, the cart might not hold it, but it would slow it down, Charlie decided, satisfied. He grinned at Constance and fished for his penlight, then got down to his knee again to look at the interior of the elevator shaft.

His satisfaction increased as he examined the side walls, and then edged inward a bit to look more closely at the back wall, the one that abutted the secret elevator. He had thought that elevator was an afterthought, and now he was certain of it. This wall had been replaced, redone. It didn't match the sidewalls in finish work, in craftsmanship; there was even a gap at the bottom. Shoddy, shoddy. And it was damn cold. He knew now that it had bothered him to find a cold wall the first time he had examined the secret elevator. In a house as well built as this one, that had been wrong, and he had been dumb not to follow up. He heard himself repeating silently, *Dumb, dumb,* and realized he was staring at his fingers, which seemed unable to hold the light steady enough. His fingers felt detached, too large. He tried to look at his hand to see if something was wrong with it, but that seemed to require too much effort. His eyes were detached, he thought, bemused at the idea.

Constance had been leaning over trying to see what he was looking at, but the effort became too great; her head was getting too heavy, she realized, and thought it might become so heavy that it would topple her over, and how would that look to be sprawled out on the floor of the cold-storage room, getting colder and colder second by second, maybe frozen stiff before anyone got around to finding her, and the—

Abruptly she stood upright and drew in a breath of air. She was dizzy, her eyes not focusing properly.

"Charlie!" she cried. "Charlie!"

How strange, he was thinking, the way the little spot of light drifted around and did not settle anywhere. He heard her call as if from a long way off and thought that was strange also, and then the light made a track down the wall and his fingers were so far removed that he no longer could use them to pick it up, even if he had wanted to do so. He wanted only to put his head down and rest at the moment. He heard the call again, frantic and shrill, and he roused.

She was tugging at him and he was trying to back out of the elevator shaft, but he was so leaden that each movement was tortured, in slow motion, and the cart was in the way. He finally got out in a tangle with the cart and Constance was pulling him upright. He wobbled and the room tilted, but he took a breath and another. Then they were pulling each other to the stairs, upward. Each step took them into better air; by the time they got to the top, they were both drawing in long shuddering breaths, very frightened and pale.

Constance reached for the doorknob, tried to turn it; nothing happened. She tried again, and then with both hands. Charlie pushed past her and tried.

"We're locked in," she whispered. "My God, we're locked in!"

"*Shhh. Shhh.*" He looked past her. The door was solid, with only the brass knob on this side. No lock. On the other side was a bolt, to keep anyone from opening the door accidentally in case they wanted to purge the air inside. He did not waste time trying to force the door now, but looked back at the room. Stainless steel walls, shelves, bins, a counter, the upended cart and another one at the far wall, the open door of the dumbwaiter, the shaft behind it, and the dumbwaiter itself on the floor above. Even if he knew which pipe was feeding in carbon dioxide, there was no way in here to turn it off again.

"Don't move," he said then. "I'm going up in the dumbwaiter and I'll come around to open the door. The air's okay near the ceiling here, so just don't move."

She did not argue. Her pale eyes were wide and very frightened, and she was the color of snow, right down to her lips. She touched his cheek and closed her eyes for a second, a blessing, transferring all the love a touch could carry, and then he took a long breath and, holding it, started down the stairs. He had not broken anything, he told himself, the mechanism would work okay. He pushed the cart aside, but on second thought dragged it back, then he pushed the down button. He had to close the door first, he realized, cursing himself for an idiot. He closed the door and pushed the down button again and stepped on the cart to keep his head as high in the air as possible. He could not remember that the infernal thing had been so slow before, but now it seemed to creak at dinosaur speed. He exhaled the air in his lungs and took a shallow breath, not certain how good it was here, then certain that he had to breathe it in, no matter good or bad. The dumbwaiter finally came and he pushed the open button, and now he had to abandon his place on the cart, lean down to enter the cage, hold himself in a bent-over position because it was not quite five feet high, and at last it began to ascend in slow motion.

At the top of the stairs Constance had taken off her shoe and was pounding on the door with it. They both knew it was a futile gesture. This room was too well insulated.

He held his breath in the dumbwaiter, certain it was filled with dangerous air. By the time the cage came to a stop, his lungs were afire, his head pounding; he could see veins in his own eyes with each beat. When the door opened, he lurched out, staggering and reeling, and tried to race through the pantry to the door at the end, into the hall. His gait was like that of a drunken man; he crashed into a wall, veered off it, and made his way to the door of the cold-storage room and fumbled with the bolt. Constance fell into his arms when he opened the door.

18

THERE had been times when Constance had glimpsed an anger in Charlie so intense that it had been frightening. The time that Stan Walinowski's wife had been beaten severely, so badly that she had lost an eye, Charlie had turned to stone. He and Stan had worked together, and following the beating suffered by Wanda Walinowski both men had worked overtime, weekends, after hours, until one day Charlie had come home with a pinched look, a haunted look in his eyes, and that night he had made love to her passionately. The following day he had insisted that she learn self-defense because, he had said, if anyone ever laid a hand on her, he would kill the son of a bitch. There had been no doubt then, or ever, that he meant exactly that. He and Stan had gone back to regular hours, and no one ever brought up the subject of the vicious attack or the guilty person. And, God help her, Constance thought, neither had she. She had been afraid to.

That afternoon Charlie had turned to stone again, she thought, and instantly corrected herself. Ice. He had turned to ice. Dwight had found them on the steps of the verandah, leaning against each other, simply breathing.

"What's up?" he asked.

Charlie did not speak, and Constance told him what had happened.

"Jesus! Are you all right?"

At her nod, he turned and hurried off with Howie in tow. He returned a few minutes later. "No prints," he said in disgust. "Oxygen turned all the way down, carbon dioxide all the way up."

Charlie did not even look at him.

"When did they all leave the library and television room?" Constance asked.

"Right after I left you two. Mrs. Ramos was making lunch. There didn't seem much point in keeping them locked up after we found the gun."

Constance shook her head at him gently. "Of course not. It wasn't your fault, Dwight. We know that." What a nice younger brother he would have made, she thought, so concerned, so . . . She realized with a start that the look on his face was awareness, and it was directed at Charlie. Another shared man thing, she thought distantly. He knew that Charlie had turned to ice and why.

"Why don't I bring out a tray of sandwiches," he said, a touch too eagerly. "You haven't eaten and neither have I."

"You go ahead," Constance said. "I want to go up to our room. I need to wash. I feel filthy."

Charlie was on his feet before she finished, and she knew this would be part of it; he would not leave her alone a second until they were well away from Smart House.

Constance took his hand; it was icy. "Well, it wasn't really a serious attempt," she said. "Not with the dumbwaiter as an escape hatch. It must have been meant to frighten us."

Dwight looked uncomfortable, glanced from her to Charlie and back, and said slowly, "It was serious. It looks like someone tried to jimmy open the dumb-waiter door in the pantry. If he'd managed to do it, the door in the cold-storage room wouldn't have opened. If Charlie hadn't already forced that one and held it open it would have worked."

Charlie's hand tightened painfully on hers.

Still Dwight hesitated. "Charlie, take it easy, okay? Don't do anything stupid, old buddy."

Finally Charlie really looked at him and grinned. "Do something stupid in Smart House? They'd toss me out on my can. Are you bringing the divers back?"

"Yeah. Six-thirty."

"Good. Let's go wash up." He tugged her hand and they went back inside, up to their room.

Constance showered and tried to scrub away the feeling of violation. This was how people said it felt to be burglarized, she thought, scrubbing, scrubbing. And rape victims. She shut her eyes hard and let the steaming water hit her face, her head. Violated. Someone had wanted her dead, had wanted Charlie dead. If either of them had fallen, no doubt that one would be dead, maybe both of them, drowned in the incoming tide of carbon dioxide that would pool near the floor, gradually accumulate to fill the room. She shook her head angrily, determined to stop thinking about it, and saw instead how Charlie had been leaning over, low to the floor, his face in the pool of poison.

He met her at the bathroom door and held her, nuzzling her wet hair. "You're as shriveled as a raisin," he said finally, stepping back to examine her. "Okay?"

"About what you'd expect from a raisin. What are you doing?"

Their suitcases were on the beds, one on each, and

a few garments had been folded inexpertly and put inside. Other things were in a heap.

"We strike our tent and decamp," he said and looked ruefully at the mess he had made. "No more sleeping in Smart House. We're heading for a hotel or motel or something."

How could his eyes do that, she wondered. At times they seemed to become flat, lusterless, like smooth rocks. "All right," she said without argument. "I'll pack, but on one condition. We get something to eat first."

"Not here." Bad policy to eat in the house of anyone who was trying to kill you, he thought. "Get some clothes on and we'll hop in the car and go find a place that knows about steamer clams and beer and civilized things of that sort." He looked at the papers on the desk. "It's actually a good idea to get the hell out of here for a while. I'll take that stuff and we won't come back until six-thirty."

They met Dwight in the downstairs hall, and he told them about a restaurant that knew all about clams, gave them directions, and said if they were still there in a couple of hours he'd join them. Five-thirty or a few minutes later.

The clams were exactly right, Charlie announced with satisfaction after the second bucket was emptied. And the booth was exactly right, with a good view of the ocean, and, more important, good lighting. A pleasant-faced middle-aged woman had served them and now returned with coffee and the dessert menu, which was the same menu they had scanned earlier. Charlie asked if anyone cared if they used the table for a spell and she looked surprised and asked why anyone would. And so they had a well-lighted table and coffee and he began to spread out the papers again.

Constance read the ones Charlie already had finished with: the corporate structure, the forensics reports on Gary and Rich, financial forecasts . . . She wished they had the inventory that Bruce had compiled, and then muttered, "Damn."

"I agree, but why?"

"Bruce has covered any missing object from his room, hasn't he? The blue whale that he says is gone."

"'Fraid so. That inventory gives anyone else an out, too. Suppose a cast-iron sea lion is missing. Our guy would say, 'I don't know what you're talking about. Never laid eyes on it.' Who could prove otherwise?"

"But why go to the trouble of switching things like that? Why not just let the object be from Milton's room?" She stopped, then said, "Oh, I see. You're right. It must have been the ashtray. We know Milton used that. It would be missed even if another object wouldn't be."

Charlie grinned at her look of annoyance. Food had done wonders for his disposition, and distance from Smart House had helped, he knew. He turned once more to the timetable they had made up for the time of the game, the night of the two first deaths.

She gazed at the sparkling water that rose and fell, rose and fell forever. The trouble was, she thought, anyone could have killed Milton and tidied up afterward, and no one could have killed Gary and Rich. She nodded to herself. That was the problem. Why hadn't Rich Schoen put up a fight, struggled to save himself? Why had Gary let someone push him into the Jacuzzi without taking the other person in with him, at the very least? Maybe Dwight's scenario was the only way it could have been done, with two people working together. Or maybe both men had been moved, after all. Milton had been moved, perhaps they had been also. The police work might have been ineptly done, a mistake made. She frowned at the blue Pacific Ocean. No matter how inept, no one would mistake death by drowning for anything else. She muttered another *damn,* under her breath this time, and Charlie's hand covered hers on the table.

"Let's take a walk on the beach out there," he said. "We'll come back by five-thirty to meet Dwight." His voice was very low, very quiet; he sounded weary.

"Charlie! You know!"

"Not yet. Not yet. I want to think about it. Let's walk."

She knew he did not see anything of the beach as they walked side by side without speaking. He could walk tirelessly in this stage, or play endless games of solitaire, or drive hundreds of miles. What he could not do was sit and do nothing. It was as if he had to give his body a task and turn it loose on it as if that controlling part of his brain might otherwise interfere with his thoughts at these times. That part of his brain needed something to occupy it just to keep it out of the way.

Here, children were playing in the sand, racing back and forth with pails of water, building forts, castles. A few teenagers were in the water, splashing happily, but no one was really swimming. The waves, even though the tide was receding, were too unruly, the water too cold, even though it was August. The air had a fresh ozone smell, good, clean air, and it was pleasantly cool, even though the sun was hot. So many contrasts, contradictions, she thought. Other strollers smiled, nodded, spoke, and she responded, although Charlie was oblivious. Runners overtook them, passed them, leaving deep prints in the wet sand, and she thought about how Sherlock Holmes could tell the height and weight of a person by examining such prints, or know if he had been carrying something, or someone.

They got back to the restaurant only minutes before Dwight arrived, tired, irritable, hungry. They had come back thirsty and already had ordered beers, and now Charlie was sketching rapidly on a napkin as Dwight ordered a sandwich and beer.

"Still nothing?" Constance asked Dwight.

He shook his head. "Oh, there's something," he said with great bitterness. "Harry Westerman and his wife have been in touch with their lawyer, who spoke to me and ordered me to get my crew out of there, to let those poor people go home. And so the bloody damn on."

"Tough," Charlie muttered without conviction. He finished his sketch and eyed it a moment, then turned it so that Dwight could see.

"Look," Charlie said, pointing to three rectangles. "This big job here is the main elevator, and next to it is the private elevator, and the last little shaft is for the dumbwaiter. Granddaddy, Poppa, and little John, all side by side."

He was so pleased with himself, he was intolerable at the moment, Constance thought, glancing from him to Dwight Ericson, whose face was a mask.

"Now," Charlie went on, "at the bottom here we have the cold-storage room. And in the cold-storage room there is a controlled atmosphere. Fifteen percent oxygen, one percent carbon dioxide, and so on, all appropriately monitored with alarms and exhausts if things get out of hand. But the low oxygen and high carbon dioxide are givens; they don't trigger alarms. And here," he said, drawing in some hash marks, "we have leakage from the little-John shaft to the Poppa-elevator shaft, an inch gap at the bottom of the wall. That whole shaft becomes part of the closed system practically."

Dwight Ericson was shaking his head. "We've done the figures, Charlie. It would take too long to build up enough carbon dioxide or exhaust the oxygen in a space that big. No one was missing long enough. And what do you think they did in there, just fold their hands and wait an hour or two to die? They would have raised a ruckus, and you know it. Someone would have heard them pounding on the walls or yelling."

Serenely Charlie continued. "I did the figures, too. If that cage were hermetically sealed it would take two men about half an hour to die of carbon dioxide poisoning. Drowning in their own waste, so to speak. But they didn't die of carbon dioxide poisoning, you see. And besides, the cage isn't hermetically sealed: There is that leakage through the bottom, and ventilation holes in the top. So, let's say the cage is up here on the second floor when they enter for whatever reason and close the door. The cage is filled with warm air, of course. As soon as they start to descend, the fan comes on and the nice warm air is replaced with cool air from the shaft, and the nice warm air starts to rise, taking its nice oxygen with it. We all felt the same thing, dank, cold, oppressive, but we opened the door and got out. Anyway, by the time the cage gets to the basement level, the air has been changed a few times—good air out, bad air in. Normally that wouldn't even be noticeable because you open the door and in comes more good air. But this time, let's say, the door doesn't open. And the cage comes to rest in a pocket of air that is very bad, very concentrated carbon dioxide, low oxygen. You know about carbon dioxide, pockets of stale air, poisonous air that collects?"

Dwight's expression had changed. He no longer looked impatient or bored or forbearing. His eyes narrowed and he nodded. "Yeah. Miners, divers, cave explorers, they all know about coming across pockets like that."

"And firemen," Charlie added darkly. "You go in a big building in any city and if the sub-subbasements haven't been used for a spell, you know. Anyway, that's what would collect in that shaft. Carbon dioxide on the bottom, because it's heavy, the lighter elements above, all of it bad."

"Dear God," Constance said softly. "Those poor men!"

"Right," Charlie said, almost brusquely. "So there they are. Their own body heat would create an updraft of air, enough to make the ventilation holes practically useless, a menace in fact, because the heavy carbon dioxide mix would be pulled in at the bottom while the better air escaped out the top. And every minute they are consuming about seven hundred cubic centimeters of oxygen, and they're producing five to six hundred cubic centimeters of carbon dioxide." His voice had become very flat now, a machine voice. "You learn things like that so you know what you're dealing with in fire situations. Are people still alive in pockets of air, breathing? Is the good air exhausted yet?" He stopped abruptly, then went on. "Anyway, by the time Gary and Rich realized they could die, it was probably too late to do anything about it. First, in only a couple of minutes, discomfort, headaches, then a condition that, I've been told, and can now attest to, is like almost waking up from a nightmare, knowing you have to move, but you can't seem to locate your body parts and do it. Five minutes at the most. By then it was too late. Collapse, unconsciousness, it happens fast."

Dwight started to speak, subsided, as if aware that Charlie should not be interrupted right now, that he was looking at something not quite visible to anyone else.

The silence endured until Charlie shrugged slightly, and said, "But, as you say, they didn't die there and get moved to their final resting places. They weren't dumped as corpses anywhere. And they sure as God didn't walk alone. The damn house was responsible for their deaths, but the final act was somewhere else. In that state, when the door opened, they both had to be alive still. Whoever found them must have had the hell shocked out of him. And instantly he knew they had to be taken somewhere else, or the house would be blamed. Maybe at that time they could have been revived, could have recovered, but if even one of them died, the house would be the killer and there goes the company. Either or both might have been brain damaged. If one did recover, he might implicate whoever closed the door on them. The killer couldn't risk any of those things. So he probably sent the elevator up to the roof, and he took the main one up. That's the only place both elevators are side by side. His first thought must have been to get them both the hell away from the secret elevator, away from the office or Gary's room where walls might be tapped, the secret elevator might be found. Or maybe he was already on the roof when he called up the elevator and opened it to find them both dying. Anyway, the next act must have been up there, someplace where he could go from one elevator to the other with little risk of being seen. I think he must have got Rich to his feet first, walked him to the big elevator, and finished him off there. Maybe Rich actually collapsed and that's how he bruised his face, on the carpeted floor. But the human killer finished him off, all right. Anything at all over his face at that moment would have been enough. He was incapable of fighting back. Maybe he marked his face and used the mesh bag to hide the marks, but probably he used it just to make certain the police didn't settle for an accidental death. Then back to Gary. Down to the first floor with him, out the rear of the elevator, and through the back hall. Gary might have been reviving by then; opening the door would have flushed out the bad air, brought in breathable air. He could walk; the original printout showed that he did walk into the Jacuzzi room, but he was dazed, stuporous; that's how victims of anoxia are, before they actually die. The killer walked him through the dark back hall, to the Jacuzzi, and tipped him in and covered the pool. He was trying hard to make certain the police would look for a murderer, not label either death accidental. But his very cleverness made him botch it. Too many directions, too many false clues pointing every which way.

"He had to have a few minutes free just to tidy up, and neither body would be found too soon. The hand-held computer would lock the elevator wherever he left it, and Gary was out of sight. He put the other control computers and the blueprints in the elevator. He didn't want anyone finding that secret elevator just then. He made popcorn and imitated Gary's wild laughter so everyone would assume Gary was alive and he would be provided with an alibi. Then, unlock the big elevator, rejoin the party, and wait."

Dwight had been eating his sandwich mechanically. He chewed for several minutes. At last he shook his head. "It's plausible, I grant you that. There are messy areas, like why did he move Gary somewhere else instead of leaving him in the big elevator too?"

"What if he was interrupted?" Charlie said. "Actually a couple of people went up to the roof at exactly the wrong time for the killer. If Gary was reviving in the cold fresh air, he would be a risk. He might start making noise. So our guy had to close the big elevator and lock it, close himself in with Gary in the secret elevator and take him someplace where he could finish what he had set out to do, and that was to clear Smart House."

Dwight sighed, still doubtful, still not accepting. "And what's that about the popcorn? How in hell do you figure that?"

"Gary took the popcorn maker from the kitchen before eleven," Charlie said. "He went out the back kitchen door, on his way, no doubt, to his little elevator that would deliver him either to his office or his bedroom. Customarily he had popcorn every night in his office. So why did he then not make it there? Why carry the stuff around with him for fifteen or twenty minutes? He wasn't in the garden during that period; too many others wandered in and out to miss him. No, he went from the kitchen to somewhere else and put the stuff down, and later the killer must have seen the perfect way to establish that Gary was still alive and hungry at eleven-fifteen. When he got the blueprints and computers to stash away in the elevator, he got them from Gary's office; the popcorn maker was probably there, and he saw his chance and took it."

"It could work," Dwight said after another thoughtful pause. "And the good Lord knows I want something that could, but there's no way on this earth to prove any of it."

Charlie spread his hands. "Neither Rich nor Gary was drugged or drunk. They probably weren't hypnotized into lying down and dying, voodoo cursed into it, or talked into it with promises of candy. You can't order a man to lie down and stop breathing, even at gunpoint. They had to have been in a stupor of some sort, incapable of resisting whatever was being done, but capable of walking with help. Anoxia stupor. Not forced on them by having their heads held in fruit bins, or by being urged to enter one of those experimental growing structures in the greenhouse. Someplace close by, accessible. A place that didn't alarm either of them enough to put up a fight. I came up with the elevator. You're right. No proof. But what else is new at this point?" He leaned back in the booth with his arm along the seat back and his hand on Constance's shoulder. "Besides," he said, "I knew from the beginning the damn house was guilty as hell."

"And I suppose you know who took a chance like that just to clear the house?"

"Sure," Charlie said. "But it's going to be tricky to prove it."

19

IT was nearly eight, and Charlie had just finished loading the suitcases into the rented car when Beth and Jake found him. Beth was deathly pale, her eyes very big and frightened. Jake seemed more concerned for her than for the fact that Charlie obviously was planning to leave.

"Alexander said you're going away!" Beth cried on the verandah as Charlie approached. "Why? What are they doing? Why did they rip up part of the balcony? Charlie, what's happening?"

He took her arm and steered her into the foyer. "Calm down. Take it easy. We would have found you to say good-bye. Where's Alexander now? Where are all the others? I thought you'd all be eating and we didn't want to disturb your dinner."

"Who can eat?" she cried.

"They're in the dining room going through the motions," Jake said soberly. "What's up?"

Charlie looked at his watch and said resignedly, "Beth, will you tell Constance I'll be in the garden bar? Let's get a drink," he said, turning to Jake.

Beth bit her lip, then darted up the stairs. "I'll be right back."

"Drink," Charlie muttered, and led the way

through the corridor into the atrium where he went behind the bar and began to look over the assortment of bottles; Jake sat on a stool opposite him. The sun was very low now, but still came through the dome on the roof, lighted up the rock wall at the far end of the room where the waterfall sparkled in its plunge. That end of the room was bright; shadows had gathered at the bar end. Charlie hummed tunelessly as he poked among the bottles and came up with Drambuie. Regretfully he put it down again and settled for bourbon on ice. Jake shook his head when Charlie offered him the same.

"I was going to meet the group in a group," Charlie said after taking a sip. "But this might be better. I think your story should be that you and Milton struggled. He said nasty things and pulled the gun on you and you hit him. When you wrested the gun away, it went off and a bullet grazed his head. And then you panicked and tried to cover up. It isn't neat, and it leaves a lot of questions, but between you and me, there are always a lot of questions without answers."

"You've gone mad!" Jake said coldly.

"Not a bad story, all things considered," Charlie went on, as if he had not heard. "Temporarily out of your mind, that usually works. That way I don't have to mention the secret elevator, or the carbon dioxide in the basement, or the unattended popcorn in the garden here, or the gun on the roof. Or even the reversed Turing test and how all of you practiced being each other to fool the computer. Of course, people will assume that you were responsible for Gary and Rich's death, but they won't be able to prove anything, and in a way that would be good. Smart House is cleared in the minds of the people who count, and you still own the lion's share of a prosperous company. You'll need it, no doubt. Defense comes in costly packages. Did you know attorneys charge for every phone call, every minute they even think about your case, even if they're on the can?"

"You son of a bitch, you're trying to frame me and blackmail me!"

"You don't have much time," Charlie said easily. "When the captain calls it off for the day, I'll tell him my story, make my report to your colleagues, and take off. Did I mention where the divers are working now? The north end of the beach. If they don't find the ashtray and sheet today, then tomorrow they'll bring in a logging helicopter and start playing jack-straws with all that driftwood, and maybe the divers will go on to the next rock pile, and then the next one. I have to admire that captain. He's got gump-tion. He'll stick with it until he finds something—sheet, ashtray, pair of slacks, shirt, something. But I want to get the hell out of here. So I'll tell him a story, and I don't give a damn which version it is, one that involves fun and games and foolishness, secret elevators and a killer house, or one that starts and stops with Milton's death."

"This is extortion and you know it, you bastard! I'll get you for this, so help me God!"

"You almost did," Charlie said mildly.

"Next time you won't be so lucky. Have you told any of the others any of this?"

"Nope. Haven't talked to the shareholders. I de-cided to let you pick the story you like best first."

Jake looked around desperately, as if searching for a weapon, a rock, a bottle, a gun, anything. His hands were white on the countertop. Charlie was out of reach on the other side. Jake flexed his fingers and said, "You're close to what happened." His voice was hard, tight, the words clipped. "I was taking a walk on the balcony when Milton went mad and attacked me. He had a gun. I hit him in self-defense and he fell hard and struck his head. It was an accident, but

I blacked out in a panic." His face was white, his expression murderous.

"It might work," Charlie said judiciously, "if the others cooperate. But after trying to frame Bruce, you lost him, and probably lost Maddie, and when Beth realizes that you were trying to win her over for her shares, I don't know. One or the other might even remember that you were out of sight when they heard that laughing they assumed was Gary."

"Beth will believe what I tell her, and the others don't matter." He leaned forward and said in an intense, low voice, "When it's over, Charlie, I'm coming for you. I'll have resources, more than you've ever dreamed of."

"Number four," Charlie murmured. "What about Laura? She saw Milton pick up your water gun on the roof. One day she might connect that to Rich's killer."

"You can speculate all you want, but you can't prove anything about Gary and Rich, and you know it, or you wouldn't want to make a deal."

"Just how far gone were they when you found them?" Charlie asked.

For a moment he thought Jake wouldn't answer, but then he drew a deep breath and said in a hoarse whisper, "Like zombies, both of them. They were dying. I know about brain damage. You can't understand, no one can, what that would have meant to a man like Gary. To see a mind like his gone, destroyed. Maybe they could have been revived, but they were dead; they would have existed maybe, but not as men with minds. Gary . . ." His voice dropped even lower until it was nearly inaudible. "He was a devil, and the other side of that is that he was a god, and I worshipped him. I did what I had to, what he would have wanted if he had been conscious enough to say so."

Charlie shook his head. "People have pulled through after accidents like that."

He might not have heard. His face was agonized, his expression black. "I opened the door, holding the water gun, aimed at where I thought Rich would be. They were out, both of them, Rich in front. I got him to his feet, to the big elevator. I was going to take him down, get help, and he collapsed. Unconscious. Gary was in the little elevator, unconscious, moaning. They were too far gone! I didn't want to finish them, but I had to or we would have been ruined, all of us, and they were already dead men, still breathing a little, but dead. Past saving."

His eyes were staring, not through space, but as if through time, back to that night. His voice was thick and low when he continued. "Rich fell down and I could see how it would work out, step by step— Smart House blamed, all the work destroyed, the dream gone, everything shattered. It couldn't appear to be accidental. I saw that before I touched him, before I even knew what I had to do. Gary would have wanted me to save the company, at any cost. Any cost. Save Smart House. His dream . . . I tried to make the police understand that the computer couldn't have done it. Anyone who knows computers would know it couldn't have done all that—the insecticide, the lights going off, the pool cover. No computer could have done it, but the fools didn't understand, no matter what we all said."

"You were too clever for them," Charlie murmured. "So that's going to be your story—two accidental deaths and self defense when Milton attacked you. It might fly."

With a start Jake brought his gaze back to Charlie. He shook his head. "I don't know a goddman thing about how Gary and Rich died. That's my story. And Milton pulled a gun on me. He must have killed them and thought I was onto him. That's my story and it'll work. I'm good at details, Charlie, remember? It'll work. I'll make it work. They'll buy it."

Tiredly Charlie said, "Dwight, is that enough yet? I'm getting rather bored."

The lights came on and Dwight Ericson stepped out from the storage area behind the bar. Two other men came from the shadows; they were carrying guns.

"You goddamn son of a bitch!" Jake cried in disbelief, incredulous. "You lied!"

Charlie shrugged. "And you tried to kill my wife." He set his glass down and the musical computer voice said, "Thank you, Charlie. Would you like another drink at this time?" He looked at Jake. "We've been broadcasting ever since we came into the bar. It's all on tape; they've been listening in the dining room. The voice prints, they tell me, never make a mistake. If you claim this one is wrong, you blow the whole security package, don't you?"

For a moment there was a glint in Jake's eyes, almost of recognition of a good end game, Charlie thought, appreciation maybe. But probably not, he decided.

Now the sun was setting, the western sky a redstreaked blaze, the ocean azure fringed with white. Charlie and Constance were in the living room with the group, Charlie at the window looking at the panorama of sea and sky, Constance in a straight chair near him. Very nice, he decided, very nice. He turned to look at the others who were still arranging themselves: Beth in a white high-backed chair that dwarfed her and bleached the color from her face; Laura and Harry Westerman at opposite ends of a sofa; Maddie in a chair drawn close to Bruce. He was ignoring her. Bruce was sprawled, his clothes a mess, his hair a mess, sneakers untied. Alexander had not yet lighted on anything, but paced around the room jerkily as if seeking a special perch. Dwight Ericson and his men were gone. Jake was gone, too.

"Alexander, if you will come to rest someplace, I'd like to get this over with," Charlie said.

"Sorry, sorry," Alexander said, as flighty as a hummingbird, and sat on the edge of the nearest chair.

Charlie nodded. "By now you've all seen that little elevator, and you know about the hand-held computers that could control just about everything in this house, including the secret elevator. I'll keep this as brief as I can. From the beginning there were several questions that seemed to need answers. Playing the assassin game, why didn't Jake kill Rich when he had a chance, several chances, in fact? He inherited his as victim early in the afternoon when he got Beth and did nothing about it the rest of the day and evening. Then, why would Gary cheat in his own game, when he tried to get Maddie to witness after she was out of it? Why did Gary laugh in the garden that night? At whom? Everyone was accounted for and no one was with him, apparently. Why didn't Gary make popcorn in his room or his office? Why didn't the main elevator work after eleven o'clock that night? Those questions all came up when you told me about the game and your movements."

They were all looking blank. He shrugged. "There were other questions that came up over Milton's murder. Why did anyone pick that night to hide the little computer? Why scatter dirt and leave a pile at Bruce's door? Why was Jake wearing his contact lenses if he had been in bed asleep? If he hadn't been in bed, why the pajamas? Why did anyone wipe prints off all the accessories in Milton's room? Why did Bruce mention a gun that night?

"We'll have to go back to the game for this,"

Charlie said apologetically. "Milton Sweetwater has gone down to the basement for a new weapon. He hears Jake and Rich, and sees the office door close. Minutes later he returns to the elevator to see Rich alone, and they ride up together. The problem is that Jake had Rich's name, and made no effort to get him either time, although when Milton came down he could have been a witness. Why not? He says that he didn't know his next victim, that he kept forgetting to check. Maybe. And remember that curious scene when Gary had a tantrum because his mother would not witness his killing Bruce. Very strange. What was that all about? Everyone insisted that Gary loved games, that he wouldn't have cheated, and yet, that was clearly an illegal move. And in front of Jake. Picture it: Gary and Jake enter a room where Bruce and his mother are and Gary uses the plastic knife to stab Bruce, but his mother won't play, and Jake has left by then. Gary has a royal tantrum. Why? Because Maddie refused to play, something he already knew, or because Jake left prematurely? What would have happened if he had entered the kill in the computer and Maddie had witnessed?" He looked at Alexander and waited.

Alexander fidgeted, embarrassed again, and shook his head. "It would not have been allowed, not if Maddie had been taken out of the game."

"But exactly what would have happened?" Charlie persisted.

"The computer would have said something to the effect that nonplayers wouldn't be allowed to participate in any way, that Gary was out of line, and he could not make another attempt at murder with that particular dagger. Depending on who made the mistake, it might have added a penalty. Because it was Gary, it probably would have given Bruce a twelve- or twenty-four—hour reprieve, a time that Gary could not attack again. That's all."

Charlie nodded gravely. "And how unusual would it have been, to have a computer respond in that way?"

Alexander looked infinitely relieved now. He brightened, his eyes gleamed. "You just don't know! That's what I've been trying to tell you. That's reasoning! Human reasoning, not just number crunching! Jake would have been plenty impressed! Plenty!" He stopped abruptly and looked panic-stricken.

"Exactly," Charlie said. "I've been listening, Alexander. I really have been." He turned to Beth. "That day after Jake killed you in the garden, you wandered down to the greenhouse, didn't you?" She nodded, her gaze fastened on him as if hypnotized. "Which door did you enter by?"

She moistened her lips and swallowed, then said, "I walked around and went in the end door."

"So Gary and Jake were at the end nearest the house. And they both ran out when you entered. I wonder why. Jake had killed you; he knew you were no threat. And Gary knew you had overheard his murder; again, no threat. Why did they duck out? What were they carrying, Beth?"

"I never said they—"

Charlie was smiling gently at her. "It's all right, Beth. I know you never said they were, but close your eyes and see that scene in your mind's eye. They were carrying something, weren't they? One of them, or both of them, Beth?"

She blinked finally, then closed her eyes. After a moment, she cried, "Both of them. I thought books, but they weren't books, were they? The little computers! It must have been the computers!" Her eyes opened. "I thought it was just the paranoia, everyone afraid of everyone else. And they had no reason to be afraid of me, neither of them. That's what I focused on. That's what was so awful. I never even gave a thought to anything in their hands. How did you know?"

"It had to be something they had that made them dodge you that way. As you said, neither of them had a cause to fear you. But a private demonstration of the computers, that was different. That was serious business that Gary wasn't ready to share with anyone but Jake yet. I suspect that sometime during that day or evening Gary programmed in a command either to keep Jake from getting a new weapon or from learning his next victim, or even both, and Jake knew it and didn't even try, and that's why he didn't go for Rich when he had a chance. You were his last victim, in the game anyway. From all accounts he was an avid game player, just like Gary. It didn't add up."

Beth was nodding. "They had been down there by all the valves and gauges and things. Holding the computers."

"And later, to add a bit of confusion, Jake used the computer again to release poison in the greenhouse. Not to hurt anyone; he chose his time, after all, but to lead the police there, to the demonstration rooms, the little experimental atmosphere-controlled rooms where people could be suffocated. He was trying hard to force them to look for a human killer. He was doing all he could to keep Smart House out of it."

"You jumped to that conclusion just because Jake didn't try to get Rich when he had a chance?" Harry looked angry and sounded disbelieving. "For Christ's sake! I never got a victim all weekend!"

"But you weren't reported closeted with either Gary or Rich all afternoon and evening the way Jake was. From late afternoon on, he seemed to be with one or the other every time anyone reported his presence. They were showing him everything, together, and separately, each with his own game plan, no doubt. Rich wanted to start showing the house to potential buyers, and Gary wanted to continue researching artificial intelligence. Meanwhile, Jake was the largest shareholder after Gary; he was the one to convince. When Rich went up in the elevator with Milton, Jake stayed behind in the office. And no one saw him again until he came back down with Beth at eleven-ten or a little after. During that time, he found the key to the main computer and began trying it out. Beth, you told us he could recreate up to ten chess moves; he had a phenomenal memory for details, and during the day he had seen many computer operations, remember. We know Gary kept the little computers in his office, and Bruce overheard him demonstrating them to someone. And Gary had made use of the secret elevator, no doubt about that, but he must have used the manual controls. Why not? It wasn't computer locked, the way the bedrooms were. Why would it have been? No one knew about it yet except Gary and Rich and Jake. So the little computers were in the office and Jake was in the office.

"And now things changed. Jake could unlock the weapons cabinet and get his new weapon. Remember, he wasn't planning murder or anything else at that time; he was playing the game."

Charlie turned to Laura. "After Rich witnessed for Milton, you all went to the library to record the kill, right? And Rich seemed to be in a hurry?"

"Yes."

"He knew Jake was in the office. So he went back, and Gary showed up with his popcorn maker and popcorn and oil, and in the next few minutes Jake managed to get Rich and Gary in the little elevator together and locked them in with computer control. He must not have had a weapon yet or he could have taken Rich out the second Gary joined them, but he didn't. So he put them both on hold and went out for a weapon. And he probably was taking his time, in no rush because he knew where his victim was, along with a witness. He locked the elevator at the base- ment level so that no one would be likely to hear if they got mad and pounded on the walls. This is the crucial time period. Everyone is accounted for except Jake. I told you people notice each other more than they realize, and they did. But Jake was out of sight for half an hour or longer. Anyway, he got his squirt gun and then went up the stairs to the roof. We know that because the main elevator was in use about then, Maddie was coming down. It takes a little time to get up three flights and he was in no particular hurry. Five or six minutes after he closed the little elevator door and locked it at the basement level, he called it up there and opened it to find two dying men."

Maddie lost her control then and began to sob. She buried her face in her hands and rocked back and forth.

Harry stood up abruptly. "This is pure fantasy. You don't have a shred of proof. Horseshit! Why not in Gary's office, if he had the computer? Or the bed- room? Any other room?"

"If anyone saw him entering the office or Gary's room, the game would be up. Remember the com- puter-locked doors. He wasn't supposed to be able to open either room. And people were milling about all over the place, potential witnesses. The first floor? He would have had to go through the garden room, behind the pool, around the back hallway, and, again, too many people. He liked fun and games as much as Gary did, I take it. He wouldn't want to give away the secret elevator any more than Gary did at that point, and he didn't want to risk having someone tag along and upset his plan to get Rich as soon as the door opened. One witness, Gary, was all he wanted on hand, because he was playing the game. He had out-witted Gary, solved the computer puzzle, got his weapon, locked them in. He must have been feeling pretty triumphant. He opened the door and found two dying men in the little elevator." He stopped and rubbed his eyes absently. His voice was tired when he resumed.

"You heard what he said about that part. He tried to revive Rich, couldn't, and finished them both off in a way that he thought would make the police go after a human killer, not link the house and computer to the deaths." He paused, then went on briskly. "And Laura and Milton came up before he was finished. He had dropped the water gun without a thought, no doubt. Milton picked it up; as soon as he mentioned it, he was tagged the next victim. This time it was a deliberate decision."

Charlie stopped and looked at Maddie. She was sitting rigidly upright watching him fixedly.

"So, now they were both dead, and Jake had to move fast. He started the automatic popcorn maker to establish that Gary was still alive at approximately eleven-fifteen, hurried back to the secret elevator and got the blueprints from Gary's office, and put them and two of the little computers in the elevator. He let himself out of Gary's bedroom on the second floor and raced to his own door and pretended to be leaving just as Beth was coming out of her room. They went down the stairs together, and he left her on the first floor long enough to go uncover the popcorn maker, to let out the aroma, and open one of the sliding doors. He imitated Gary's laughter, and went into the library where he remained until the first body turned up."

"You couldn't have proved any of this," Harry said. "If the fool had kept his head, he would have been home free. That goddamn fool!"

Charlie shrugged. "He framed Bruce, you know. And I suppose he had plans for an untimely death for Laura, just in case she ever began to piece it together. She did see Milton pick up that water gun on the roof. If the fool had kept his head he might have ended up sole owner of the Bellringer Company eventually."

Beth flushed and ducked her head.

"Anyway, we don't have to prove any of it. He's tagged for Milton's murder, and that's plenty."

Harry took a deep breath. "That goddamn fool! You might as well finish this. How did you guess?"

Charlie looked aggrieved. "I deduced it," he said. "Jake killed Milton on the balcony, wrapped him in a sheet, and trundled him to the cliff where he shot him and then rolled him over the edge. But it all raised questions. Why pick that night to hide the little computer? There hadn't been any need before there was another death, more searches in store. He could have kept it forever, except for that. Suddenly it was a liability. He could have stashed it in the little elevator, but he needed a victim to frame. So he planted the computer in a pot and made a mess generally with the dirt, left some outside Bruce's door. He was to be the goat. By then Milton had to be dead, you see. Jake knew Bruce was up all hours, and it was a good bet that he'd be down in the garden before the night was over, to get dirt on his shoes. He was watching to make certain, and when Bruce did go down, he followed in time to see Constance and me in there, too. That made it even better. But then Bruce said something about a gun, and that got a very strange reaction from Jake. He laughed, for him a wild laugh, in fact, because he was shaken by the mention of a gun. He passed it off rather well, but still I had to wonder. And I wondered why he had his contacts in if he really had been sleeping. No one puts in contacts just to get up and get a drink, they simply put on glasses. But if he hadn't yet been sleeping, why lie about it? And why the pajamas if he hadn't been in bed yet? What if, I thought, he somehow had messed up the clothes he had worn earlier? Whoever wrestled Milton off the balcony, down to the cliff might well have messed up his clothes. Changing clothes in the middle of the night would have been like pointing a finger at him, so the pajamas and robe, but he forgot about the contacts. Sure enough, his gray slacks are missing, the ones he wore yesterday. And Bruce mentioned the gun, not because he had one, but because he had heard a shot and had not consciously identified it as a shot, but part of his brain knew. By the time we met them both in the garden, Milton was already dead.

"So there it is," Charlie said with an air of finality. "He switched stuff from his room to Milton's room and wiped off his prints, but his ashtray is missing, a heavy mahogany ashtray with a crystal bottom. Mrs. Ramos assures us that the inventory about which accessories were in the various rooms is correct. Eventually she might have noticed the switch, but no one asked her. I expect that Dwight Ericson will find the sheet, Jake's slacks, and the ashtray off the rocks at the north end of the beach." He glanced around at them all and added without expression, "No one knows about that stupid game of murder. I'll send you a written copy of my report, and God help you all. Satisfied?"

Harry closed his eyes briefly, then glared at Charlie. "He could have beaten it. A good lawyer would have got him off."

"And left Bruce holding the bag," Charlie said dryly. He held out his hand to Constance. "Let's hit the road."

"Beth, don't leave yet," Harry said sharply when she stood up also, a look of revulsion on her face.

"There's the company to consider, our plans for the future . . ."

"Go to hell," she said. "You can talk to my lawyer as soon as I sign one on."

"He killed my son," Maddie said suddenly in a cold, furious voice. "I intend to cooperate with the police in any way I can to have him found guilty, even if it means talking about that insane game." She stood up and walked out.

Bruce began to laugh.

At the door of the room Constance glanced back once. Harry was seated on the deep couch, scowling at nothing in particular; Laura was across the couch from him, frozen faced. Behind them both the immensity of the Pacific Ocean stretched out forever, and for the first time Smart House looked small, insignificant. The shareholders of Bellringer Company looked like motes against that infinity. Constance took Charlie's hand and they walked out to their car.

Beth was waiting for them. She held out her hand, first to Charlie, then to Constance. "Thanks." She looked past them at Smart House. "Gary, Rich, Milton, Jake. They were the real brains of the company. It's over and done with now. All of it." She stepped closer and swiftly kissed Charlie on the cheek, and then said gravely to Constance, "I won't forget you. I owe you a lot." She turned and ran to her car, got in, and drove off fast.

"There goes a potential millionaire. Millionairess? Anyway, thirty, eligible, rich, pretty."

Constance held his hand firmly. "Free," she said. "None of the rest matters very much." They went to the rented car and got in, started out the wide driveway, up the hill. "I'm just glad to be away from that place," she murmured when they made the curve that took Smart House out of view.

"I knew it was a killer the minute I set eyes on it,"

Charlie said, and started to hum in the tuneless way he did.

"Before you set eyes on it," she said lazily, and rested her hand on his thigh the way she did.

"Right. You know the trouble with geniuses?"

"Tell me."

"They think they're so damn smart."

He looked at her sharply, because in his head he heard her soft voice saying, *Yes, dear, but I forgive you*. She was gazing out the window at the sculptured grounds, smiling slightly.